THE RETURN OF THE
COWBOY

And The DIAMONDS OF LEGION

Engineered by the Lord

AUTHORED BY

G.S.CREWS

Crews Publications Presents, The Return Of The Cowboy

This novel is a work of fiction. Any resemblance to real people, dead or living, actual events, organizations, establishments, and/or locales are intended to give the fiction a sense of reality and authenticity. Names, characters, places and incidents are either products of the author's imagination or are used fictitiously, as are those fictionalized events and incidents that may involve real persons and did not occur or are set in the future.

The Return of the Cowboy Copyright © 2009 by G.S. Crews

Published by:

Crews Publications

PO Box 1201

Jonesboro, GA 30237-1201

Phone: 770-617-9688

Email: crewspublications@yahoo.com

Edited by: Asta Editorial Services

Library of Congress Catalog Card No: In publication data

IBSN-10:

IBSN-13:

Dedication

Mom, thank you for showing me all of those westerns. Now, I will show them something new. Rest in Peace, Ellen.

Preface

Of Ms. Ellen & the Diamonds of Legion

A sleek, moss green mini-submarine emerged from the dark water of a vast underground lake and silently maneuvered around an island of jagged rocks that loomeds in the deep darkness. The hyper-white lights on its bullet-shaped nose beamed on the walls of the underground cavern, exposing dark brown pointy rocks hanging from the ceiling like the teeth of a dragon. The land formation of rocks stretched out into the depths. The mini-submarine docked at a group of jetties that protruded from the water, and the protective, bubble-like cover of the air-tight cockpit slid apart.

The pilot of the vessel was a young black woman in her early thirties. She was dressed in SWAT team body armor. On her curly head rested a golden tiara with silver flared wings on each side. The woman nimbly leapt from the cockpit, skipped across three tiny rocks, then somersaulted through the air, landing on a nearby flat rock.

She wore one weapon that was strapped to her back— a golden double-bladed battle-axe.

To men and women of the world, this lady was known as Ms. Ellen. To the monsters in the world, she was known as Axe-Murderer.

Ms. Ellen called out in a proud voice, "Lady of the Lake, Ms. Ellen is here!"

There was only silence and darkness. She yelled again.

"Lady of the Lake, Ms. Ellen is here! I heard you in my dreams!"

The woman wheeled around, toward the sound of swirling water, with her golden axe extended. Suddenly, she became aware of a golden light emitting from her axe.

"My axe is glowing."

"Yes, Ms. Ellen. My creations glow in the presence of their maker."

Ms. Ellen turned toward the voice that had a Russian accent. Standing on the surface of the water was the majestic Lady of the Lake with her diamonds sparkling within her cream-colored gown and a crown of running water floating over her golden hair.

"Lady of the Lake!"

"Yes, my darling. It is I."

"The dream was so real! Your voice…your voice was so strong!"

The Lady of the Lake pointed her finger at Ms. Ellen. Glimmering sparkles twinkled from her fingertips and onto the surface of the lake.

"Ms. Ellen, I have a warning. The final confrontation between man and monster is coming."

"Final confrontation?"

The Lady of the Lake strode across the surface of the still water with her radiance beaming softly.

"The order has been given to the Banshee to lead an army of undead to destroy Bonanza."

"The Banshee? Who is she?"

"The Banshee is a hideous creature who hides behind a façade of beauty and wields a terrible voice that can drive anyone into madness."

Ms. Ellen nodded her head.

"Do you remember, five years ago, when the earth quaked and was flooded with goblins, werewolves, ogres, and other evil creatures?"

"Yes, the earth's plates shifted and raised my community one-hundred feet above sea level. Mountains became valleys and forests turned to deserts in one day."

"The axis of the earth did not move. The same one who caused the earth to quake has ordered your destruction."

Ms. Ellen narrowed her eyes and shook her head in disbelief.

"No one can make an earthquake."

"Au contraire, mon ami."

"How do you know French?" Ms. Ellen asked.

"I am a water spirit who has lived among men of all races. I am fluent in all languages, but this thing cares not for this world or its ways."

"How? How can this be?"

"This thing is not of this earth; it is of the Underworld."

"The Underworld?"

"You may also know it as Hell. This thing is a powerful member of the Legion."

"Jesus battled the demons of the Legion and cast them into a herd of swine."

"Yes, the tradition has been to cast those demons into swine and other animals, but, one-hundred years ago, an Indian shaman discovered that he could cast the most dangerous members of the Legion into three diamonds with the power of the Wand of Existence."

"Fascinating, but disturbing."

"The demons escaped but were cast back into their prisons by a courageous cowboy and his wolf as they passed through the country."

"Jumpin' Jehosophat! My father spoke of a cowboy coming to our rescue! He said that the cowboy was the only person who could save us!"

"I can not foresee this champion coming to your aid in the nick of time, but I can give you an idea of what type of foe you are up against."

Ms. Ellen nodded her head and listened intensely.

"The most dangerous member is named Desire. She was cast into a yellow diamond. Immediately, the diamond was changed into the likeness of the head of a giant cat with large teeth."

"So, what do the other diamonds look like?"

"Death is the black diamond that is shaped like a jackal's head, and Deprivation is the blue diamond that is shaped like a ram's head."

Ms. Ellen tossed her golden axe from her right hand to her left hand.

"Great! So where are these diamonds at so that I can hack them to smithereens?"

"Deprivation is trapped in the Pyramid that serves as the

Master Gate."

"The Pyramid right smack in the middle of our community?" The Lady of the Lake nodded her head.

"Yes. Desire got him to go inside by tricking him and triggered the force field that surrounds the structure, trapping him there for all eternity."

"I—"

The Lady of the Lake interrupted Ms. Ellen's sentence.

"There is no time for you to understand. If knowledge is power, then touch my hand and become powerful!"

Ms. Ellen reached out and touched the Lady of the Lake's hand. Instantly, images of the past flooded her mind. Ms. Ellen's head began to throb and blood trickled from her small nose as she became inundated with information.

"My head…it hurts."

"If you let go of my hand, all you know will perish. Desire has ordered the children to be eaten alive and everyone else turned into the undead."

Despite the pain, Ms. Ellen tightened her grip. She could not let her people down. Finally, the episode was over, and the Lady of the Lake released Ms. Ellen's hand. Ms. Ellen wiped her teary eyes and let out a deep breath.

"How much time do we have?"

"Be prepared to fight by the second sunrise or be slaughtered!"

"Lady of the Lake, thank you. I have to get back and prepare my people."

"Go, Axe-Murderer, and write down what you have learned. Remember that the tiara will heal all your wounds and the Golden Axe of King Arthur will not tarnish."

"Thank you again."

Ms. Ellen did a series of back flips and landed in the cockpit of the mini-sub. The glass doors slid back together and sealed the cockpit. The sub sank as the engines were put to full throttle. Ms. Ellen sped back to her community as fast as she could.

2

The deep gray storm clouds broke, and a wide glare of sunlight splashed over a dry dusty plain. Here and there were the skeletons of eighteen wheelers and cars. This plain, now a corroded cemetery, was once a busy stretch of road known as Tara Boulevard. Their husky iron hides had been greatly corroded by the reaping whirlwind that damaged much of the earth's environment.

The reservoirs that helped nourish the wetlands and creeks had long evaporated.

No birds flew in the sky.

No trees or bushes grew there.

Downed telephone poles and twisted wire rested here and there.

The entire area was deprived of life and filled with fear.

The glare of sunlight sped across the desert plain as if it had just escaped from prison. The terrain changed from desert to rocky. Here and there a small stunted bush grew in the shade of brown flat rocks. A bundle of tumble weed rocked from side to side in an unfelt breeze.

The landscape was alien.

The sunlight stretched across the stony terrain as the landscape rose in elevation. It crept over treacherous rocky slopes and toward a plateau that towered one hundred feet above sea level. The light reached the base of the plateau then moved up the side of the plateau, via a well-made path, until it reached a tan twenty-foot wall that bordered the top of the plateau.

The wall was not made by bricklayers or architects. It was made by an intelligence greater than man.

The sunlight illuminated the path until it reached a set of iron gates that were imbedded on the wall. Above the gates, a sign was posted that read:

BONANZA, the Last City of Man

The light broadened around the great wall, enveloping it. Suddenly, the light leapt up the wall and spilled over into a neighborhood of ranch and Victorian homes that were red-bricked with vinyl siding.

More corroded pickup trucks, sedans, and motorcycles were parked in the driveways. Even the surface streets had deteriorated. Weeds busted through the cracks and crevices.

A strange silence filled this impoverished neighborhood.

The glare of sunlight spread across the community and passed the largest army supply and sporting goods stores in the southeast.

The store was empty.

All of the sniper rifles, shotguns, hunting bows and arrows, and ammunition had been taken from their cases. There were no green and brown army fatigues hanging from the racks or folded on the shelves.

The store was derelict.

The sunlight continued its trek. It traveled across a park until it reached the concrete stands of a high school football stadium that was packed with more than twenty thousand people.

However, the football stadium was not quiet.

There was a loud clamor of excitement. Just one hour before, Ms. Ellen had returned from her meeting with the Lady of the Lake and asked to meet with all its residents.

Now, she stood in the shadowy end zone that had the fading words Lovejoy Tigers written in the grass.

In Ms. Ellen's right hand was wrapped around a microphone that was hooked up to a generator.

She stood with her eyes closed, contemplating the ill news the Lady of the Lake had given her earlier in the day.

"How can I tell them? How can I tell them that the Banshee is leading an undead army of zombies to Bonanza to slaughter us in two days," Ms. Ellen muttered.

Ms. Ellen glanced upward at the reddish brown peak of the Pyramid that loomed over the stadium like a figure of doom. She could not see the deadly invisible force field that surrounded the structure, keeping whatever was inside trapped. Ms. Ellen closed her eyes in despair.

"Some people have a bad dog in their neighborhood, a liquor store, or even a crack house, but we have a Pyramid that is the Master Gate to the Underworld in ours. No wonder the property value went down."

Ms. Ellen licked her small lips. She had not worn any lip gloss or eye shadow in five years. Going out with the guys for a beer at Fox Grill in Atlantic Station or just text messaging her cousin were things of the past. The world had changed overnight. Things that were myths had become truths, and truths had become harder to identify.

Ms. Ellen tried to calm the heart that was thudding under her shirt. She glanced down. The microphone shook in her right hand.

"How can we fight against something that can open the Gates of Hell and flood the earth with monsters?"

Ms. Ellen took another deep breath, but it did her no good. The microphone was still shaking.

"I have to calm down. I can't speak to them like this. Lord, give me strength!"

At that moment, sunlight washed over Ms. Ellen. She felt its warmth on her closed eyelids. She felt renewed. The audience gasped as the light flickered on Ms. Ellen's tiara. She resembled Titian from Greek mythology. Ms. Ellen gripped the microphone. Her hands were steady. She began to hum into the microphone.

"Hmm! Hmm! Hmmmm! Hmmmmmm!"

"Hmm! Hmm! Hmmmm!" hummed the audience in response.

Ms. Ellen opened her brown eyes and gazed upon the multitude of people sitting in the stands and standing around the football field, humming the tune. The sight empowered her. The sight reenergized her and removed her heavy load. There was hope.

Ms. Ellen cleared her throat and sang through the microphone, "*Precious Lord,*
Take my hand
Lead me on, let me stand.
I'm tired, I'm weak, I'm alone.
Through the storm, through the night.
Lead me on to the light.
Take my hand, precious Lord, lead me home!"

The audience was mesmerized by the vocals of Ms. Ellen. Someone yelled out in the crowd, "Sing it, girl! Sing your song!"

Ms. Ellen obeyed and reached into her stomach to release deep soul stirring notes. She placed her finger on her left ear and leaned forward.

The crowd went wild. A nearby brunette lady, dressed in a pair of dirty jeans and yellow blouse, chanted as she held her newborn child.

"Lead me on, Lord! Lead me on!"

Ms. Ellen leaned back and let her vocals explode across the stadium.

Ms. Ellen whirled around and threw her left hand in the air with her two fingers extended in a peace sign. The audience took up the song with her and the stadium was magnified by their voices. This was more than a glorious sound. It was a hopeful sound!

Ms. Ellen began to prance around the end zone, and the crowd went into a frenzy with people hugging each other, crying, and sending praise up to the Heavens. Soon the song ended. Ms. Ellen wiped her teary eyes and cleared her throat. It was time to address her people. She spoke into the microphone in a powerful voice.

"Good evening, my beautiful people of Bonanza! I have news for you! We are alive!"

"Yeah! We are alive! We are alive," chanted the people.

"For five long years, we have fought monsters that only existed on the movie screen! Zombies! Werewolves! Lizard-men!"

"Yeah! Yeah!"

"We have had to conserve our ammunition and use other weapons because these monsters keep coming back! It's almost like they have no end, but today, Bonanza, I am here to tell you that their end is coming!"

Ms. Ellen upheld her double-bladed golden axe.

"We have fought! We have survived!"

"Yeah! Survived," replied the people.

Ms. Ellen let the crowd die down as she continued to address the people with her fiery spirit.

"We have fought without guns, electricity, technology, and we have won! We have won because we have each other!"

The audience went wild as cheers and praises of appreciation flew up and into the air.

"Ms. Ellen! Ms. Ellen!" the people chanted.

This time, Ms. Ellen did not let the crowd die down. She spoke louder and more powerfully.

"Bonanza, I have a message from our friend, the Lady of the Lake! She warns us that, in two days, the Banshee is coming with an army of the undead to destroy us, to murder our children, and to eat those they capture alive!"

Ms. Ellen could see the concern on their faces. Some frowned. Some stared with blank expressions, while others wept. Ms. Ellen continued. Only this time, she spoke not from her stomach but from her soul.

"Bonanza, I say let them come! Bring the Banshee and all the zombies because they will not find a sleeping city but ferocious Lovejoy Tigers who are hungry for freedom, hungry for liberty!"

Every person heard her proclamation. Even better, everyone felt the proclamation. The audience erupted in applause! It was a strong sound. It was a necessary sound. Ms. Ellen smiled, but, as the applauding subsided, a young black man dressed in a white t-shirt and blue jeans spoke out in a strong voice from a nearby stand.

"When is the cowboy coming?" the young black man cried out.

Ms. Ellen did not reply. She was beginning to doubt her father's revelation of a cowboy coming to their rescue. Ms. Ellen pointed the spiked golden tip of her axe toward the men and women who were sitting in the nearby stands. They were dressed in army fatigues from the largest army surplus store.

"Golden Arms of Bonanza, stand up," Ms. Ellen ordered in a loud voice.

The men and women, who were dedicated to hand to hand combat, leapt to their feet. They stood as still as statues with M-16's and M4 Carbine machinegun rifles strapped to their backs. The guns were decorated with and other

"Golden Archers of Bonanza, stand up," Ms. Ellen ordered.

Hundreds of men and women, who were dedicated to hitting their targets from long distances, leapt to their feet with their sniper rifles and bows and arrows strapped to their backs, courtesy of the local sporting goods stores.

"Sons of Bonanza, stand up," Ms. Ellen ordered.

The final group of ladies and gentlemen leapt to their feet. Their number was only ten, but their courage was of ten thousand! These ladies and gentlemen were dressed in SWAT team body armor like Ms. Ellen but were armed with Carbine 15's and AR-15 machine guns with rocket launchers. They were the last remnants of the organized force once known as the Jonesboro SWAT Team.

"Bonanza, do you see these ladies and gentlemen?" Ms. Ellen asked in a loud voice.

The audience did not respond. They looked upon the men and women with respect and reverence.

"These men and women will protect and serve you! I will protect and serve you! For Bonanza!"

"For Bonanza!" the mass of people shouted.

There was a grand applause. Ms. Ellen saluted the people and the men and women before leaving the end zone. She hurried to the police station that was two blocks away from the stadium and the neighborhood. She sat at a rectangular table in the break room that was lit by candlelight. The orange light reflected on her oval face as she began to write in her composition notebook every detail the Lady of the Lake had revealed to her.

"In the foothills of the Appalachian Mountains lies Pine Mountain," Ms. Ellen wrote in her cursive handwriting as she recorded how the three most dangerous members of Legion had escaped their diamond prisons.

Hopefully, this recording would survive the test of time and be a testimony to those who would read it in the future. Hopefully, they would survive this last battle and be able to add more information to the record.

In the southern foothills of the Georgia Appalachian Mountains on the outskirts of a small resort town known as Pine Mountain, a distressed woman dressed in khaki pants, brown hiking boots, and a white t-shirt that verbalized the attitude "Spirit" hiked through the woods. The woman's name was Jane Wright, and she was not enjoying this beautiful Fall day of full fluffy white clouds and mild temperatures. Jane's ice blue eyes were red from intensive crying. Her golden blonde hair was wrapped in a ponytail, and her lightly tanned cheeks were flushed from raging emotions.

"Why did he have to cheat on me? Why can't I have someone who desires me like I desire him?" Jane mulled as she climbed a grassy hill.

So what caused this beautiful model, who was accustomed to gracing the runway while wearing the latest fashions, to become this disheveled hermit hiking through the woods by herself? On that Fall day, Jane had fled to her father's remote mountain cabin with the hope that the untainted sounds of nature would calm her nerves, soothe her trampled heart, and mend her broken hopes. So far, her therapy was proving effective. Suddenly, her cellular phone rang, and, instinctively, Jane flipped open the device. The calm voice on the other end took her breath and caused her world to stop spinning. The voice belonged to her fiancé, Mann.

"Jane, are you there?" Mann asked in a calm voice as he leaned on his desk.

The sleeves of his navy blue blazer stretched just past his silver watch and his nails were slightly manicured.

There was no reply. Mann listened closely. He could hear the ambient sounds of birds chirping. However, Jane did not answer. She only breathed, listening to the owner of this calm voice. Disgust for this shell of a man lined her mouth, but she held her peace. Perhaps, her nonverbal language would send Mann the message.

"Where are you? Can you quit playing these childish games?" Mann asked in a stern voice.

The condescending tone of Mann's voice placed Jane into battle mode. She licked her pink lips, preparing to issue a verbal assault. The only language Mann understood was violence.

"Like you haven't played games with me? You practically played me like an Xbox," Jane coldly replied as she squatted on a nearby flat rock.

Mann sighed as he rubbed his hands through his short brown hair. He knew that it was not going to be easy. However, cutting edge technology always made the most complicated tasks simple. He clicked the mouse of his computer. The flat screen illuminated and displayed a dynamic database with fields such as social security number, first name, last name, and phone number. Mann swiftly keyed Jane's cell phone number into his GPS database. Serving the city of Atlanta as its Chief Information Officer had its perks. Immediately, a green topographical map of Georgia appeared on his computer monitor. In half a second, a pink triangle flashed to an area known as Pine Mountain that was about one hour south of Atlanta.

"Jane, nobody has heard from you in two days! You missed a photo shoot for *Eyez* magazine yesterday! You haven't missed an appointment since you were three years old," Mann said as he aligned his cellular phone with the GPS database and signaled for his helicopter to be made ready.

"I don't want to model anymore! People like you treat models like trophies, not humans! I am not an award on your shelf," Jane lividly replied.

An instant message popped up in the lower right corner of Mann's computer screen. It read, "Chopper ready in five minutes."

Mann ignored Jane's emotional rhetoric and clicked the 'OK' button on the screen. Today, he was going to get back what belonged to him. As long as Jane's cell phone stayed on, Mann knew he could track her whereabouts. Mann knew he needed to soothe things over between Jane and himself. However, he was not accustomed to requesting forgiveness. Mann swallowed and gave it a try.

"Jane, I miss you. You're the woman of my dreams, and I am coming to get you."

Mann stood up from his chair and straightened out his blue blazer.

Jane smiled, but the smile quickly faded. What Mann had done to her last Thursday was totally unacceptable. Mann had left her sitting alone at the dinner table at The Sun Dial restaurant that overlooked every building in the city. She had sat there as the restaurant slowly rotated, not enjoying the telescopic view of the surrounding cities, and watching the busy traffic on interstate 75 dwindle as the orange sun disappeared in the west. The city lights came on as the sky darkened. Quincy, the waiter, had poured several glasses of wine. When she could not take anymore of the waiting, he provided her with a free bottle. Jane had not forgotten that terrible feeling.

"On Thursday night, you stood me up. A fiancé should not stand up the lady of his dreams."

Jane stood up from the rock and made her case to an invisible jury.

"I sent you a text message," Mann replied as he entered the elevator. "My cousin's birthday party ran—"

Jane snapped at the admission.

"Mann, your text message said that you were working late on a city project!" Jane Wright yelled as her heart skipped.

"Umm! Uhh," Mann stuttered as he pressed the letter 'H' on the control panel of the elevator.

"Stop stuttering, and get your lie straight!"

Mann cleared his throat and gathered himself to make his response without stuttering. However, his voice still cracked when he spoke. He had told one lie too many. In essence, Mann felt it was time to come clean. At least he could enjoy the alluring nightlife of Atlanta without a guilty conscious.

"I...I...I have been seeing a lot of people," Mann confessed as the door of the elevator opened and he walked towards the helicopter that was waiting for him.

"You bastard," Jane screeched as she broke into a sprint, dashing through the woods like a fleeting deer.

As she ran, thoughts of how she had been faithful to Mann for years flowed through her mind. She ran and cried until no more tears could drip from her stinging eyes. The only thing that remained in her was the desire to make Mann hurt worse than any man had ever been hurt before. Suddenly, she became aware that Mann was still on the phone.

"Jane! Jane! Jane!" Mann shouted through the phone.

Jane stopped running and slowly raised her cell phone to her ear. Her arms were shaking and her lips trembled. Jane listened.

"Jane, speak to me," Mann cried out as he heard her raspy breathing. "Jane, talk to me, baby," Mann pleaded.

"I am going to kill you," Jane slowly spoke in a threatening manner.

Mann licked his lips as he heard the seriousness of the threat. However, he could not let Jane suffer by herself. There was no telling what harm she would do to herself in such an isolated place. He nodded his head for his pilot to take off. The least he could do was bring her back to civilization where she could be around friends, family, and, of course, sign that multimillion dollar contract with *Eyez* magazine for next year.

"Jane, I'm—"

Jane did not wait to hear the pathetic apology. She pitched her cell phone at a heap of rocks. It slammed into a million little pieces.

"Jane, are you okay?" Mann shouted as he heard the crash of the phone.

There was no reply. Bad thoughts began to manifest in Mann's selfish mind. What if he had caused her to jump into a ravine? He could go to jail for murder! Mann quickly accessed the GPS database on his cell phone. The pink triangle of Jane's whereabouts had shifted about a mile west of her original location. That was where he would begin his search.

"Rice, how long will it take for us to make it too this location?" Mann asked as he downloaded the coordinates to the pilot's navigation system.

"Thirty minutes. No more, no less," Rice replied as he lowered his dark shades.

"Make it happen," Mann responded.

The helicopter sped away. Mann gazed out the window of the helicopter as the towering buildings of the Westin Peachtree Plaza, the Promenade One, and Inforum become a blur. As the helicopter skimmed away from the skyline of the city, Mann reminisced about all of the good times and the bad times. Even after all of the lies, he did care. Mann just hoped he had the chance to tell Jane how he felt in person.

Jane hurried to see if she could put the device back together. The phone was her only form of communication while out in the wilderness. She picked up the shattered pieces of the phone and attempted to put them back together, but the attempt was futile.

"Agggh," Jane screamed in frustration.

She wiped her eyes and discovered that she was in unexplored territory. In her twelve years of visiting her father's cabin, she had never seen this part of the mountain. The bushes were thicker and wilder, and no animals lingered there.

"I hate you, Mann," Jane shouted as she held the broken pieces of the phone in her hands.

Only one word echoed throughout the woods.

"Hate! Hate! Hate!"

Jane collapsed to her knees, sobbing until the warm sun broke through a fluffy cloud and beamed on her neck. It was hotter than ever. She jerked her hands from her face and shielded her eyes from the glare. Suddenly, the bushes around her faded from green to yellow.

"What in the world?" Jane muttered.

She watched as the grass withered away, revealing a heap of stones that had been covered up over the years. Suddenly an object at the base of the heap of rocks caught her eye. It was two feet high and two feet wide. The object resembled a marker shaped like an arrowhead. Jane crawled on her hands and knees toward the object, drawn by its mysterious presence.

"An ancient arrowhead marker," Jane spoke slowly as she studied its triangular shape and ran her fingers along its sides.

The arrowhead nicked the side of her finger.

"Ouch! Still sharp," Jane muttered as she put her finger in her mouth.

Jane's eyes focused and she looked past the arrowhead marker and became aware that the heap of stones actually covered a larger granite stone. She could see strange markings at the top of a chunk of granite. Jane studied the strange markings and was intrigued.

"These markings are of an ancient language," Jane muttered as she began to recall her archeology class at Georgia Tech before her model career had blossomed.

Jane leapt to her feet and commenced pushing the smaller stones away. After half an hour, the full surface of a granite rock was revealed. After a short moment, she quickly identified the language of the Iroquois civilization.

"This is a sacred burial site of the Cherokee Indians."

She ran her fingers over the scratchy characters, feeling the shallow grooves of the characters.

Jane completely understood the importance of this find and knew that she needed to make sure she had the best translation. The find could earn her the Nobel Peace Prize. She carefully studied the characters, seeking the best translation.

"Behind this rock rests the cowboy named Life and his wolf known as Midnight. They are servants of the wheel within the wheel," Jane translated, speaking softly.

Jane briefly reflected on the symbolic representation of the 'wheel within the wheel', the unbreakable force within a force. The sun became hotter, but Jane continued with diligence. The moment was hers and hers only.

"The arrowhead marker represents their bravery," Jane continued to translate as she wiped the sweat from her brow. "They restored peace to our land and saved the world from destruction. They put the most dangerous members of the Legion, known as Death, Deprivation, and Desire, back into the diamonds."

The last sentence sent chills down Jane's spine. She wiped

her brow again. The sun seemed to be right over her, beaming only on her.

"Who could put Death, Deprivation, and Desire back in the diamonds?"

At that moment, a cloud passed over the sun, casting an eerie shadow across the rock. The sun lost his power, and Jane felt no more heat. The shadow had taken over.

A mountain lion roared somewhere in the woods.

It was a sound that made the strongest man feel vulnerable, and Jane became scared. However, she was persistent. She had to finish the translation no matter what dangers were near.

"The diamonds must be de—," Just as she was about to say the word 'destroyed', the large boulder crumbled to dust. Jane leapt back, eyes wide and heart pounding as the rising cloud settled.

"Narley, dude," Jane gasped as she peered at the opening of the cave.

She quickly extracted her flashlight and pocket recorder from her backpack. She shone the beam inside the cave. It was dark and a rotting odor escaped from within.

Jane gagged from the vile scent.

Jane wiped her mouth and prepared to proceed with the documentation procedure.

"Jane's log: It is approximately 12:45 p.m. on October 11, 2001," she spoke in a calm voice as she started the documentation process. "I have just discovered an ancient Indian burial cave. I am about to enter."

She entered the cave, shining the light here and there. She noticed the walls of the underground void.

"Jane's log: The giant granite rock tightly sealed the cave and provided a perfect environment to slow decay," Jane recorded.

Jane traveled deeper into the cave. She had not gone far when she discovered deep grooves on the floor of the cave. She looked closer and saw something white on the cave floor. Jane inched nearer and discovered that it was the skeleton of a canine and not too far away was a bundle of tattered clothing. Jane grimaced at the skeleton of the canine.

"Jane's log: I have just found the skeleton of a canine and, based on the size of the animal's bones and fangs, it was a wolf," Jane speculated as she examined the skeleton closer.

Jane concentrated. The backbone of the wolf seemed to have been crushed in three places near the middle region.

"Only massive blunt trauma could have crushed the vertebrae in such a way," Jane said.

Jane bit down on her lower lip and turned her attention toward the clothing. The clothing seemed to have once been black leather.

"This was probably a nice get-up. It probably predates the 1850s but was just in time for the 70's...wait, there seems to be the remains of a cowboy hat." Jane carefully cast aside the deteriorated material.

She examined the effects closer. She found two rusty .45 caliber revolvers, a tarnished sword, a bag of ball bearings, and a rusty s-shaped glaive like the vampire hunter used in the movie *Blade* to hurl at fleeing vampires. Jane removed the items from the clothing and discovered something remarkable— the remains of a human skeleton.

"Oh, my God! The skeleton is still intact," Jane gasped into the recorder as she viewed the brown-stained skull, sternum, ribs, pelvis, femur, fibula, and bony feet.

This was definitely the find of the century. The old revolvers and the language on the rock confirmed an approximate date around the 1800s. Jane steadied her voice and held the recorder closer to her mouth. She wanted this recording to be as clear and concise as possible.

"I want this to be clearly understood. A cowboy and a wolf were buried alive."

Suddenly, the skeleton's bony hand opened and revealed three small diamond figurines: a black diamond shaped like the head of a jackal, a sky blue diamond shaped like the head of a ram, and a yellow diamond shaped like head of a saber tooth tiger. This latter figurine attracted Jane's eye.

"I wonder who could have made this beautiful jewelry. There wasn't a diamond sculpting machine until the early 1900s,"Jane pondered as she picked up the yellow diamond figurine and placed it in her pocket.

Suddenly, Jane felt the need to want, to wish, to crave all things as the power of the yellow diamond took over her.

"I-I feel all that is in the world!" Jane shouted in the dimly lit cave as she felt a rush of energy in her body.

The spiders, centipedes, and scorpions that lurked in the darkness were drawn toward her. However, Jane did not take heed of the creeping arachnids. She desired more of the feeling of domination. All of a sudden, she became aware of the presence of the other two diamonds. Immediately, Jane felt threatened and wanted to destroy them!

"The Diamonds of Legion will serve me or be broken," Jane bellowed as she glowered over the crystal figurines not sure which one to grasp first.

Then, she made up her mind. Jane grasped both of them.

Right when her hand touched the figurines, the cave spun into a blur, and she passed out. Bearing more than one diamond of Legion was a burden that no mortal could carry. Jane laid there on the ground floor of the cave with arachnids biting her. Unbeknownst to her, Jane had uncovered the most dangerous members of Legion, and one of the monsters was on the verge of being released from its prison.

Jane opened her eyes then closed them. The light was not golden like sunlight but was artificial, lacking the essence to sustain life. Jane was in a private wing at the Center for Disease Containment. The director at the CDC, Dr. Francois, owed Mann a favor from the past. When Mann had called him up, frantically talking about how he needed to bring his girlfriend in for the emergency treatment of arachnid bites, he almost packed his bags and left town. However, paybacks for under the table governmental allowances sometimes included things such as secret medical attention. Now, Jane was almost conscious.

"She is coming to, Mann. Her vital signs are picking up," Dr. Francois spoke in his proper medical voice that he used when advising patients of the results of their tests.

Dr. Francois stood up from his computer terminal. He was a man of medium height and was slim with narrow shoulders. He walked over to the nearby mirror and glanced at his balding head. There seemed to be new growth. His miracle hair tonic was working!

"Hair is happiness. In about six months, I am going to be six times happy," Dr. Francois said as he pulled a stick of gum from his coat pocket and watched Mann approach the monitor.

"Doctor, have you ever heard of anyone trying to commit suicide by crawling into a hole full of spiders and scorpions?" Mann asked as he remotely observed Jane's recovery.

"Who knows what happens upstairs in these models' heads when they gain a pound or two," Dr. Francois replied as he pointed to his baldhead. "Everyone knows true beauty comes from within."

"Not true," Mann responded. "True beauty comes from doctors who can perform cosmetic surgery!"

"You should have married my fourth wife! She was practically made in China," Dr. Francois laughed.

Mann patted the doctor on his back and turned around.

"Keep her sedated until I come back."

Dr. Francois nodded his head and pressed a red button. A cloud of sleeping gas was jetted into the room. In seconds, Jane had fallen back to sleep.

"And where are you going?" Dr. Francois inquired.

"I am going to personally notify Jane's parents in Bonanza about her condition," Mann said as he picked up his briefcase.

"Her parents still stay in that decaying place? Those houses were built in the 1970's."

"Yeah, they still stay there. The property value has been going down due to crime. The city even put a police precinct with a SWAT team on the edge of the neighborhood."

"That's a super-neighborhood watch. Why doesn't Jane just buy her family a new house?"

"Sometimes it's hard to leave the ghetto, even when you have a one-way ticket out," Mann replied as the automated doors opened.

Dr. Francois nodded his head and continued to monitor his

high-profile client. In the meanwhile, Mann trotted toward his red Mercedes Benz. He tossed his suitcase in the front seat and turned his music loud as he sped out of the parking deck.

"It's my birthday! It's my birthday! I have diamonds! It's my birthday!" Mann ridiculously rapped as he maneuvered his vehicle into the left lane, heading towards I-75.

Earlier, when Mann had loaded Jane onto the helicopter, he had discovered that Jane clutched two beautiful diamonds in her hand. Greed filled his heart at the sight of the priceless jewels, and Mann secretly scooped the jewels into his briefcase. Now, he was headed to an esteemed jeweler in the suburbs to have them appraised.

"These beauties might buy me a yacht and a villa in the Mediterranean Sea," Mann shouted out as he sped south on the interstate from Atlanta.

However, Mann was not aware that the evil powers within the diamonds were organizing a trap for him even as he drove. They were waiting for the chance to make him choose his fate. Mann glanced in his mirror and saw the city fading away. That was the last time Mann would ever see the city of Atlanta and the beautiful model named Jane.

"BEEP! BEEP! BEEP!"

Buzzers blared!

"WERRREEEO! WERRREEEO!"

Fire alarms rang throughout the Center for Disease Containment, but the employees of the wonderful institution cautiously walked through the hallways towards the designated exits as they were trained. However, Dr. Francois stood at his computer monitor, sweat beading up on his baldhead as his fingers raced across the keyboard. Nevertheless, his override codes were producing error messages. The security system had gone haywire!

"C'mon! C'mon, you bastard," Dr. Francois urged as he rolled up the sleeves of his lab coat.

In his moment of panic, Dr. Francois glanced over at the monitor that was connected to Jane's room. The hospital bed had crumbled like a piece of paper, and her room was demolished. The one-ton automatic metal door was crumbled in the adjacent hallway.

Dr. Francois mouthed an obscenity. Jane was nowhere in the room. Unexpectedly, the monitor went black.

"Who could have done this? Who could have freaking done this? I am supposed to be in Switzerland next week," Dr. Francois demanded as he quickly tapped on the keyboard, bringing up more cameras in the private wing.

As the various cameras came up, Dr. Francois could see massive claw scrapes along the walls of the hallways. He studied the trail of abrasions until they reached the door that lead to where he was standing. Immediately, Dr. Francois felt someone standing behind him.

"Hah! Who's there?" Dr. Francois yelled as he wheeled around.

There was nothing but the door and a couch in an adjacent sitting area.

"Whew, I need to rebook my flight for tomorrow," Dr. Francois sighed.

"R-r-run while you have a chance," a feminine voice urged behind him.

Dr. Francois almost jumped out of his skin when he heard the powerful voice behind him. Crouching on the desk behind him was Jane! Dr. Francois stared at her, crouching there in her dirty khaki pants, tee shirt, arms and face littered with bites from the insects that had covered her.

"H-h-how did you get there?" Dr. Francois asked.

"H-her powers of teleportation are minimal while the other diamonds exist," Jane replied in a distant voice as she stretched like a cat.

Dr. Francois frowned as Jane's hands scraped the desktop with her dirty nails. He noticed that her ice blue pupils were fully dilated.

"J-J-ane, snap out of it! You are hallucinating," Dr. Francois begged.

Instead of her expression changing, Jane reached in her pocket and extracted the yellow colored diamond. She held it in her hands as her hair began to flutter in a rouge wind. The yellow diamond began to grow until it was the size of a helmet. Dr. Francois did not believe what he was seeing. He was witnessing an object expanding massively without altering its physical composition.

"The age of man is over," the voice of a little girl from within the large diamond said.

Another alarm went off.

That one was louder and required Dr. Francois's immediate attention. He snapped his head toward the display on another computer monitor. The bold word **'CRITICAL'** flashed in red across the screen. The storage facilities of the most dangerous diseases in the world had been breached. The death toll would be in the millions if he did not reset the system!

"Jane, please stand aside. I have to reset the system or lives will be lost," Dr. Francois pleaded as he rushed forward.

"Jane is no more. There is only Desire," a childlike voice from inside the diamond responded.

Suddenly, Jane snatched Dr. Francois by the shoulder and hurled him across the room.

"WHAM!"

Dr. Francois crashed into a small table and tumbled head over heels.

"Put on the helmet, Jane, and I will grant your wishes," the voice of the little girl advised.

"I only wish to be loved," Jane spoke as she placed the helmet on her head.

"Greater than love, you will be feared," the voice of the little girl responded.

Dr. Francois stared as Jane's clothing morphed into a deep purple robe, and her healthy hands became yellow diamond encrusted claws. Her blonde hair became yellow flames, and her beautiful face became that of a yellow saber tooth tiger. Dr. Francois cringed as yellow flames wreathed around this creature's head that was both beautiful and terrible.

"After one-hundred years, I have returned to the earth," Desire caterwauled as her flaming tail rose.

Dr. Francois glanced at the monitor. The time limit had expired, and the world's most dangerous diseases were released at that very moment. The State Department would soon send troops to bomb the city to keep the deadly contamination from spreading.

"You have doomed us! The army will be here soon to bomb the city," Dr. Francois shouted at the monstrosity.

"Your army is no match for mine," Desire responded as she produced a large golden key from within the deep sleeves of her robe.

"What is that key for?" Dr. Francois yelled as he scrambled to his feet and knocked down a bookshelf.

"This is the Key to the Gates of the Underworld. Today, I will open these Gates of the Underworld, and the monsters will over run the earth! No one will be able to stop me," Desire purred in a sinister voice.

Dr. Francois saw a golden keyhole form in mid-air, and golden energies began to whirl around the key as Desire inserted it in the keyhole.

"Pitiful human, I need servants who can spread quickly," Desire growled.

The monster grabbed Dr. Francois by his lab coat and pulled him closer to her burning face.

Dr. Francois cringed from the heat of the flames as Desire scanned the good doctor's mind for his greatest fear. What she discovered would be excellent for her scheme.

"Human, I will transform you to the undead, and you shall hunger for man-flesh. Those who you scratch or bite will also rise with the hunger," Desire purred.

Dr. Francois cringed as Desire drew him closer.

Her flames singed the skin on his face.

"Before I end your world, tell me something, human," Desire growled.

Her flaming jeweled tail twitched as it tilted in the air behind her.

"A-anything," Dr. Francois responded as he trembled in fear and lost control of his bowel movements.

"Where did your friend take the other Diamonds of Legion?"

Desire roared.

The roar of Desire beat upon Dr. Francois like a headwind and tortured more than his physical form. The roar itself peeled away portions of the doctor's flesh, damning Dr. Francois to become a zombie.

"South! He's heading south," Dr. Francois answered as purple sores began to form on his baldhead. His eyes transformed from brown to yellow.

"Then, that is where I will bury them until I can break them," Desire mumbled as she tossed Dr. Francois to the side.

"Man flesh!" the doctor roared as he sprinted out the doors.

Desire's red eyes gleamed like rubies as she gazed through the walls of the building, watching as the good doctor leapt on a man's back then bit him. In seconds, the man had leapt to his feet, slobbering, and yelling in rage.

"Go and spread, my children," Desire purred.

She intensified her gaze. Her eyesight zoomed across buildings, pedestrians, and settled upon the fast moving interstate. Her feline pupils locked onto the zooming car that carried the precious stones. Then, she peered ahead of the car. There was a bridge that spanned across a river. A watery tomb was sometimes better than a rocky tomb.

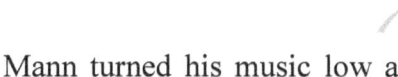

Mann turned his music low as he neared the bridge. For some reason, he felt as if someone was in the car with him. He glanced at the briefcase. There was a need for him to open the briefcase and take out the diamonds. He could not resist the temptation. Mann let go of the steering wheel and opened the briefcase. The two diamonds were glowing!

"Choose or die," the voice of a little girl from the black diamond that was shaped like a jackal's head spoke.

Mann chose, but, as he reached toward the black diamond, his car veered toward a sports utility vehicle. The driver reacted too late.

"Watch it, you moron," the driver yelled in his Bostonian accent as his wheels locked.

Mann's car careened into the adjacent sports utility vehicle!

The impact caused Mann's car to flip over and smash through the guardrail on the bridge. His air bags deployed, busting his nose as the compartments struck his face. However, the front end of Mann's car hung over the edge of the bridge.

"Heeeelp!" Mann screamed as he felt the car tilting forward.

His head was hurting, and his vision was blurred from the smoke of the airbags.

All around him, he heard the sound of cars coming to screeching halts. Mann remotely heard the doors slamming and people loudly talking.

A siren went up in the air.

"Hurry and pull him out before the car falls off the bridge and into the river," a lady cried out.

"Check to see if the other guy is okay," a man cried out.

Mann sensed himself about to lose consciousness. He reached forward and grasped the sky blue diamond of Deprivation. As Mann placed the diamond in his blazer pocket, two men seized him and jerked him out of the wrecked car. Just before he passed out, the car slid off the edge of the bridge and plummeted into the river along with the black diamond. Soon, Deprivation would awake and open the master gate to the Underworld.

"Raise the Pyramid and open the master gate. Then, I will trap you there for all eternity, my love! There can be only one ruler!" Desire purred from miles away.

Desire watched as Mann was hauled into an ambulance and carried away. As this event transpired, all media attention converged upon the city of Atlanta where a humanitarian disaster was unfolding. People were falling dead by the droves because of airborne diseases. The president ordered the city to be destroyed.

"I want to get this part as close to right as possible," Ms. Ellen contemplated as she continued to record in her journal.

Ms. Ellen slowed her writing. She bit her lip as she recollected her father's last moments with her. Ms. Ellen got up from the table, poured herself a glass of water then sat back at the table. She closed her eyes and remembered before she began to write.

Inside a ranch-styled house in the neighborhood of Bonanza laid a man on his deathbed. Sitting at his side was his daughter, Ms. Ellen. It was the man's final hour on this earth. Old age had come to claim him at the age of 105. Among the accolades of his lifetime, the greatest was that he was a very respected clairvoyant.

"What is that on the monitor, Ellen?" Mr. Scott inquired in his raspy southern voice where the "th" sound was replaced with a "d" sound.

"Something about the diseases being released and people dying in Atlanta," Ms. Ellen replied as she picked up her radio and pressed the button to speak on all channels.

A crisp alert chirped, indicating that her signal was ready to be broadcast.

"E-Ellen, I dreamed last night! It was as clear as day," Mr. Scott spoke in his raspy voice.

Ms. Ellen nodded her head and put the radio down. She knew that if her father had a dream it was important and that she needed to listen. His dreams had assisted her with completing unsolved cases and even helped her avoid dangerous situations.

"What was the dream, Dad? Was it bad?" Ms. Ellen inquired as she rubbed her father's baldhead.

Her father swallowed and his Adam's apple moved like a buoy in ocean water. Her father had survived heart attacks and other debilitating ailments, and there was no shame in the way he was passing today. He had seen his daughter grow to be a very respected woman.

"I dreamed of thangs with shiny heads! One had a shiny head like a jackal, a ram, and a saber tooth tiger! Shiny like them earrings I bought you fo' yo' birthday," Mr. Scott said.

"You mean shiny like diamonds," Ms. Ellen replied.

"Yeah, like diamonds."

Ms. Ellen pulled out a notepad and began to write down her father's vision.

"Notify your SWAT to take all the guns from the Army surplus and the sporting goods store. Take them to the precinct."

"Dad—"

"Just listen, Ellen! Stop bein' hard-headed! Get as many people to Bonanza as possible before 3:30 p.m. today."

"What about the basement of the church?"

"Use dem contraptions only for the final battle."

"What about the diseases in Atlanta?" Ms. Ellen asked.

Mr. Scott closed his eyes and took a series of deep breaths. Ms. Ellen became afraid. The nurse had warned her to be aware of the deep breaths. Deep breaths always preceded the final breath.

"My time has come," Mr. Scott said in his raspy southern tone. "Ellen, God will take care of the diseases, but there is something else."

"W-what is it?" Ms. Ellen inquired.

"Give me a pencil and paper."

Ms. Ellen quickly picked up a nearby pencil and pad of paper. She handed it to her father, and he quickly began to draw triangles that looked like the roofs of houses.

"What is that, Dad?"

"It is the neighborhood, Bonanza. The land will rise from Panhandle Road to Tara Boulevard to Tara Road."

"What do you mean 'rise'?"

"It will look like those rocks out west…the kind John Wayne used to stand on to see the land."

"Umm, a plateau."

"Yeah. Then, the pyramid will rise and a wall will surround Bonanza. The earth will shake at 3:30 p.m. today," Mr. Scott warned.

"Great. An earthquake." Ms. Ellen rubbed a hand through her curly hair.

However, Mr. Scott held her other hand.

"The earth will shake, and the monsters from the Underworld will come," Mr. Scott gasped.

Ms. Ellen jotted down the information as she held her father's hand. His grip was strong. Ms. Ellen glanced at the monitor that evaluated her father's heart rate. His heartbeats were spreading further apart.

"WHEN THE COWBOY COMES WITH HIS WOLF, TAKE THEM TO THE BASEMENT OF THE CHURCH. HE IS THE ONLY ONE WHO CAN SAVE THE WORLD," Mr. Scott gasped one final time.

Ms. Ellen briefly reflected on the mural that her father painted along the basement walls of the church. The mural depicted a cowboy dressed in black, leading a cavalry against an army of monsters.

"G-good bye, D-dad," Ms. Ellen wept as she held her father's hand while he passed away.

Suddenly, her radio began to chirp. Ms. Ellen quickly picked up the radio and answered the call.

"This is Ms. Ellen."

"This is Sgt. Steve. We need you in Bonanza where an ambulance has crashed into a building," Sgt. Steve reported above a loud rumbling sound.

"The ambulance is making all of that noise?" Ms. Ellen asked as she pulled the sheet over Mr. Scott's face.

"You won't believe this! A Pyramid is rising from the ground! It's coming up out of the ground right now!"

"Sgt. Steve, get a hold of your nerves!"

"Yes, ma'am."

"Go secure the army surplus store and the sporting goods store! We are going Code Red! I am about to broadcast on all channels! Ten-4!"

"Ten-4."

Ms. Ellen ended the call and then glanced at her deceased father.

I promise to give you a funeral, Ms. Ellen thought to herself.

Ms. Ellen put on her bulletproof vest and strapped her rifle to her back. She clicked on the radio and made the announcement that caused Bonanza to be the last refuge of mankind.

"Code Red! The Bugle is blown! Direct all civilians to the neighborhood of Bonanza! Bring all weapons and ammo to the precinct! This is Ms. Ellen speaking! I repeat. The Bugle is blown! Withdraw from other areas! Direct all civilians to the neighborhood of Bonanza where it is safe! My father has just given me his last vision. The monsters are coming," she announced as she walked out of her home and hopped into her squad car.

10

Tears were in Ms. Ellen's eyes as she dotted her last period, ending the narrative that she had lived and was living. She laid her head on the table and cried herself to sleep. Not too far away, something magical was happening. Not only would these next two days be days to remember but also days to die for.

Chapter 1

The Return of the Cowboy and the Wolf

The day was dreary. Dark gray clouds were scattered across the sky, and the rain clouds blotted out the sun as the rain fell steadily. The muddy streets in the southern antebellum town of New Hampton were as empty as a ghost town. Inside a newly reconstructed grand saloon, known as the Insane Kitty, a green-eyed gunslinger stood on a wobbly table as he boasted of his success before a crowd of cut-throat bandits and their notorious leader.

The gunslinger was dressed in dark brown jeans and a tan shirt with the image of the grim reaper crawling from a dark hole. Along his slim waist were additional clips of bullets; on each hip loosely hung a black nine-millimeter. The gunslinger knew if the leader of this elite band of misfits was amused by his tale, then he would be the newest addition to the Fifty Marauders. However, if the leader of the misfits was bored, then he would be hanging from the gallows by sunrise. The gunslinger raised his voice an octave and delivered the punch line that would hopefully make him famous.

"Ten men of the law cornered me in an alley. I slapped two in the face with a broom and when they drew iron, ten men got shot dead with my two little girls, Nina and Mina," the gunslinger shouted as he gestured with his two pistols.

"Yeah," an onlooker cried out.

"The only thing faster than my bullets is my hand turning up a liquor bottle!"

The crowd of misfits began to murmur as they sat under the light of a grand chandelier. The gunslinger heard one of the misfits ask another what his name was. The gunslinger grasped a flask of brown liquor and took a swallow to clear his throat. The liquor that rushed down his throat was hotter than summer heat.

"Ten Shot's the name until the world shakes again!"

The phrase 'until the world shakes again' had become popular among the citizens of New Hampton. However, other phrases like 'Slave' or 'Shine' held an opposite polarity. As some survivors of the earthquakes had attempted to restore their normal way of life, others, like Ten Shot, had slid deeper into the abyss of hatred, committing the most gruesome crimes against humanity. In New Hampton, slavery and genocide were occurring at a rapid rate. The slim green-eyed gunslinger knew that slavery was the new vehicle for the town's economy, but even more valuable would be a hired gun protecting the cargo.

"Master Pau, if you choose me as your gun, then I will bring New Hampton stronger slaves. New Hampton will become the slave capital of the new world," Ten Shot assured the older man with thin white hair who sat in the midst of the bandits.

The downpour intensified outside, and more people began to stream into the saloon where playing cards had become synonymous with playing with your life.

"Ahh choo," sneezed the older man who was dressed in a collared shirt that fit tight around his plump belly.

No one blessed the man. Ten Shot watched the man wipe a blot of yellow phlegm and snot on his pants. Ten Shot stared at the man, and the man stared back. Suddenly, the man broke his stare and addressed the gunslinger in a heavy southern accent where the 'th' sound was pronounced as 'da'.

"Ten Shot, I require you to join my Fifty Marauders," Master Pau said after careful consideration. "We need a gunman with your expertise! Munsters are everywhere in dem bushes and what not!"

The Fifty Marauders nodded their heads in agreement and a low murmur of gratitude grew among the crowd. Ten Shot also nodded his head and, like a well-conditioned speaker, he waited until the murmur died down before responding.

"Much obliged, Master. I will consider the offer," Ten Shot responded as he took another swallow from his bottle of liquor, hoping to gain some ground for negotiation.

"Consider it fo' what? Dis is why you requested an audience with me, boy."

Master Pau shoved a barely clothed female Asian slave to the floor and forcefully pressed his muddy boot on her head, smashing her face against the filthy floor.

"Uggh," the woman cried out.

A cold chill ran down Ten Shot's spine as he saw the woman's face being pressed against a piece of chewed tobacco. Ten Shot could actually see the brown juices seeping from the wad of tobacco and onto her soft cheek.

"I am Master Pau, da man in New Hampton! No one considers my offers!"

Ten Shot flashed a sinister grin, displaying a portion of his teeth.

"Just know that if I bring you stronger 'Shines', then I will be number two in command," Ten Shot ordered as he hurled his empty bottle of liquor against the batwing doors of the saloon where it shattered into little pieces.

"No one has ever made a demand to Master Pau, not even my mother when I took my time coming into this wicked world!"

"Thanks for the tidbit about your mother's pregnancy, but I really don't care."

The token of disrespect was felt throughout the crowd, but, rather than let his anger explode, he simply dug up his nose with his forefinger.

"I could have you broken into beaucoup pieces like dat bottle you just smashed."

The Fifty Marauders' hands cocked their pistols and shotguns, ready to put more holes in the disrespectful gunslinger than a slice of Swiss cheese. In the corner adjacent to the sixty foot wide elongated bar that housed plenty of alcoholic beverages, a slim brown haired piano player ceased his wonderful playing.

"Finally, a break," the piano player said as he heard the unified clicking of the guns.

Ten Shot pivoted around with his back toward the bandits and crossed his thin arms.

"If you are going to shoot me, then do it. Send me to the next world!"

Ten Shot gazed outside the saloon and into the stormy weather. He was not afraid of dying for what he wanted. Master Pau wiped a green booger on his shirt. He liked this kid for one reason. The kid had nothing to loose.

"Fifty Marauders, you may relax," Master Pau declared as he lifted his boot up from the woman's head.

The Fifty Marauders put away their weapons. However, the slave did not get up. She knew that if she moved without permission Master Pau would cut off her hand or worse.

"Ten Shot, you drive a hard bargain," Master Pau advised in a loud scruffy voice.

"I live to die for what I want," Ten Shot replied.

Master Pau quickly signaled for the servants to serve him.

"Live you shall! Welcome to the Fifty Marauders, you sly fox! Come and sit under the chandelier with us!"

Ten Shot turned his attention to the magnificent brass chandelier and beheld the hundreds of crystal shards and kerosene lanterns that were held in place by a thick steel cable. No one but the Fifty Marauders were privileged to bask in its brilliance.

"Much obliged," Ten Shot replied to Master Pau.

A group of malnourished slaves quickly answered the summons of Master Pau. Eight men and four females of various nationalities carefully walked to and fro each table, careful of not letting any of their dirty garments touch the Marauders. They were emotionally battered and physically malnourished. Master Pau had labeled them 'Shines' because of how their foreheads gleamed with sweat when toiling.

"Ten Shot, I give you dese 'Shines' to serve you. If dey do not serve you to your liking, they will be lynched from the Trees

O'Life," Master Pau proclaimed in a proud voice.

"Certainly," Ten Shot replied.

"Don't thank me. Thank the piano player," Master Pau spoke in his scruffy voice. "I want to hear 'Camp Town Doodah'!"

The piano player commenced to play the classic Camp Town ragtime music on the rickety grand piano.

"Camp Town girls, sing this song," Master Pau joyously sang as tobacco spit flew out of his mouth. "Camp Town races five miles long...Do Dah...Do Dah Day!"

His bandits took up the song, crashing bottles and spilling liquor onto the floor without a care. The 'Shines' would have plenty of work to do that night. Ten Shot did not participate in the shenanigans. He rubbed the black diamond that was in his pocket. Ever since he had found the good luck charm on the banks of the Flint River, his life had changed for the better.

"Ten Shot, you shall bring me da strongest 'Shines' from here to Timbuktu and dey will work under moonlight and sunlight," Master Pau shouted as he stood in the midst of his bandits.

Ten Shot smiled as he felt the sensation of success. He sat down in a nearby chair, grinning from ear to ear.

"Even God will turn away his eye when he sees the empire of New Hampton," Master Pau continued to boast.

Outside the saloon, a loud clap of thunder boomed. The patrons inside the saloon do not take heed of the thunder. They continued to party. Ten Shot leaned back in his chair and glimpsed a fat curly red-haired wheelchair bound bartender drunkenly bursting out in laughter as she gave one of her patrons the middle finger. Ten Shot liked the bartender's rude behavior. She was the type of woman he needed in his life— handicapped, rude, and a master at mixing drinks!

"Dance to the music! Dance to the music," Master Pau chanted as he did the jitter-bug.

"For a person who is overweight, Master Pau has moves, but watch me," Ten Shot shouted as his competitive nature took control.

"Yeee haw!" Master Pau shouted as he began to swing his arms out in a circular fashion.

"Yeeee haw!" Ten Shot shouted as he leapt on the table and performed an uncoordinated two-step.

Suddenly, a cowboy strolled through the batwing doors and stood in the elevated foyer of the saloon that overlooked the dinning room where the party raged on. He was a tall black man with a brown skin tone. He was dressed in black leather pants, black shirt, black cowboy boots, and a black cowboy hat with a genuine black leather trench coat. Around his neck was a black triangular shaped scarf. A slight discoloration spanned from one side of his cheek to the other. The discoloration appeared to be an uncanny birthmark.

"Greetings and salutations, partner," the cowboy politely spoke.

Everyone heard the voice. It was strong. It was true. Ten Shot whirled around on the wobbly table at the same time the piano player ceased his playing and beheld the cowboy standing in the foyer. Ten Shot noticed the cowboy's amber colored eyes beneath the shadow of his hat. They had an eerie glow about them. However, Ten Shot was undaunted. He licked his lips as he dropped his right hand to his nine millimeter. Either the 'Shine' was here to serve Master Pau or he was here to die!

"Do you know where you are, cow**boy**?" Ten Shot asked as he emphasized the word 'boy'.

Ten Shot was ecstatic when he discovered that the cowboy

wore no pistols or any other weapons. Ten Shot was ready to give lesson 101 in 'Why You Should Not Bring a Gun to a Gunfight'!

"Is this the wonderful town of New Hampton?" the cowboy asked as he popped his knuckles that were covered in black leather gloves with holes along the knuckles.

"The 'Shine' has some type of intelligence," Ten Shot answered as he grabbed a nearby slave by the back of his head.

Ten Shot spit in the face of the slave.

"Stranger, we have plenty of work in the Hole with the other 'Shines'! So go ahead. Hang up your coat and take a load off!"

Everyone laughed except the cowboy. Master Pau let the laughter die down and then called out to the bartender.

"Betsy Sue, get your gut-buster out if you want to shoot with the Fifty Marauders! It's going to be fireworks for you, cowboy!" Master Pau yelled as he jerked out his 30-30 rifle from beneath his table.

There was a loud clicking noise as the Fifty Marauders cocked their guns. Betsy Sue swiftly reached up under the bar and removed her sawed-off shotgun from under its secret place. She flipped it open to make sure it was loaded.

"Let the good times roll," Betsy Sue screamed as she slammed her shotgun closed and aimed at the cowboy.

"Master Pau, let me rid you of this rat," Ten Shot requested.

"Be creative or else," Master Pau said as he gave his men the signal to stand down.

Ten Shot speedily thought of how he would cripple the cowboy. In the meanwhile, the eldest and wisest 'Shine' known as Ms. Pook had called for all of the 'Shines' to meet in the largest dirt floor shed. She had ordered a single candle to be placed on a windowsill, facing toward the town. Not only had a storm come to Hampton, but also the savior of mankind had come to give them freedom.

"Now, you 'shine'—"

Ten Shot's ignorant sentence was stopped short as a jet-black wolf with yellow eyes waltzed under the batwing doors and stood beside the cowboy.

A low ferocious growl resonated from the wolf as it bared two large fangs.

Ten Shot noticed that both the cowboy and the wolf were as dry as a wood chips.

"Who are you?" Ten Shot gasped as he drew his pistols.

The unarmed patrons of the Insane Kitty took cover.

"Put your guns down, Ten Shot," the cowboy ordered as thunder shook the structure of the saloon.

Drinking glasses and plates fell from the shelves and broke as a whirring wind howled outside.

"You and your dog are about to be put in a pine pox," Ten Shot yelled as he clicked the safety on the guns.

"A pine box sounds lovely compared to sealed in a cave, doesn't it, Midnight?" The cowboy patted the wolf on its head.

The wolf snarled and displayed more than forty-two sharp teeth.

"Ten Shot, the plague is on you, and those towns you traveled through are now filled with the living dead! Do not condemn this place," the cowboy demanded.

Master Pau snapped his head toward Ten Shot. He had encountered the undead before and barely escaped. They were quick, agile, and hideous! He always wondered if there was a carrier who infected others.

"Ten Shot, you're da dag gone carrier," Master Pau charged as a stream of slobber flew from his mouth.

"No! This cowboy is off his freaking horse," Ten Shot retaliated.

"Ten Shot, destroy the black diamond and reclaim your humanity," the cowboy instructed.

Ten Shot was shocked. How did he know about the black diamond? No one had ever seen his good luck charm.

"The black diamond is mine," Ten Shot yelled as he aimed at the cowboy's chest.

"Ten Shot, the power of the black diamond is already changing these people into the undead! What would a man profit if he gained the world but lost his soul?" the cowboy reasoned.

"Cowboy, perhaps you will be a priest in the next world," Ten Shot replied.

"The next world is not for me or you," the cowboy spoke. "Ten Shot, let me reintroduce myself. My name is Life, and this is my friend, Midnight!"

At the sound of the names, Ten Shot's facial expression tightened and contracted.

"Cowboy, I really don't care who you are, but thank you for coming! Good- bye," Ten Shot replied as he braced himself while standing on the table as he began to apply pressure to the triggers.

"Sic'em, Midnight," Life ordered.

With a burst of uncanny speed, the wolf darted through the air and pounced upon Ten Shot before he could fire his handguns.

The wooden table was flattened from the impact. Quickly, Ten Shot dropped the gun that was in his left hand and grasped the nape of the wolf's neck just in time. A second later, the wolf would have ripped him another.

"Ten Shot, that mutt almost bit yer neck," a drunken bystander yelled.

Ten Shot jerked his head to the left.

Ten Shot snapped his head to the right.

Warm saliva dripped down Ten Shot's hands as he held off the lunging wolf with his left hand while trying to aim with the other.

"Toss' em off yer gut, Ten Shot! He only weighs 'bout two nickels and one dime," the drunken bystander laughed as he gulped down a mug of beer.

"H-he's t-too h-heavy," Ten Shot gasped as his arms shook from the tremendous weight of the wolf.

"You're weak! There is no room in the Marauders for weaklings," Master Pau angrily yelled as he aimed his rifle at the wolf.

Ten Shot was not about to miss an opportunity to join this exclusive group. He pulled together all of his remaining strength and shoved the gun in front of the wolf's muzzle!

"E-eat on this, y-you m-mutt."

However, the wolf was fluent in all languages, and it understood what Ten Shot's intentions were. It slapped Ten Shot's gun into the crowd. The drunken bystander who had been laughing at the foray picked up the weapon. It was mangled beyond comprehension!

"Somebody help Ten Shot! Marauders, help him," a lady

screamed in the crowd as Ten Shot barely dodged another snap.

"Grrrrgghh! It's time to end this," Midnight snarled.

"Oh-h my God! The wolf talks!"

"I do more than talk! Watch!"

Suddenly, the wolf bit down on Ten Shot's left forearm and viciously shook its head from right to left.

"Aggh, it's scraping the bone! Somebody shoot the mangy dog before it rips off my arm," Ten Shot screamed.

The wolf's fangs ground against the bone in Ten Shot's forearm.

"I don't want to die!" Ten Shot screamed.

This fear of dying triggered the hidden power within the black diamond, awakening the monster known as Death.

The black diamond briefly flashed in Ten Shot's pocket, and those standing nearby were affected by its power as they were transformed into the living dead.

"Now, I won't feel guilty," Life muttered as he noticed the skin tone of the Fifty Marauders alter from a lively hue to a dead gray color.

Even as Master Pau aimed his rifle at the wolf, his eyes glazed over as they bulged from their sockets. His gray skin rotted away as puss oozed from the sores on his face. An undying hunger for man-flesh filled his body.

"Maaaan fleeeessh," Master Pau moaned.

At that moment, another crack of thunder shook the saloon. Midnight leapt off of Ten Shot as Betsy Sue jerked in surprise and wildly shot with her eyes closed. When she opened her eyes, she became aware that she had blasted Master Pau's right shoulder! However, there was no bloodshed. There was only a fiery ash of hellfire that was released!

"My shoulder! My shoulder!" Mater Pau screamed as his white hair withered away.

"What is going on?" Betsy Sue spoke in a low voice as she saw the ashes drift from the devastating wound.

"Human, I will bite off your head! Rgggh!"

Master Pau's mouth stretched wide enough to decapitate her. Betsy Sue closed her eyes and shot again as Master Pau lunged at her. When she opened her eyes, there was a pile of smoldering ash.

"Heaven, have mercy! The dead walks," Betsy Sue muttered as she lowered the sawed off shotgun onto her lap.

Ten Shot slowly opened his eyes. As his eyesight refocused, he saw something frightening. Above him, sparks flew as the cowboy sawed away at the thick steel cable with a sword.

"Marauders, stop him before he crashes the chandelier," Ten Shot exclaimed as he stared upwards with quaking eyes.

Life was aware of Ten Shot's request. He spun around and swung his sword in a side chop. Ten Shot's eyes widened as Life leapt from the falling chandelier.

"Make wayyyy," Ten Shot shouted as he scrambled to his feet and leapt into the crowd.

The giant chandelier crashed upon most of the Fifty Marauders. Slicing glass shards pelted the bystanders as incinerating flames began to spread across the wooden floor. Around Ten Shot's neck, the black diamond began to glow. After a century, Death was about to be released from its prison.

Betsy Sue dropped her sawed off shotgun as she witnessed

Life somersault from the raised foyer in a single bound, twist through the air, and fire two revolvers similar to the ones in the old westerns. The tail of his black trench coat fluttered in the wind like a cape.

"The cowboy has a gun!" Betsy Sue screamed.

"The cowboy has a gun!" the bystanders echoed as they fled.

Betsy Sue cringed as the cowboy crouched low and blasted the zombie Marauders with a hailstorm of bullets. The barrage of bullets sliced arms, severed legs, and busted heads. Piles of burning ashes were left in the wake of the aftermath.

"He is only attacking the monsters," Betsy Sue spoke as she witnessed the cowboy dart here and there, gunning down the zombies.

The flames and smoke grew, and the people stampeded toward the back door. The scene was surreal for Betsy Sue. No more than twenty minutes ago, she had been serving drinks. Betsy drifted into a daze as she witnessed the mayhem. Just then, the scream of a nearby zombie snapped Betsy Sue from her trance.

"Agghh!!! Get it off of me!!! My leg!! The wolf has me," a zombie Marauder cried out.

Betsy Sue jerked her primitive wheelchair to the left to see the black wolf cruelly gnashing the leg of a zombie Marauder with one devastating slash of its paw then vanish into thin air only to appear before another Marauder, leaving piles of fiery ash.

"Mary, mother of God," Betsy Sue cried out as she crossed her forehead with her forefinger and searched for a quick escape route besides the backdoor where a gruesome bottleneck effect was beginning to occur.

The wheels of Betsy Sue's wheelchair screeched as she

maneuvered toward the crowd.

She stopped when she viewed people being shoved against the walls and trampled on. Right when she was about to give up hope, Betsy Sue spied a narrow path that lead to an unnoticed side door. Betsy Sue would have rather been shot to death than face the black wolf!

"C'mon on, Betsy! Go as fast as you can," Betsy Sue motivated herself in a wavering voice.

Betsy's obese arms began pumping as she quickly traversed across the hardwood floor, swerving left then right and around the burning heaps of ash and bodies. Just as she was about to reach the door, Ten Shot dashed through the tendrils of smoke. He saw the door also, and Life saw him!

"I'm glad to see you are finished playing possum," Life growled as he locked Ten Shot in his sights.

Life zoomed in ahead of Ten Shot and was about to blast the door handle when he heard a door bang against the wall.

Immediately, Life took evasive action as a group of zombie Marauders appeared on the stairway.

They cocked their rifles and fired.

Betsy Sue glanced over her shoulder to see Life quickly holster his guns and somersault backwards, dodging the gunfire.

"Where did his guns go?" Betsy Sue screamed as the weapons vanished.

Life hurled a silver disc at the riflemen on the stairway.

The zombie Marauders exploded in a fiery heap of ash, and the silver object returned to his hand!

"What does the cowboy want?" Betsy Sue frantically inquired as Ten Shot pushed her wheelchair.

"He came for me, Betsy Sue! I should have given him the

black diamond," Ten Shot answered as a tear trickled down his cheek.

"W-what black diamond?" Betsy Sue frantically asked as Ten Shot brought her wheelchair to a halt.

Ten Shot snatched the diamond from his pocket and held it in his hands, watching it glow and dazzle. Betsy Sue could see the black outline of Ten Shot's bones in his hands as a pale light radiated.

"This is what he came for! He came for this!"

Betsy Sue shielded her eyes as she pleaded with Ten Shot.

"Please throw it away! Please!"

Ten Shot did not heed her. His green eyes were distant as he stared into the pale glow of the black diamond.

"I-I feel the power! The power of Death calls to me," Ten Shot exclaimed in an exasperated voice as he anxiously clutched the precious jewel.

Suddenly, the black diamond that was shaped like a jackal's head expanded in size but not in weight. In seconds, the black diamond had grown from the size of a pendant to the size of a helmet.

"Diamond Bearer, you will not die! Put the helmet on and become Death," the voice of little girl from within the crystal spoke.

Ten Shot obeyed the voice and slipped the black diamond over his head. As soon as he had, a mammoth surge of cylindrical black energy encapsulated Ten Shot and hurled Betsy Sue from her wheelchair.

Betsy Sue's neck broke as she crashed against the wall.

Before she gave up the ghost, she watched Ten Shot's slim body become muscular and encrusted in rocky black diamonds.

His head turned into a jackal's head with a gold and blue helmet protecting his head. Around his massive torso appeared heavy black armor that left his bulging black diamond arms exposed. Along his waist was a red leather belt that held a gigantic black double bladed axe His leather wristbands and thigh pads were embedded with tiny skulls, and the soles of his black sandals were plates of steel.

"The cowboy is not the monster. Ten Shot, you are the monster," Betsy Sue said as Ten Shot's head became a diamond jackal with green eyes and black flames wreathing from its structure.

At the sight of the transformation, Life retreated to a shadowy corner of the smoky saloon where Midnight lingered. They had to regroup on their strategy. Death had been released from the diamond.

"Life, I told you that we should have burned the building down! Now, we have the undead running around, biting people, and making more undead people," Midnight growled.

"So, you were right, and I was wrong. I will give you some beef jerky later," Life replied as he scratched Midnight behind his right ear.

"It's payback time for Death for putting that blemish on your face and breaking my back before you could lock him away in that diamond one hundred years ago," Midnight growled.

Life did not respond to his comrade. He distinctly remembered yelling for help after the avalanche had sealed them inside the cave. Life remembered hoping that the Cherokee shaman would dig them out and the realization that no one was coming to help them. Today, there would not be a replay of those events.

"Midnight, if the gates of the Underworld have been opened, why is Death the last one to escape his prison?" Life whispered.

"That means Desire is up to her old tricks of world domination. She always wanted to be the head honcho of the three," Midnight said as he wiped zombie slime from his muzzle.

"Exactly. We cannot let Death notify them that we have returned and risk a bipolar alliance," Life said.

"Next option: Sneak attack," Midnight snarled.

"That's the best play in the book, partner," Life replied as he rubbed Midnight on the head.

Life stood up, but before he could make his move, Midnight asked him a very important question.

"Life, who brought us back from the Outside? Surely, the Shaman is pushing up daisies by now."

"I don't know, but whoever it was granted us the qualities of the Wand of Existence: superhuman strength, superhuman agility, and you can even become a shadow."

"And you're only weakness is thirst."

Life tapped his side where a canteen of water was stored.

"That's right. With all these strengths, we will crush the diamonds once and for all."

Midnight stood up on all his fours.

"Now, you're speaking my language," Midnight growled.

"Your Moon Glaive," Life said as he reached into his invisible weaponry belt and produced the Moon Glaive.

Midnight gripped the polished 'S' shaped blade in his jaws. The blade could cut through anything and was laced with Cherokee magic that allowed its user extreme speed and agility. Life and Midnight rushed into battle. Even after a century in limbo, the cowboy and the wolf were ready to savor the taste of revenge.

4

Steam rose off of the black armor of Death and blackish flames wreathed around Death's diamond jackal head. Death marveled at its massive diamond hands and arms. He felt his hard diamond curved teeth, his diamond pointy ears, and his diamond muzzle. He was as before, and Death was pleased. The physical world was once more at his mercy.

"From this day forward, I will reap my harvest of mankind," Death roared.

Suddenly, something crashed into Death's jaw and back. The impact knocked him through the wall of the saloon and into the muddy streets of New Hampton where a deep groove was embedded in the earth from where Death had skid out of control.

The falling rain sizzled on the black armor as Death rose to a bent knee position. He rotated his flaming head toward the gaping hole in the side of the building and spied his assailants standing in the gap.

"The cowboy called Life, we used our remaining strength to cause a landslide, trapping you and your mangy canine to starve to death," Death gasped as he beheld his attackers.

"You can never keep a man and his dog down," Midnight snarled.

"Midnight, let's send Death back to the Underworld where he belongs," Life spoke to Midnight.

Death was not afraid of the cowboy and the wolf. He knew he would be victorious.

"Life, I know that you remember my black axe, Plague," Death roared as he unlatched his axe that was on his red belt.

"Yes, I remember your little toothpick," Life replied as he

withdrew his sword.

"Then, you will remember that the dead follows it." Death roared, thrusting the head of the axe into the earth.

The ground splintered then cracked. The crack gaped open into crevices and a scent similar to a mound of feces drifted upward.

"Maaannnn! Fleeesh! Aggrrrgh!"

Cries and moans were heard.

"The dead lives," Life said as he sneered at the red sinews and tendons of a decaying hand pulling itself up from the crevice.

Zombies dressed in torn rags with their decaying muscles and tendons exposed crawled from within the earth. A pale light is in their eye sockets and a hatred for the living was in their decayed hearts.

"Rise, my servants, and feast upon these imbeciles!"

"Run for your lives!" A group of bystanders screamed as they fled the scene.

Life and Midnight stood their ground. They were not afraid of the undead.

"Another day at work," Life said as he drew his sword and leapt into battle with Midnight behind him.

"Man-flesh," a zombie whose spine and shoulder bones were visible gnashed.

The zombies sprinted toward the cowboy and the wolf.

"Send them to the next world," Life yelled.

Life spun and chopped three zombies. The zombies exploded as their bodies slid apart at the mid-section into fiery heaps of ashes.

"Here's a one way ticket," Midnight snarled as he smashed a zombie with his paw then decapitated another by leaping high in the sky and slashing with the Moon Glaive.

Just a little ways off, two men watched the destruction of the zombies.

"The cowboy is fast like a ninja! Look at how he flips and swings his sword sideways! That thing is sharp," one of the men said.

"Nah, he is more like a samurai! Look at his proper posture—legs shoulder width apart and sword under chin," the other man debated as Life sliced downward then upward.

"No matter if he is a ninja or samurai, that jackal guy is gonna toast the bread and cut the cheese," the first man said.

"What does toast the bread and cut the cheese mean?" the second man asked.

The first man shrugged his shoulders. Suddenly, the cowboy flipped above the heads of the zombies and landed in front of Death.

Behind Life, the zombies exploded into burning heaps as Midnight rammed into them with the glaive. The two men cheered.

"Ahh, man! Did you see that?" both men shouted.

The two men fell silent as Death turned his head toward them and snarled. His hot saliva dripped to the ground and sizzled.

"Sorry, Mr. Monster," the men yelled as they ran away.

Suddenly, Death swung his axe sideways, and Life swung his sideways.

The impact of the axe and sword sent shockwaves through the air collapsing several nearby buildings. Death reared back to swing his axe but before he could do that, Midnight flew through the air with his Moon Glaive clenched in his jaws. Death was vulnerable and could not block the slashes of Midnight.

Silver and green sparks flew, yet the Moon Glaive could not

breach the armor of Death.

"Nothing can penetrate the Armor of Death," Death boasted as he reared back and laughed.

"We'll put some ketchup on those words and make you eat them," Midnight snarled.

"I laugh at your idle threats! Cease your prattling and prepare to perish!"

"Prattle this, you bag of hot air," Life yelled as he cart wheeled forward with his cowboy boots, striking Death in the forehead.

Death stumbled backward, and Life nimbly leapt sideways and hurled a handful of steel ball bearings at the monster. The speeding ball bearings struck Death's armor and burst.

The ball bearings were laced with holy water and the drops of water melted away Death's armor like acid!

"Arrgh," Death roared in agony.

Life noticed a flicker of blue light seeping through the damaged armor.

"Death, you broke my wolf's back and put this mark on my face," Life angrily yelled.

"Rrrrgggh! I have lost only once and that was to the one who is self beginning! You are nothing," Death snarled as he displayed his sharp diamond crusted teeth.

"My name is Life, and Life is me!"

"Today, Life, you will learn to fear Death!"

Death's black claws extended five inches, but Life did not falter.

"Fear is a result of doubt. I have no doubt that I can beat you now," Life replied.

"Then, I will pound you with the Fist of Death until you fear me," Death roared.

"VOOM!"

His black flames exploded about him and hardened the muddy ground!

"Stay behind me, Midnight, and wait for the counter attack. You did good last time," Life coached as Death dashed toward him.

"I'll do better next time," Midnight snarled as he stepped back one paw at a time.

Suddenly, Death swung his axe with the intent to swipe Life's head from his shoulders. However, Life crouched very low as the axe rushed over his black cowboy hat. Life quickly rolled to the right and leapt high into the stormy sky.

"Where did you go, cowboy?" Death inquired as he wildly looked left and right.

At that moment, Death caught a glimpse of Life's reflection in the blades of his axe. Life was descending from the clouds with his sword drawn back behind his head! Death whirled and blocked the downward strike with his axe.

The force of the blow brought Death to one knee and dented the earth. However, Death was not so easily defeated. He shifted leverage and snatched Life by his trench coat and hurled him toward a marble fountain erected in the middle of town.

Life crashed into the marble fountain.

"Silly, cowboy. Death is the finale of all outcomes," Death roared.

Before Death could fully enjoy his moment, Life burst from the rubble and sprinted towards Death, firing his guns. Death blocked the bullets with his axe and returned the favor.

"Burn, you infidel, burn," Death growled as he spit swirling black fireballs at Life.

"You need to cool off," Life said as he quickly holstered his revolvers and dodged the incinerating balls of fire.

Life moved at the speed of a blur and suddenly leapt across the distance. Death swung a claw at him.

Life ducked and swung his elbow into the damaged armor.

"Arrgh," Death roared in agony.

Life concentrated all actions on the damaged armor, letting loose a flurry of punches in that one location.

"One for the money," Life yelled.

Death clumsily swung an open claw again.

Life ducked and, at the same time, spun around, kicking Death in the same spot.

"Arrrrrggggh," Death roared louder.

Death maladroitly swung again and missed his target.

"Two for the show," Life said as he delivered a smashing knee to Death's armored chest.

Death lunged at Life, but Life slid through his open legs and thrust his elbow into Death's lower back. As his elbow crashed into Death's lower back, Life winked at Midnight.

"Three for the show," exclaimed Life as he jumped in the air and performed a backwards kick.

Suddenly, Death grabbed him by the ankle and jerked Life upside down with an incredible strength. Instantly, Life's body went limp. The Fist of Death had taken him!

"Infidel, I will pound you with my Fist of Death just as I promised," Death growled as he heaved Life upward and prepared to thrust him into the earth head first.

Just as Death raised Life above his waist, Life reached beneath his trench coat and extracted his sword.

"Three to let the souls free," Life exclaimed.

With all of his might, he thrust the blade through the damaged armor and wrenched it right to left.

Life's blade cracked but did not break.

"Do it now, Midnight," Life shouted as he kicked Death in the muzzle with his free leg, breaking the icy grip.

As Life fell to a kneeling position, Midnight lunged over his head and through the air with the glistening Moon Glaive.

"Midnight Shadow Strike," Midnight snarled as he unleashed a flurry of strikes along the damaged armor.

"Noooo," screeched Death.

The black armor faded to a dull gray as purple orbs of souls spewed forth from the fatal wound. Life stood up and examined his sword. There were tiny cracks in the blade, but he sheathed the sword without any further ado. Revenge had never tasted better.

"Ahhhgggghhhh! Deprivation, release the gremlins! The cowboy has returned," Death shrieked as he exploded in a blinding light.

After the explosion, not only was there the steamy body of Ten Shot lying on the ground but also a black diamond that was shaped like a jackal's head. The rainfall returned harder than ever.

"Nice trick," Life said as he stooped down and picked up the black diamond.

Last time, the diamonds had used their remaining strength to trap him in a cave. Now, Death was trying to use the rainfall to wash him safely away. Suddenly, a voice of a little girl called out from within the diamond.

"Don't hurt me, mister," the voice of a little girl said. "I am no threat. I could serve you! I am—"

"You are crushed," Life replied as he squeezed the black diamond, crushing the evil jewel.

Life let the diamond dust sift through his fingers. The rain ceased and a breeze blew. Change was in the air.

"Good job," Life said as he took the glaive from Midnight's jaws and returned it to his invisible sheath.

Life rubbed his best friend's head back and forth, causing Midnight to stutter.

"Yy-you haven't f-f-forgotten the slaves have you?" Midnight asked.

"I never did. Today, freedom rings; we will be carrying the bell," Life said.

Life and Midnight walked away from the town. Death had been returned to the Underworld, but there were two other members of Legion to deal with. Hopefully, they had not heard Death's warning.

Chapter 2

The Battle at the Hole and The Gremlins of Legion

Life and Midnight walked away from the center of the town by way of a rocky dirt road that led into a valley. The thin green trees gave way to thin dead trees. The grass became higher and higher. Abundance was absent from this valley. As Life and Midnight traveled, a group of spies observed their every move from a safe distance.

"Life, I can smell the sweat of the people on these stones," Midnight snarled as he trotted beside Life. "Please let me rip the legs from the person responsible for this!"

"Anything for you, my canine friend," Life replied as he kicked aside a heavy rock. "This road was purposely made to weaken the spirit! The plantation is just on the other side of the rocky slope."

"Have you heard the voice again?" Midnight asked.

"Not since we left the cave," Life said.

"Hopefully, it will speak again. Do you think it is God?" Midnight asked.

"If not, then it is of God," Life replied as he glanced at the purple clouds in the evening sky.

The magic Wand of Existence had endowed him with extensive knowledge pertaining to omens, and he automatically knew why the sky was purple. Peril was upon them. Deprivation had heard Death's last cry.

"Deprivation has released The Gremlins of Legion! Midnight, can you grow?"

Midnight nodded his head and began to expand until he was the size of a young horse. Life hopped onto Midnight's back, and they swiftly sped down the road. As they rode away, a mob of horsemen met up with the small group of spies who had been spying on the cowboy and the wolf. A sandy haired young man dressed as the sheriff nudged his stallion forward.

"They are headed to the Hole, Master Goodman," the captain reported of the spies. "I think they are going to free the 'Shines'!"

The sheriff's star, even though slightly tarnished, glinted in the dim sunlight.

"Thinking is not part of yer job description, Skillet," Master Goodman scowled as he cocked his 30/30 rifle and spit a stream of tobacco juice onto the ground. "I'm going to bury that cowboy and his wolf in the Hole with the rest of the vermin! Follow me, men!"

The mob moved forward. They were armed with torches, guns, and various farm equipment. The audacity of the cowboy had to be checked, and Master Goodman was ready to administer capital punishment for the cowboy's actions.

2

Life rode Midnight down the dirt road until they came to a great live oak that sat on a stony hill. Its strong twisting limbs stretched outward like greeting arms, and its girth cast a great shadow on the land. Life saw the flock of black birds and asked Midnight to slow down.

"Is it about to get cold?" Midnight asked as he came to a halt.

The black birds soared around the tree.

"Under normal circumstances, yes, but these birds are carnivorous. Why would they be flocking around a tree?"

Life felt Midnight's muscles in his shoulders tighten.

"What do you see?" Life asked.

"The birds are not swarming around the tree for berries. The birds are feasting on the flesh of dead people!"

"Take me closer," Life ordered.

Life and Midnight left the dirt road and traveled through the short grass until they came to the hilltop. The black birds screamed at the cowboy and the wolf.

"CAW! CAW!"

Life dismounted and ignored the rude birds. He stooped down and read a weathered wooden sign that was posted in front of the live oak.

"Here is the Tree O' Life," Life read aloud as he ran his fingers along the words of the inscription.

"More like the tree out of my worst nightmare," Midnight muttered as he stared at the hanging corpses of men, women, and even children.

They were about to leave when they heard a whisper from

the heights above.

"P-please, he-help me, mon!"

Life jerked his head upward to see a middle-aged man with salt and pepper dreadlocks tied between two limbs of the tree. He was dressed in a dirty light blue blazer and some raggedy dark slacks. Both of his arms were extended and his wrists were tightly bound.

"X marks the spot, Midnight. Let's play catch," Life said to Midnight as he pulled out the glaive and hurled it at the ropes.

The rotating glaive circled the man, snapping the ropes without even touching a hair on his wrists. As he fell, Midnight caught the man on his back then returned to the ground. Life performed a behind the back catch as it returned to his hand and utilized the blade to cut free the bonds.

"Hold on, partner! Everything is going to be as good as good can get," Life said as he freed the man.

"Water…please," the man spoke in his island accent as he clutched the cowboy's arm.

The man's lips were parched from the harsh elements. Quickly, Life extracted an oval shaped canteen from beneath his coat and placed the bottle to the man's cracked lips. After a moment of drinking Life's water, the man was reenergized and his wounds were healed!

"Thank you! Lord a mercy! You be a saint," the man shouted as he marveled at his rejuvenated strength.

"Thanks for the vote of confidence," Life said.

Before the man could stand up, Midnight addressed him.

"Who did this to you?"

"What! The steamy wolf just talked," the man exclaimed as he scuttled backward.

"Easy there, fellow," Life soothingly spoke as he grabbed the man by his ragged pants and held him down. "Let's make a long story short. I'm a good guy, and this is my talking wolf."

The man slowly relaxed. The cowboy and the wolf were the first people he had seen in the last three days! The man gazed into their eyes and determined that they were good. He took a deep breath and told them who put him in the tree.

"Master Pau and Master Goodman did me this wicked ding," the man confessed as he stood up.

"How did you earn this fate?" Life asked.

"Dem wicked mon did me this 'cause I would not tell dem how I got out the Hole, mon! Dem wicked mon beat me then sentenced me to be pecked to death," the man stated.

"That bastard," Life said as he looked at the numerous corpses above them.

"Aye, mon," the man agreed. "I was going to sneak into town and steal the Scroll of Liberty 'til I was caught!"

Life raised an eyebrow at the mention of the scroll. There were magical trinkets within the world but all were hidden in very secret places. Perhaps this one was revealed when during one of the earthquakes.

"Why would you risk your life for a scroll, and why would you think it was in town?" Life inquired.

"This scroll is magical. Whoever possesses it has the ability to give freedom or deny it, mon," the man said as he looked around. "That is why them monsters never attack New Hampton and why no one has ever escaped the Hole!"

Life listened intensely. The power of a scroll that granted freedom would also have the ability to take freedom away from others. However, if the scroll were in the town, he would have sensed it.

"Master Pau has already been sent to the crossroads, and I am eager to help Master Goodman on his way," Midnight snarled as he licked his huge fangs.

"What is this Hole I keep hearing about?" Life asked as he continued to gaze upward at the numerous victims.

"The Hole is the plantation where dem wicked mon keep us 'Shines'," the man informed.

Suddenly, the man dropped down onto his stomach. However, Life and Midnight did not take such actions.

"What is it?" Life asked.

"It is Master Goodman," the man fearfully whispered. "It is the bumbla clot in the flesh!"

Life peered toward the dirt road and saw a mob riding with torches. Midnight growled, but Life held him back.

"Easy, partner."

"He is going to set fire to the Hole! I have to save the people," the man shouted as he leapt to his feet again.

Before he dashed away, Life grabbed the man by the arm.

"My name is Life, and this is my wolf, Midnight. Can you show us how to get in the Hole? We will help you."

"Aye, mon, there is another way across the field to an underground tunnel that I shoveled with me bare hands. I will show you it. My friends call me Danny Boy," the man said as he shook Life's hand.

"Nice to meet you," Life replied.

"I will take you to see Ms. Pook. She will know what to do!"

Danny Boy and Life leapt onto Midnight's back, and they quickly rode toward the Hole. Above them, the purple clouds deepened in color to a sullen black against the fading sunlight.

The Gremlins of Legion were closer.

Master Goodman slowed his horse to a light trot while traveling over the wooden bridge that lead to the shambled tin-shack community known to all as the Hole. For the past five years, every 'Shine' of New Hampton had resided and died there unless they had earned a special trip to the Trees O' Life. Surrounding the Hole was a stagnant creek that reeked of decaying fish. The residents of the Hole bathed in that creek, washed their clothes in that creek, and even gathered their drinking water from that creek. On the banks of this smelly creek, a large stone wobbled and tilted over, revealing the entrance to a tunnel. Emerging from the hole were three heroes: Danny Boy, Life, and Midnight.

"That's enough wire to cover a farm," Midnight snarled as he noticed the triple layer of barbed wire surrounding the wooden spiked fence that bordered the creek.

"Shhh," Life whispered as he heard someone speaking. "Somebody's coming across the bridge toward the gate. You go ahead to Ms. Pook and tell her the plan while I investigate."

Danny Boy and Midnight went their separate ways as Life snuck through the surrounding brown brush and moved silently toward the gate.

"Boss, he's a witch, ain't he?" Skillet asked as he reached inside of his overalls and extracted an iron skeleton key.

"Yea, but instead of a broom the jerk rides a wolf," Master Goodman replied as his horse trotted a couple of feet behind Skillet.

Master Goodman put on his sheriff's hat and brushed his sandy hair from his eyes. Behind him, the mob shouted threats.

"Bring out the cowboy or we'll burn your houses and make you rebuild them," one mob member threatened.

"Yeah," the mob resonated in one voice.

"Bring out the cowboy, or we'll starve you then feed you poison," another mob member threatened.

"Yeah," the mob echoed in one voice.

"Bring out the cowboy, or we'll chop off your feet and make you stand up," another threatened.

"Yeah," the mob resonated in one voice.

"Boss, can I be the first to put the torch under his dirty feet?" Skillet begged as he unlocked the wooden gate with the iron skeleton key.

"Right under the vermin's stinky toes," Master Goodman assured. "Now open the door and quit yer babbling before I turn you from a deputy to a log in this creek!"

"Boss, what about the wolf? Can we burn him alive, too?" Skillet begged as he heaved on the heavy wooden gate.

Before Master Goodman could answer, an arm swiftly reached out from the shadows of the gate.

"He's got me! He's got me," Skillet screamed as the grip tightened.

Suddenly, a knife pressed against Skillet's throat, and Skillet's body tensed up.

Master Goodman and the horsemen drew their guns and cocked them. They were ready to shoot to kill.

"Twenty women to the person who brings me that arm," Master Goodman ordered.

"D-don't shoot," Skillet pleaded as numerous barrels pointed at him.

"You might want to sound a little more convincing," Life hinted in Skillet's ear.

"P-put yer guns down! Stand down! Stand down," Skillet screamed as he urinated in his pants.

"In the past, you have enjoyed making others feel insignificant. So tell me. Does the shoe fit?" Life murmured in Skillet's ear.

Master Goodman tilted his rifle and stared into the shadows, searching for a target. There was nothing to lock in on. The cowboy had placed himself in a very strategic position.

"Too smart," Master Goodman muttered.

Master Goodman did not panic. The cowboy had sealed his fate by visiting the Hole. If the cowboy did not surrender, then Master Goodman was prepared to burn the Hole down. That was what his father called a win-win scenario.

"Cowboy, come out. We can talk this out around a campfire! You can bring your dog, too," Master Goodman announced with a grin on his face.

Laughter generated within the mob, but Life did not lower the knife. Life noticed the beads of sweat on the back of Skillet's neck.

Life lightly breathed on Skillet's neck, and Skillet panicked. He assumed the sweat that was trickling down his neck was blood.

"Father, please forgive me of my sins," Skillet prayed.

Life hid his laughter and spoke in a stern voice.

"Tell Master Goodman to take his friends and leave now, or he will pay with his life. The Gremlins of Legion are almost here," Life warned in a low voice.

"G-go home because The Gremlins of Legion are almost

here," Skillet summarized to the best of his ability.

"You shouldn't have come here, cowboy! Now, everyone in the Hole will suffer," Master Goodman retaliated.

"Oooh, Momma, I'm sorry for talking to you like a spoiled brat," Skillet trembled as tears began to rush from his clenched eyes.

"After I deal with you, cowboy, I am going to burn alive everyone in the Hole," Master Pau said as he swung off his horse and took a kneeling position.

Suddenly, everything became quiet. Life glanced upward to see the black clouds intertwining with the purple clouds.

"The Gremlins of Legion are here," Life shouted as he jerked Skillet over the threshold.

Master Goodman sprinted toward the gate, but it slammed in his face!

"Ugghh! H-he jammed it," Master Goodman strained as he tugged on the gate.

"Master Goodman stopped tugging on the gate and glanced over the side of the wooden bridge to see a green medium height creature emerge from the water. The creature had one yellow eye, large floppy ears, black talons, and sharp teeth. The creature was none other than a gremlin.

"Eat hot lead, you gremlin," Master Goodman bellowed as he squeezed the trigger of his rifle.

"Yrrrreeekkk," the gremlin shrieked from the fatal wound as its body withered away in a burning heap of hell-fire.

Master Goodman's horse dashed away at the sound of the numerous splashes. There were swirls in the water below.

"Yee haw! Get ready, boys. The gremlins are out the bag," Master Goodman yelled as he prepared himself to shoot at the first thing that came out of the water.

There was no battle cry, no cheers for bloodshed. Master Goodman glanced over his shoulder to see the mob galloping back toward town, leaving him to fight alone.

"You yellow belly cowards," Master Goodman cried out.

Master Goodman peered over the edge of the bridge. Hundreds of one-eyed gremlins emerged from the creek and scrambled up the bank to the bridge.

"Grrrggh," the foremost gremlin growled.

Master Goodman waited until the gremlins corralled the bridge. Then, he shot for his life.

"BLAM! BLAM!"

One fell, then another fell, but twenty more scrambled toward him with their talons extended. Master Goodman squeezed the trigger of the rifle.

"CLICK!"

The gun did not fire. He squeezed the trigger again.

"CLICK!"

"No! I am out of ammo," Master Goodman hollered as he swung the rifle like a club.

The Gremlins of Legion tackled Master Goodman, and the gnashing of the gremlins drowned out his cries. The gremlins commenced to find a way past the barbed wire. They would not rest until the cowboy was destroyed.

Life and Skillet were halfway to the shed when they became aware of Master Goodman's terrifying screams.

"W-what was that?" Skillet fearfully spoke.

"That is what happens to you when you betray me or my friends," Life advised as he half-dragged Skillet.

"Who are you and your friends? Please don't kill me," Skillet pleaded.

"I am a preserver of life. It is not my decision for who should have it or who shouldn't," Life explained.

They stopped in front of a tin roofed rectangular shaped shed. It was silent and one candle burned in the window.

"The preserver of life-that sounds like the name of a bank," Skillet said as he scratched his head.

Life opened the door then politely nudged him forward.

"The wire should delay the gremlins for the time being. You will be safe inside here. After you, my friend," Life politely spoke as he beckoned Skillet to enter the room.

"You're a pretty kind fellow, you know," Skillet remarked as he walked inside the shed with a feeling of relief.

"Thanks for the compliment. Please show the same courtesy to Ms. Pook and my friends," Life grinned as he slammed the door shut and leaned against it while cocking his pistols.

Life gazed at the black and purple clouds twisting together against the golden sky. He closed his eyes and listened to the talons of the gremlins dismantling the barbed wire. The terrifying sound put the number of gremlins at a dreadful one thousand. However, Life was no ordinary cowboy. This was the perfect opportunity to test his newly acquired skills.

The door slammed, and Skillet realized that he was not

inside the shed alone as he saw the light of the makeshift torches reflecting off the sweaty faces of the 'Shines' sitting on bales of hay. At their sides were customized spears, knives, and axes. His heart was beating so hard that it almost climbed up his trachea and leap out of his mouth. Skillet slowly pivoted around and viewed the makeshift torches lining the hallway.

"I don't have anything against you people," Skillet cried out as he leaned up against the door, fidgeting with the handle.

The 'Shines' huddled in the hallway in an intimidating fashion.

"What do you mean by 'you people'?" an Asian man asked.

"Who are 'you' people?" a black man asked.

Skillet was terrified as he stared at the various races of people he had just subjected to his hatred. One particular 'Shine', dressed in a dirty light blue blazer with dark slacks, came forward. This 'Shine' had salt and peppered dreadlocks, a round face with high cheekbones, and a dimple in his chin. This was the same 'Shine' he had beaten, tortured, and tied to the Trees O' Life three days ago!

"You look like you just saw a ghost," Danny Boy said.

"I-I am s-sorry," Skillet stuttered.

"Come with me, batty boy! Ms. Pook waits," Danny Boy said as he seized Skillet by the collar and dragged him across the dirt floor.

"What are you going to do with me?" Skillet inquired.

"Don't worry, be happy, mon! We be taking good care of you like you took care of me," Danny Boy replied as he shoved Skillet and tripped him at the same time.

Skillet fell on the dirt floor of the shed. He shook his head from left to right as he tried to stand up. As he struggled to his feet, Skillet heard the soulful voice of an elderly lady singing the spiritual "Swing Low, Sweet Chariot". Her voice rose an octave, finessing rhythm and timing to create a masterpiece. The sound of the lady's voice took away Skillet's worries. For a moment, he was at peace.

"Swing low, sweet chariot, coming for' to carry me home," the elderly lady sang.

"Ain't no angel taking you home," Danny Boy said as he heaved Skillet to his feet, shoving him toward the stables of the shed.

As they walked around the corner, the elderly lady pitched her voice into an amazing octave that caused all eyes to water.

"I looked over, and what did I see? A band of angels coming after me!"

Skillet wiped his eyes as he saw the singer of the song. Sitting on a bale of hay was a frail elderly lady of about 70 years old. She was dressed in a blue button-up plaid shirt with a pink floral printed dress and dirty white sneakers. At her side was a gnarled wooden walking stick. Her hair was styled in two short gray braids that curled by the lobe of her ear. She wore a pair of oversized glasses that loosely fit her tiny face.

"Don't be afraid, Skillet," the elderly lady said in her feeble voice.

"H-how do you know my name?" Skillet asked in astonishment.

"Know your name! Baby, I gave you the name when you took a piece of fat-back out of the skillet and burned yo' hand up," the elderly lady laughed as she pointed a crooked finger at Skillet.

Danny Boy smiled as he saw the bewildered look on Skillet's face.

"It took a lot for me to talk the fire out of your hand. Probably 'cause you were so greedy," the elderly lady continued to laugh.

Skillet stared at his right hand. The burn scar he had received twenty years ago was lightly visible. Until then, he had forgotten the pain of the burn and the housekeeper who had healed him.

"Nana Pook, is that you? I remember you now," Skillet exclaimed. "You took the fire out my hand!"

"You were a fat lil' boy back then. Always stayed in the kitchen, sneakin' whateva I cooked," Ms. Pook said as she nodded her head and rocked from side to side.

"You made the best blackberry pies, fruit preserves, and macaroni cheese for Sunday dinner," Skillet excitedly articulated as he drifted on a memory.

Danny Boy rolled his eyes at the comment. He remembered like it was yesterday how Skillet and the others went from house to house, rounding up those who were different and placing them in the Hole. The memory enraged him, but, somehow, Danny Boy held his peace.

"Skillet, thank you for the kind words, but, just as God's green earth needs light, I need some info from you," Ms. Pook said as she leaned forward.

Skillet became uneasy as he looked past the oversized glasses on the elderly lady's face and at the deep care lines under her eyes.

"I need you to show us where the Scroll of Liberty is."

Skillet's smile vanished at the request of Ms. Pook. He had been with Master Pau when they discovered the scroll in a twisted dead tree. The scroll gave Master Pau the power to dominate and oppress. Then, one day, the scroll simply disappeared. That was when Master Pau organized the Fifty Marauders to maintain order in New Hampton. The scroll was a secret that only he,

Master Pau, and Master Goodman shared.

"I have never heard of such a scroll," Skillet lied while staring Ms. Pook in her eyes.

"WHAM!"

Danny Boy punched Skillet, and he fell to the ground.

"You wicked, mon! Ms. Pook, he doesn't deserve to live! Let me cut him up into tid bit pieces," Danny Boy shouted as he jerked a machete from the holster at his waist.

"Baby, your anger is getting the best of you. Let's use some of God's good sugar instead of the devil's vinegar," Ms. Pook remarked.

Danny Boy relaxed and took control of his emotions. After all, Ms. Pook knew best.

"Shine, you will get nothing from me but some hard work! That goes for all of you," Skillet coldly replied as he spit on Ms. Pook's shoes.

"So much for God's good sugar. Now, its time for some hot vinegar," Ms. Pook stated.

Ms. Pook whistled two times, but the sound was not acute. It was dull like a dry cough.

"Your dry lips can't even whistle! I bet you bleed dust," Skillet disrespectfully yelled.

Danny Boy raised his machete with the intent to hack Skillet, but Ms. Pook held her hand up.

"Skillet, there is a way that seems right to a person, but its end is the way of death," Ms. Pook said as she quoted a proverb.

"Save your stinking breath, old lady, and learn how to whistle."

"My friend doesn't need me to whistle loud. He can hear me from anywhere," Ms. Pook laughed.

Skillet's heart skipped a couple of beats as he saw the massive wolf step out of the shadows. Skillet's bottom lip trembled as he saw the five-inch fangs of the wolf. The yellow eyes of the wolf were menacing, and Skillet was filled with fear.

"You will tell us where the scroll is or I will bite off your fingers one at a time," Midnight threatened.

Skillet gulped at the severity of the ultimatum as he glanced down at his fingers. Having ten fingers was a good thing. Perhaps he could cooperate.

Life stood in the middle of the plantation with his guns drawn. The sun had set. A purple haze lingered in the night sky. Among the hovels of the Hole, a foreboding presence filled the air. The Hole was as silent as an abandoned mine.

"Come on! What are you waiting for?" Life yelled as he became impatient.

A hair raising howl went up, and Life could see hundreds of one-eyed gremlins, smashing through the barbed wire surrounding the walls of the plantation. Life's pupils dilated, and his mouth went bone dry. His heart beat slowed as he viewed the tide of gremlins scrambling into the plantation. The battle fire had ignited within him, and the only thing that would cool its ambers was the annihilation of his enemies.

"Welcome to the after party," Life laughed as he blasted the monsters with his pistols, reducing them to fiery heaps of ashes.

Several monsters were disintegrated by his supreme marksmanship, but the whole did not cease their attack. They attacked more ferociously. Life whirled around just in time to shove the barrel of his left pistol into the leering mouth of a gremlin.

"Shhh, be quiet," Life said as he squeezed the trigger.

"BLAM!"

"Rggh," the gremlin shrieked as it became a mound of fiery ash.

Life spun in the opposite direction with a roundhouse kick and smashed the heads of two gremlins while shooting three other gremlins that were at arm's length. Life pivoted in a half circle as two gremlins leapt at him from opposite directions.

"Banana split," Life yelled as he slid into a horizontal split.

The gremlins crashed into each other in mid-air. Before they could fall to the earth, Life blasted them. Then, he rolled forward. As he rose to one knee, he blasted a gremlin as it ran toward him with his right pistol and without turning around. He aimed with his left pistol then blasted a leaping gremlin from behind. As Life jumped to his feet, a gremlin leapt onto his back. Its lashing talons tore at his forearm and ripped his coat.

"I got you now, cowboy," the gremlin hissed.

"Oh, yeah? Go ahead and bite me then," Life urged as he continued to blast the lunging gremlins without worrying about the gremlin that was on his back.

The gremlin bit down. The gremlin's teeth shattered.

The gremlin fell off Life's back, squirming on the ground while holding its injured mouth.

"Oops. I forgot to tell you to watch out for the sword that you couldn't see," Life laughed as he performed a backwards flip and blasted the gremlin that was wriggling on the ground as six more leapt at him.

If he didn't do something fast, the gremlins would overwhelm him. Life performed a quick spinning leg sweep, knocking down four more gremlins and quickly leaping in the air, delivering a smashing sidekick to two more gremlins.

"Time to end this meeting," Life said as he swung a crushing elbow into the face of a gremlin and leapt sideways and into the air, kicking two gremlins in their hairy chins.

As he landed on his feet, Life put away his gun and extracted his sword that was strapped to his back.

With three quick swings of his blade, Life sliced through the hideous crowd and dashed toward a narrow alley. Shortly, Life came to a dead end and whirled around, slicing a pursing gremlin's head in half with his sword.

"Didn't your gremlin ma tell you not to follow cowboys?" Life asked in disgust as the gremlin smoldered in ruins.

The mob of gremlins lingered back and crowded the narrow side street, blocking all avenues of escape.

"Ha! Ha! We have a fish in our nets! Cowboy, you should not have come back," the gremlins laughed.

"I belong here. Maybe you should go back to the Underworld where you belong," Life replied as he pointed the sword at the gathering gremlins.

"Your annoyance ends today, and Deprivation will give us a reward," one gremlin chuckled as he exposed a mouth full of tiny sharp teeth.

"You should have asked Deprivation for two eyes instead of one 'cause you didn't see this coming," Life shouted as he flipped out his glaive and hurled it toward the crowd of monsters.

"Too fast," the gremlin croaked as he dodged the spinning knife.

The blade plowed into the other gremlins and didn't stop.

"I wasn't playing with you. I was playing catch with him," Life remarked as the glaive chopped its way to the end of the street where Midnight caught it in his massive jaws.

Standing behind the wolf were the people. They were armed with their customized weapons and ready to fight.

"Show no mercy," Midnight growled as he dove into the crowd of gremlins.

The residents of the Hole sprinted from behind Midnight, hacking away at the gremlins. Before the first gremlin could flee, Life hurled a lasso at it.

The rope automatically hogtied the gremlin, sending him crashing to the ground.

"Stay right there, and enjoy the show," Life said as he leapt into the battle with his sword, cutting the bewildered gremlins down like a scythe in a field.

After the gremlins had been eliminated, Life returned to where he had bound the first gremlin. Life extracted two ball bearings from his jacket and clicked them together.

"Tell me what I want to know, and I will return you to the underworld as fast as possible."

"You will get nothing from me," the gremlin hissed.

Life dropped one of the ball bearings.

The knee of the gremlin sizzled from the holy water.

"Agggh, it burns," the gremlin roared.

"Out with the bad and in with the good," Life said in a sarcastic tone.

"Agggh! Grrgh! Gaer Graew Graed," the gremlin cursed in its monstrous language as it struggled to get free.

Life reached inside and picked up a hand full of ball bearings.

"I would hate to drop a fist full of these things on you,

especially in the eye area," Life threatened and positioned his hand above the gremlin's eye.

"You are wastin'—"

Life dropped a ball bearing onto the gremlin's chest.

"Grrrrgh," the gremlin shrieked as the blessed water blistered his scaly chest.

"Where is Deprivation?"

"Deprivation is trapped inside the Pyramid northeast of here," the gremlin screamed as smoke rose from its chest.

"Thanks. Now it's time for you to go," Life said as he stabbed the gremlin with his sword.

The gremlin went up in fire and smoke.

"They smell like sulfur," Midnight snarled as he stood beside Life and dropped the glaive from his mouth.

Life picked up the glaive and cleaned its slimy edges.

"Did Skillet tell Ms. Pook where the Scroll of Liberty is?" Life asked as he tossed Midnight a bundle of beef jerky.

"He said they found it in a dead tree after the earthquakes. He said the scroll disappeared afterwards," Midnight growled as he gobbled up his treat.

"My ashy friend here told me that Deprivation is held up in a Pyramid," Life said as he returned the lasso and the glaive back to his invisible utility belt.

"Perhaps the scroll is with Deprivation," Midnight replied as he licked his muzzle.

"You should have been a detective instead of a sidekick," Life replied as he patted his friend on his head. "Take me to see Ms. Pook."

Midnight led Life toward the shed. As they walked past the embattled people, a cry of gratitude went up.

"Long live Life and Midnight," the people shouted.

"Thank you, friends of freedom," Life acknowledged in a loud voice. "Today you are no longer 'Shines', but the free beings you were meant to be! Let freedom ring!"

Life followed Midnight to the shed. If he failed to retrieve the scroll, then mankind would never have hope in this disastrous world.

7

Life thrust open the wooden doors of the shed and found Skillet sitting on the ground, being held at knife-point by Danny Boy. On a bale of hay sat an elderly black lady. She was about seventy years old and her silvery black hair was styled in two braids. Life stood before the elderly woman as she sang a hymn entitled "A Charge to Keep".

"A charge to keep, I have a God to glorify," Ms. Pook sang in the fashion of the old Negro spiritual where every syllable was sung for more than three seconds. "A God to glorify, a never-dying soul to save and fit it for the sky!"

Ms. Pook finished the song and beckoned for Life to come closer. As Life drew nearer to her, he saw a gnarled wooden walking stick. He assumed this was the woman's walking aid.

"Your song is true, old mother. We do have a God to glorify," Life acknowledged as he knelt before her.

"Rise, servant of the will within the will and have a seat at my right hand," Ms. Pook said in her tiny voice.

"How do you know that I am a servant of the Will?" Life asked as he rose to his feet and sat on a nearby bail of hay.

When he was younger, Life and a group of his friends had formed a law enforcement organization known as the Will. Life and his friends rode here and there spreading justice. One day, a gang of bandits ambushed them. Life was the only one to escape. That following night, while wandering in the wilderness, he met his best friend— Midnight.

"Your name is Life, and I know all there is to know about you," Ms. Pook replied.

Life raised his left eyebrow.

"Old mother, you are mistaken. I am over 100 years old. You can't know all about me."

"There is no mistake. Lil' ole me with all these muscles rolled back the stone," Ms. Pook sarcastically spoke as she flexed her sagging arm muscles.

"Riiiight, and I invented the duck bill platypus," Life replied in a skeptical voice.

Life briefly reflected on how he used all of his strength to try to move the stone. How could an elderly woman of her size move the stone?

"Baby, the Wand of Existence gave me the strength," Ms. Pook revealed as she grinned.

Life's mouth dropped in awe at the mention of the Wand of Existence.

"I just love to see a man dressed in black with invisible guns and a water canteen that when drank from can heal anything!"

Life became very suspicious of the elderly lady.

"Old mother, how do you know about the Magic Wand of Existence?" Life inquired as he ran his finger across the edge of his hat.

"It runs in the family," Ms. Pook said as she tipped her

oversized glasses.

Life noticed that people were beginning to gather in the stables. He did not want this conversation to get blown out of proportion.

"How did you make it to the mountains?" Life asked.

"And passed the large meat-eating scorpions. It was a day before I caught the scent of a human," Midnight growled.

There was enough silence in the room to fill twenty-five bottles of beer on the wall. However, Life and Midnight shared a unique bond that allowed them to communicate mentally. They now utilized this talent.

"Only a monster can move among monsters," Life mentally spoke.

"She is not a monster. She has a normal heartbeat," Midnight responded.

Suddenly, Ms. Pook spoke to both of them telepathically. It was the same omnipotent voice that they heard when exiting the cave.

"I am the great granddaughter of the Cherokee shaman you helped 100 years ago. I am here to help you finish what was started."

Life gazed at Ms. Pook in surprise. Ms. Pook reached into her small purse and extracted a golden artifact that looked like an eye with no pupil. She placed it on her forehead where it glowed in an eerie light.

"The Good Eye! The Shaman wore the Good Eye," Life shouted as he bowed before the elderly lady.

Midnight dwindled to his normal size and laid down on all fours with his head between his paws. The Good Eye donned its wearer with superhuman abilities. The Good Eye and the Wand of Existence would have provided Ms. Pook the strength to move the stone and restore them from the Outside.

"Stand, champions! I am not God," Ms. Pook proclaimed.

"Still, we are in your debt. Thank you for restoring us," Life sobbed as he stood up.

"The debt was reimbursed when you saved the world from Legion," Ms. Pook said.

Midnight and Life were appreciative for their sacrifice. Life did not hesitate. He asked the question that had been on his mind.

"Why did it take you so long to restore us?"

"It was not until I found a detailed map of your whereabouts in my grandfather's chest that I knew where to look,"

"So you used the power of the Good Eye to project yourself there and the Magic Wand of Existence to restore us?" Midnight growled.

"Yes, but I also have another talent that my descendents did not possess. I have the song of power," Ms. Pook stated.

"Your songs can make things happen," Midnight growled.

"Yes, the day I receive the Charm I will speak it, and it will happen. For now, I can only do little things," Ms. Pook said as she snapped her crooked finger and a bundle of beef jerky appeared under Midnight's left paw.

Life checked the left pocket in his trench coat and found it empty.

"Good trick," Life laughed.

"A better trick will be when you crush the remaining two diamonds," Ms. Pook said.

"Where are the blue and the yellow diamonds?" Life inquired.

"They are afraid."

She stood to her feet and placed her hand on Life's shoulder.

"Afraid?"

"They are afraid of he who lives and was dead, but lives evermore," Ms. Pook said.

"Revelations: chapter one, verse eighteen," Life replied.

Ms. Pook was amused at the extent of the cowboy's biblical knowledge.

"He that has an ear, let him hear," Ms. Pook said as she took the Good Eye from her forehead and placed it in her small purse.

"Tell us about the Scroll of Liberty," Life stated as he turned toward the people who had gathered around.

"The Scroll of Liberty is a scroll that contains a powerful spell. Whoever controls this spell can give freedom or take it away."

"Sounds like the steamy government," Danny Boy said.

Life nodded his head in agreement.

"If Deprivation or Desire get the scroll, then they will be able to enslave the world," Midnight said.

"One already has the scroll but is reluctant to use it," Ms. Pook prophesized.

"What do you mean?" Life asked.

"Whenever power is abused, betrayals emerge. Even as we speak, the blue diamond seeks to overthrow the yellow diamond for more power," Ms. Pook explained.

"That is why Death called to Deprivation. They were in cahoots to overthrow Desire," Midnight growled.

Life nodded his head again. He always appreciated Midnight's ability to pick up the pieces of a puzzle.

"Yes, they are allies for the moment. Death was supposed to free Deprivation from the Pyramid," Ms. Pook revealed.

"We must capitalize on this unhealthy relationship. I'm going to the Pyramid tonight to crush the blue diamond," Life said as he stood up and straightened the collar of his trench coat.

"Patience, cowboy. You will travel to Bonanza where you will meet the Axe-Murderer of Monsters known as Ms. Ellen" Ms. Pook urged.

"Who is this Ms. Ellen? And what is Bonanza?" Midnight asked.

"Ms. Ellen is the leader of an army, and Bonanza is the last free city of mankind."

"Very well, we will meet this axe-murderer," Life agreed.

"Danny Boy, are the buses ready to move?" Ms. Pook asked.

Ms. Pook had seen two school buses not too far from the Hole that had a little gas still inside their tanks.

"Ahrie, Ms. Pook. Two school buses ready to move," Danny Boy shouted in a loud voice that echoed throughout the shed and the plantation.

"What about him?" Life pointed at Skillet as he cowered in a corner.

"Let his conscious be his guide. Tomorrow, the Good Eye returns to Bonanza," Ms. Pook spoke as she leaned on her walking stick and hobbled toward the door.

Life and Midnight followed Ms. Pook out of the shed.

"Look at the smiling faces. We are heroes," Midnight growled as he noticed all of the happy people holding torches.

"Tonight is the beginning of a new hope, but who knows what the dawn will bring," Life said as he assisted Ms. Pook onto the back of a cart.

Ms. Pook did not reply. She had seen the near future. It was hazy and foggy, but the sound, oh the sound, was that of a glorious battle. Hopefully, they would be victorious at the end of the day. Hopefully.

Chapter 3

The Sons of Bonanza and The Deadly Scream of the Banshee

The two school buses traveled west from the Hole on a broken asphalt road that traversed through a field of stunted grass. They passed numerous abandoned vehicles along the road. Soon, the broken asphalt road led them into a thin wood that was over run by kudzu and deteriorating buildings.

"We are entering what used to be Lovejoy," Danny Boy said as he noticed the city limit sign.

One building caught Life's attention as he and Midnight sat in the front seat behind the driver. It had a broken faded green sign with the deteriorating word, Bucks. A large strand of slime dripped from the sign.

"Be ready. Live people don't drip slime," Life whispered to Midnight.

"These could be the zombies that Ten Shot's diamond

created," Midnight snarled.

"Or the ones that used to be human," Life replied as he wiped the sweat from his brow and drank a swallow of water from his canteen.

Life noticed that his trench coat had mended itself after his battle with the gremlins.

"Impressive," Life said to himself.

Just before midnight, Ms. Pook ordered for a halt near the remnants of an old tin roof shack and a broken cement bridge. The campfires were made and sentries were posted around the camp. Everyone within the camp rested, except Midnight. He sensed a great danger beyond the dense pockets of kudzu.

"Life, the zombies are moving! The scent of their rotting flesh is in the wind," he growled.

"Are they headed this way?" Life asked as he stooped down and patted Midnight's head.

"No, but they are headed in the direction Ms. Pook is directing us. The people won't make it. When the zombies catch their scent, they will hunt them down," Midnight warned.

"Then, we will have more undead people," Life concluded as he stood up.

If there were any monsters that he hated the most, they were zombies. They were quick, hungry, and could easily turn you into a member of the undead with one bite or scratch!

"We should turn around," Midnight advised.

"To where?" Life asked as he gazed into the mists.

"The smell of the zombies is enormous. They are gathering for something," Midnight advised.

"Good, I might get to see an old family member," Life remarked as he touched a dead tree.

The dead tree bloomed colorful buds where Life touched.

"Your tree is blooming," Midnight growled as he witnessed the miracle.

"The power that is in us makes us responsible to make a difference! Just as this dead tree just came back alive, we can do the same thing for hope! Freedom will prevail," Life encouraged as he smashed his fist into his open palm.

Midnight agreed. He elevated his muzzle and inhaled again just to confirm what he sensed earlier. The horrible scent was still there. It was fouler than the other dead scent. Such aromas belonged to only fiends from the Underworld.

"Life, there is a fiend from the Underworld with the zombies," Midnight growled

"How strong is it?" Life asked.

"The funkier they are, the stronger they are! This fiend is very strong," Midnight growled.

Life gazed up into the night sky and made a final decision.

"I will distract the army of the undead while you lead the people to Bonanza," Life decided.

"If you think that I am going to send you off to get turned into a zombie, you had better think twice," Midnight growled.

Life reached into his pocket and pulled out a bundle of beef jerky.

"Chicken teriyaki," Midnight moaned as he smelled the flavored meat.

Life extracted another bundle of beef jerky.

"Hickory smoked," Midnight moaned as the tantalizing aroma aroused his taste buds.

"You can have both of them if you show me the direction of the zombies," Life persuaded.

"Okay, they're that away," Midnight growled as he pointed his left paw.

Life tossed him the two bundles of beef jerky.

"Midnight, make sure you are on the move before morning," Life advised as he dashed into the night mists without making a sound.

"Don't call me to help you," Midnight growled as he gobbled up the beef jerky.

Life did not hear his friend as he rushed through the overgrown terrain with two thoughts in his mind: (1) Who was this fiend from the Underworld? (2) And how could he defeat it?

Life ventured forth with the stealth of a panther, leaping behind trees, half crawling, and half crouching. He did not possess the super senses of smell like his comrade, but stealth was one of his strong points. Hours had passed, and Life had not seen any signs of zombies. These creatures were usually chaotic and clumsy, not caring how much destruction they caused during their activities.

"Midnight, your nose may need to be checked," Life muttered just before the hour of the dawn.

He crouched behind a large mossy tree that leaned at an angle on an embankment. Life's head swiveled right to left, then he bounded from around the tree and sprinted through the thin wood. Suddenly, the dense pockets of kudzu withered away and a desolate plain stretched out before him.

"Where are all of the undead that Midnight sensed?" Life

pondered as he darted from behind a tree and leaped behind another.

A cloud of dust appeared on his left. Life scurried behind a mossy boulder as he became aware of hooves thudding on the ground. As he peeped past the boulder, Life viewed hundreds of zombies galloping on undead horses and bulls. He could see that their empty eye sockets were filled with pale lights. Thick strands of green slime dripped from their torn clothing, and they waved curved swords. The undead were riding.

"Let's see where everyone is hanging at," Life whispered as he cocked his guns and slowly rose to his feet.

Just then a sharp object pricked Life in the middle of his back. Life froze in his tracks.

"Give my spear the pleasure to end your life, despicable Son of Bonanza," a deep voice harshly spoke.

"H-howdy, partner," Life slowly greeted.

"Save your breath, Son of Bonanza. It is will be your last on this earth," the assailant growled as he nudged the tip of the spear.

"I-I'm not even from Bonanza," Life said.

"You lie! Only the Sons of Bonanza wear such clothing! Die for your impudence!"

Before the assailant could thrust the spear through Life's back, Life cart wheeled forward. Life's boots knocked the spear away from his back. Then, he somersaulted through the air and landed in a standing position. Life whirled, cape moving in the wind, and beheld a zombie dressed in a raggedy lab coat with his rotting chest exposed. Life squinted past the gruesome dead flesh and read the name on the faded nametag: Dr. Francois.

"You sure are ugly," Life spoke.

"I will feast on your appendages in a steamy broth," the

zombie croaked as a strand of white slime dripped down his stark white ribcage.

"You need some iron in your diet, you bag of bones," Life yelled as he squeezed the trigger of his left revolver.

"BLAM!"

The blast of his gun was deafening. The passing zombies wheeled around to see a burning heap of ash near a group of boulders. Standing near the fiery heap of ash was a cowboy. His trench coat blew in the wind. A stream of gray smoke wiggled from his gun. The sight enraged the zombies, and they quickly rode toward him.

"Don't quit now. This is why you took the job," Life contemplated to himself as the horde of zombies surrounded him.

Life stood still as the zombies surrounded him with their spears extended. Life looked upon his adversaries with distaste but hid his emotions. At that moment, a zombie dressed in a filthy purple blazer nudged his undead black stallion forward. He had long stringy hair, and his face had rotted away. Life could see the zombie's purple cheek muscles.

"Greetings to the head zombie in charge," Life said.

"Son of Bonanza, put down your thunder stick," the leader of the zombies commanded in a hellish voice.

"That was my last bullet, so I tossed it into the forest," Life said. "Besides I am the King of Bonanza! Where are my sons?"

"You lie! Bonanza has no king, and those infidels are suffering a fate worse than death," the leader roared as his rotting hand moved for his sword.

Life prepared to take evasive action. However, his actions were stopped abruptly when a zombie with half a head interjected.

"Zeus, let's take him to the pit," the zombie with the half

head whispered. "The lady will reward us for capturing another one! Bonanza is already ours!"

Life played into the zombie's hands, reenacting a scene from *Briar Rabbit*.

"Please not the pit! Anything but the pit," Life begged as he kneeled before the leader of the zombies.

"Yes, it is the pit for you! String him up, boys," the leader of the zombies roared.

A lasso looped around Life and slid down to his ankles where it contracted into a knot.

"Say goodnight, cowboy," a zombie roared from behind him as something smashed against his head.

Life fell unconscious. Hopefully, his sacrifice had not been in vain.

"BLAM!"

Midnight jerked his head into the direction of the gunshot and listened for another shot. After awhile, the silence returned, but the rancid smell grew stronger in all directions.

"Hey, mon, is Life okay?" Danny Boy asked as he stood beside the wolf.

"One shot is good. Two shots are bad. Three is worse," Midnight replied. "We must keep going."

Danny Boy beckoned for the buses to follow him and Midnight. He had opted to scout the land with Midnight, just in case of any ambushes or booby traps. They had seen nothing or heard anything to stop their advancement. From Ms. Pook's calculations, Bonanza should have been within sight.

"Can't Ms. Pook use the Good Eye to see where our enemies are?" Danny Boy asked as he leapt over a small bush.

"It would be like looking at a beach for a grain of sand. Monsters are everywhere," Midnight growled as he cautiously stalked through the thin forest.

"Well, it's good she found us two champions," Danny Boy said in his islander accent.

"Thanks," Midnight growled as he searched for any signs of trouble.

"Hey, mon, there be no more heroes," Danny Boy continued to speak. "One day the world was fine, and the next day it was over!"

"It happened that fast?" Midnight asked.

"Oh, yes, mon. Like a snap of the finger," Danny Boy said. "The monsters appeared right after the earthquakes! I still remember a zombie leaping onto a news reporter on television! When she got up, she was all chewed up. Then, she jumped on the camera man!"

"What is television?" Midnight inquired as he hopped over a stump.

"It is almost like the Good Eye, but everything you see isn't real," Danny Boy said.

"Sounds like television is a bad thing," Midnight growled as he became uneasy.

The trees were thinning. Soon, anything would be able to see them. They continued their trek but stopped in their tracks when they saw a troublesome sign.

"Look at the brown slime that is dripping from the trees! Wicked, mon," Danny Boy said.

The slime dripped from the bows of the trees that spanned for about a mile. The slime was not on the lower boughs but on the boughs that were eight feet from the ground. Only one type of zombie had that height.

"Ogre zombie slime," Midnight snarled as his body began to become translucent like a shadow.

"Where are you going?" Danny Boy asked as he became afraid.

"Stay here with the people! It is not safe from this point forward!"

Midnight transformed into a shadow and dashed through the woods until the dawn came. The thin woods disappeared and a dusty plain came into view. Midnight came to a halt and cringed. Upon the desert plain were organized phalanxes of thousands of zombies besieging a walled neighborhood that had been elevated like a plateau. Rising in the midst of the neighborhood was a great pyramid.

"I should have seen this coming," Midnight snarled as he saw undead ogres with hammers and hundreds of undead horsemen madly galloping around the city.

The monsters had dug trenches and built fires that issued black smoke to hide their numbers.

"We can not get in," Midnight concluded as he gazed upon the army of the undead besieging the city.

He sprinted back into the woods to tell the people the bad news. There was no way they were going to make it to Bonanza that day.

4

Life slowly opened his eyes, but his vision went in and out. When he finally focused, Life discovered that he was in a dark cave. He stared at the limestone rocks in the ceiling, threatening to fall upon him at any moment. Life tried to move and discovered something else more frightening. His forearms and legs were free, but he could not move.

"The Underworld sorcery is strong here," Life contemplated as he looked around the cave.

Fortunately, his amber colored eyes gave him the ability to see into the dark as well as in the daytime. He was not the only prisoner in this pit. There were five other men imprisoned there. They were dressed in navy blue tactical armored vests with black helmets. Dark bags were under their eyes, and their faces were gaunt. Across the chests of the vests were with the words SWAT. Their heads were slumped down with grief. These men were not dead. They were defeated.

"Hey, you, wake up," Life whispered.

The men did not move, but he could see that they were breathing. Whatever this draining force was had a total grip upon them.

"You guys have been down here a long time," Life spoke in awe as he saw mold beginning to spread on their vests.

"It has just been two days since we were captured by her," a weak voice said.

Life rotated his head to see a man sitting in the corner. His attire was slightly different. This man had a baldhead and an untidy gray beard. He wore a golden helmet that was stained with dirt and grime. Life assumed that he was the leader of this disenfranchised group.

"You look like you've been down here longer," Life replied.

"This cave has a way of weakening a man. It preys on the suffering," the leader of the men weakly replied.

"Who are you and your friends?" Life asked.

"My name is Sgt. Steve, and I am a Son of Bonanza."

"You know, I've heard about you," Life said as he displayed a high level of interest.

"These men around you are all my brothers by blood and shield. You follow me," Sgt. Steve faintly replied. "We serve all mankind and are the long-arm of Ms. Ellen."

"I am on my way to see her," Life exclaimed.

"You and what army?" Sgt. Steve asked.

"Huh?"

"Bonanza must be surrounded by thousands of undead zombies by now," Sgt. Steve sorrowfully explained.

"Well, I was escorting Ms. Pook and the Good Eye to Bonanza to close the master gate to the Underworld," Life coolly replied.

The name of the matriarch stirred the captives. For the first time, a murmur was heard throughout the dungeon.

"The Good Eye is coming! Ms. Pook is coming!"

The murmur grew as the men began to discuss the vision of Ms. Ellen that involved an elderly lady with a magical eye.

"It was almost a month ago when Ms. Ellen revealed this vision to us. She said that when Ms. Pook comes with the Good Eye, we will be free," Sgt. Steve said in a weak voice.

"Don't be faint in the presence of adversity. We will prevail," Life assured.

Sgt. Steve looked upon Life with teary eyes.

"She is there! She is there, and she will take the Good Eye!

Her voice! Oh, her voice is so terrible," Sgt. Steve sobbed.

"Who is this lady you keep talking about?" Life asked as he began to gather his strength to undo the magic of the cave.

"It's useless. The magic of the Banshee is strong in this pit and will be stronger when she gets the Good Eye," Sgt. Steve said as he became depressed.

"The lady's name is the Banshee?" Life asked.

"No, she is the Banshee, an evil creature with an exotic beauty that hides a fierce beast underneath. She is from the Underworld," Sgt. Steve fearfully spoke.

"Enough is enough. Now, I know what I am dealing with," Life shouted as he struggled to his feet.

Suddenly, a tremor shook the chamber, sending strands of dirt sifting from the ceiling.

Life strained as he rose from his kneeling position.

The pressure of the cave was stifling, yet Life persevered.

Streams of dirt and small stones fell from the ceiling of the cave. Sgt. Steve shielded his eyes. Then, all became quiet in the dark cave, but another noise was heard.

There was a sound of crushing footsteps descending from the heights above. Sgt. Steve cringed. The footsteps belonged to the cruel undead ogre known as Overseer.

"Our Father, who art in heaven, hallowed be thy name," Sgt. Steve prayed as he shut his eyes and prayed for everyone in the cave.

Before he could finish the prayer, the iron door of the dungeon opened.

Overseer stepped into the dungeon, and Sgt. Steve risked a glance. He saw the monster's green tattooed baldhead, its orange eyes, and thick leather chest armor that protected its torso. The ogre wore a brief that was created from human hair and wielded a huge double blade axe in one hand with a flaming torch in the other.

"Who is making all of that racket?" Overseer roared.

Sgt. Steve smelled the ogre's reeking breath and gagged.

Overseer was furious. He tossed the torch on the ground and rushed over to Sgt. Steve.

"You ugly Son of Bonanza! I am gonna pop your head off for making that racket," Overseer shouted as he grasped Sgt. Steve by the throat with his huge hairy hand.

"Agggh," Sgt. Steve choked.

A brown centipede scurried around the ogre's hand and down Sgt. Steve's arm.

Sgt. Steve was helpless. He braced himself and looked Overseer in his orange eyes as the ogre squeezed harder.

"SHING!"

A silver blade sliced the ogre's arm at the wrist. The ogre's arm disintegrated, and Sgt. Steve was free!

"You should keep your hands to yourself," Life advised as he stepped into the torchlight with his sword extended just below his chin.

The ogre's orange eyes bulged as he saw the cowboy standing in the torchlight.

"The Banshee's magic should have left you powerless, cowboy," Overseer shrieked as he clutched his wounded arm.

"Not even Underworld sorcery can render me powerless," Life said.

His fiery orange eyes glanced at the giant axe that was on the ground between him and Life. They steadied the sharp curved edges of the blade. He could grab the axe and meat-cleave the cowboy!

"Go ahead and pick up your little toothpick!"

The ogre sneered at Life, showing his chipped teeth that were covered in green scum.

"Go ahead. Don't be scared," Life taunted as he took a step backwards and lowered his sword.

Sgt. Steve looked in disbelief.

"Are you crazy? What are you doing?" Sgt. Steve frantically asked.

"He is making this dungeon his grave! I will season my soup with your bones," the ogre roared as he grasped the axe and swung it with all of his might.

Life blocked the flying axe with his sword, sending a sheet of yellow sparks across the cave. Sgt. Steve stared at the cowboy, who seemed unharmed. A blow like that would have gutted ten men!

"Who is this man?" Sgt. Steve gasped as he watched Life rush forward, leap into the air with both feet first, and drop kick the ogre in the chest.

As he descended from the drop kick maneuver, Life swung his sword diagonally left and right across the chest of the ogre then horizontally across the ogre's knees. When Life landed safely on the ground, he sheathed his sword and walked over to Sgt. Steve as if nothing had happened.

"Ha! Ha! Your sword needs sharpening," Overseer harshly laughed in his hideous voice.

"He's not dead! He's not dead," Sgt. Steve yelled as Life stooped down and extracted his canteen.

"You're right! He's not dead. He's destroyed," Life said as the ogre reared his axe back to chop him in half.

Suddenly, the body of the giant ogre splintered from the incisions of Life's sword.

"Aggh! How did you do thisss?" the ogre shrieked as his body disintegrated from the precise incisions of his sword.

"Who are you?" Sgt. Steve asked as he stared past the flaming heap and into the amber eyes of the cowboy.

"My name is Life. Drink and be restored."

Sgt. Steve drank from the canteen of Life and quickly felt his energy return. His untidy gray beard turned black and neat while his gaunt face became youthful as his brown skin tone returned. The grime on his golden helmet vanished. The curse of the Banshee was broken!

"Help me free the Sons of Bonanza! We have a war to win," Life said as he assisted another person.

"Life, go to the upper level and free the other prisoners," Sgt. Steve cried out as he poured water into the mouths of his friends.

Life quickly scoured the dungeon, freeing hundreds of prisoners that the Banshee had captured. After Sgt. Steve had gathered his soldiers, Life blasted the last dungeon door open. At that moment, Life received a premonition. He leaned on Sgt. Steve.

"Take it easy, Life. You are overdoing it," Sgt. Steve spoke.

Life wiped his brow from the moment of intense perspiration. The premonition that he had just received was devastating.

"Sgt. Steve, I have to go save my best friend, or he will die," Life said as he leaned on Sgt. Steve.

"I understand," Sgt. Steve responded.

Sgt. Steve watched as Life dashed away. Then, he turned to his men. He did not see men who had been held prisoners or tortured. Sgt. Steve saw men waiting to be led to victory. His golden helmet gleamed in the sunlight. Soon, the battle cry of the Sons of Bonanza would be heard on the battlefield even if the city of Bonanza was lying in ruins.

Meanwhile, Midnight was arguing with Ms. Pook and urging them to use the little gas they had left to go back to New Hampton. However, Ms. Pook was not budging. She insisted that they continue to Bonanza, no matter what the peril was.

"Ms. Pook, there is something out there more dangerous than giant zombie ogres," Midnight growled as he stood defiantly before Ms. Pook.

"The Good Eye must return to Bonanza, and don't you growl at me," Ms. Pook urged as she stared at the morning sky.

"Why is it so important to go to Bonanza! It's not like it's a villa by the beach," Midnight snarled as he became frustrated.

"The Gates of the Underworld were cast open. That is why you had earthquakes and hungry zombies running amuck," Ms. Pook explained.

Midnight stared back at Ms. Pook.

"The Good Eye is the key to close all the gates!"

Midnight stared back at Ms. Pook. She clearly saw that he was not making the connection.

"Baby, the Master Gate is in the Pyramid. Around the world, there are invisible gates that connect us to the Underworld! One might walk into a cave, dive into a pool of water, and find themselves in the Underworld!"

Midnight continued to stare at Ms. Pook, causing the elderly woman to become frustrated.

"We can close all gates to the Underworld at one time and free the earth from the monsters!"

"There must be another way," grumbled Midnight.

"If you will not escort us, then I will go alone," Ms. Pook said as she walked toward the nearest bus.

"Then, I will go alone," Midnight mocked as he glanced at the people.

Midnight could smell the fear that emitted from their pores. It was an oily scent.

The mood among the people had gone from joyous to doubtful as he debated with Ms. Pook. Midnight decided to place his fear aside and give freedom a chance.

"Are you sure the Good Eye will close the gates?" Midnight inquired before Ms. Pook could board the bus.

"Was Brer Rabbit born in the briar patch?" Ms. Pook asked with a smile on her wrinkled face.

"Umm, yes," Midnight uneasily responded as he cocked his head to the side.

"Then, that's your answer," Ms. Pook laughed as she saw the confused look on Midnight's face.

Midnight chuckled and so did the people. After the laughter died down, Midnight spoke to the people.

"The undead will wish that they had remained dead when they see us coming!"

The people shouted with joy and loaded up into the buses.

The engine of the first bus revved as Danny Boy pulled his dreads back into a ponytail.

"Danny Boy, keep up with me if you can," Midnight snarled.

"I'll be on you like sunlight on the big blue ocean! Big up!

Booyaka! Booyaka!"

Midnight's body trembled as he expanded in size. When his transformation was complete, he sprung forward.

"We fight for love! We fight for freedom," Danny Boy yelled as he pressed the accelerator and shifted the gears of the bus.

The wolf and the buses sped from the thin woods and across the dusty plain. Midnight knew failure was not an option, even if it meant sacrificing himself so Ms. Pook and the others could be free.

6

The sky was tumultuous from the gray smoke of the trenches filled with fire. Zombies rode undead beasts around the elevated neighborhood of Bonanza, causing billows of dust to fly into the air. A zombie dwarf, with a decayed trachea, rushed to a pavilion that had been set up just out of the range of the archers that were camped along the walls of the neighborhood. The zombie was loyal to Desire, Queen of all monsters, and would see that this city of mankind would be obliterated.

"Banshee, your city awaits you," the zombie dwarf hoarsely spoke to a beautiful young woman with slanted eyes and tan skin.

The young woman laid on a bed of pillows in a pavilion that sat upon the battlefield. The young woman was dressed in a pink full-length kimono and had a red rose fitted into her long black hair.

"It is not my city nor is this my world," the Banshee coldly responded in her pleasant voice.

This was not the reply that the zombie dwarf had expected

from the Banshee.

"We will serve the will of Desire, and her will is to burn this city," the zombie dwarf hoarsely spoke.

The young woman rolled over on a pillow. She looked on the raggedy monster and the gray bone of its rotting throat. In her opinion, Desire had wasted her time in choosing the undead as her personal monsters.

"When I release Deprivation from the Pyramid, he'll do away with you rotting corpses," the Banshee said in her pleasant voice.

The zombie dwarf was furious at the comments of the Banshee.

"You are a traitor to all monsters," the zombie dwarf shouted.

"Me, I was born in the Underworld, but someone bit you and turned you. Your kind is just an infection," the Banshee said as a breeze ruffled her pink kimono.

Beneath her beauty, her anger swelled and became as dangerous as a flame near a can of gasoline. However, the zombie dwarf continued to sound off, oblivious to the danger at hand.

"Desire will strip your elegance from you," the dwarf scowled as he extracted his dagger.

"Once I release Deprivation, we will crush Desire and all fake monsters. Then we will make room for the monsters from the Underworld! The reptile-men have already joined the cause," the Banshee spoke as she rolled over on her pillows, looking at the dwarf with her beautiful green eyes.

"Perish, you traitor," the undead dwarf screamed.

Suddenly, the Banshee's smooth tanned skin tone transformed into a wart-filled grayish hide. The red rose in her hair withered to dust as her black hair was replaced with lashing serpents. The Banshee's pleasant voice became madness.

"Listen to me," the Banshee shrieked as she directed her voice toward the undead dwarf.

The sound of the Banshee's voice bombarded the zombie dwarf, and he drove himself crazy. He ran around in a circle with his hands in the sky.

"Y-yes! Y-yes," the zombie dwarf frantically responded as he continued to run around in circles.

"Run toward the city," the Banshee shrieked.

The zombie dwarf ran directly toward the wall of Bonanza. A young woman adorned with a silver winged golden tiara was positioned among the wall with the Golden Arms of Bonanza that were dressed in army fatigues. She was dressed in her black SWAT team uniform with tactical body armor and her tiara gleamed in the dim sunlight. The woman was Ms. Ellen, the Axe-Murderer of monsters.

"Do you think he wants to come over to play cards?" Ms. Ellen asked her brother, Kent, who was standing to her left.

The sun shone off of Kent's baldhead as he smiled at his sister's sarcastic remark. Before the earthquakes, Kent was a body builder who trained several pro-wrestlers. Then, he received another calling and became a preacher. Now, he was the captain of the Golden Archers.

"Sis, that sap suka might beat you in a game of Spades," Kent laughed.

To her right, her other brother, Robert, pulled his curly hair back into a short ponytail. Before the earthquakes, Robert was an ordinary person who helped ordinary people when the police could not. Some people called it street justice. Others knew it as peace of mind. Now, he was the captain of the Golden Arms.

"That lil' zombie is about to see more than a big joker," Robert said as he drew back the string of his compound bow.

Robert aimed the tip of the sharp arrow at the zombie's chest. The shot would be clean. It would be true.

"At ease, Robert," Ms. Ellen commanded as she leapt onto the edge of the twenty-foot tall wall.

"What are you going to do?" asked Robert.

"If we are going to win this battle, the people will need some inspiration."

The brothers stared at their little sister. They both remembered her taking care of them when they were sick. Kent remembered Ms. Ellen jacking up his mischievous girlfriends. Robert remembered giving her the nickname of 'Broke Back' to encourage her to get over the complications of a back surgery. Both of them knew that there was no stopping her. They knew that this was necessary for their survival.

"We will cover you, sis. May God be with you," Kent said.

"Do what you do, Broke Back," Robert said.

"For Bonanza," Ms. Ellen yelled as she flipped off the wall.

The monsters ceased their preparations for battle as they saw the woman descending from the wall. Ms. Ellen landed on the ground and backhanded the crazed zombie dwarf.

"Rgggh," the dwarf screamed as he scratched at Ms. Ellen.

She knew of the dangers of scratches and bites from zombies. She easily dodged the lunges of the zombie like an experienced boxer in the ring.

"Rggggh!"

Ms. Ellen spun left and extracted her military knife that was attached to her forearm. The knife sliced the zombie dwarf at his neck. He exploded into a fiery heap. Instead of cheers going up, warnings echoed from the wall.

"Watch out, Ms. Ellen! Behind you! Behind you!" Kent and Robert cried out.

Ms. Ellen wheeled around just in time to dodge a downward swing from a zombie with a large hammer. The hammer crashed into the earth, and Ms. Ellen flipped over the zombie at the same time she swung her axe in an upward arc.

The blade of the golden axe hacked the knees and torso of the zombie.

"You are a hot mess," Ms. Ellen said as the zombie slid apart in a burning heap.

Two more zombies scrambled toward her. Their faces were half chewed away. Ms. Ellen threw her military knife and struck the first zombie in its left eye. The second zombie was bigger and wore a dirty purple blazer and had a badly decomposed face.

"You need a make over, honey," Ms. Ellen said as she saw the purple muscles along the rotting cheekbones.

The zombie's white hair flowed in the wind as he brandished a crooked sword.

"Axe Murderer! My name is Zeus, and I am here to dismember you," he cried out in his hellish voice.

"With that can opener? Honey, please," Ms. Ellen scoffed.

Zeus knew the range of the archers, and he dared not take another step forward. Therefore, he did the next best thing. He made Ms. Ellen come to him.

"Your Sons of Bonanza are dying, suffering in a pit! My ogre is making a victory soup with their bones!"

"Dog gone your soul," Ms. Ellen yelled as she rushed toward Zeus.

Her visage was menacing. Her pain was overwhelming. Ms. Ellen swung her golden axe, and it crashed against the zombie's sword.

The sword broke, and its tip ricocheted into the zombie's shoulder.

"Rgggh," Zeus roared as he punched Ms. Ellen in the face.

The punch busted Ms. Ellen's nose and her upper lip. However, Ms. Ellen didn't feel the pain. She only felt fury.

"Didn't they tell you never to hit a lady," Ms. Ellen shouted as she thrust the handle of her axe into Zeus's jaw, knocking him three feet back.

In her rage, Ms. Ellen leapt forward, pivoted around, and kicked the zombie in the knee.

The zombie's leg bone broke, and Zeus collapsed. Ms. Ellen stood above him with her golden axe half raised.

"Raagh," Ms. Ellen screamed as she repeatedly hacked her axe between the zombie's neck and shoulders.

The zombie burned away, and Ms. Ellen looked around. No more than ten yards away was the army of the undead creeping toward her.

"Maann! Fleessshh!"

She could see their raggedy clothes, rotting bodies, and the pale light in their eyes. Behind them was a large ogre with a spiked helmet. In his green hands was a large spiked mace!

"Get the Axe-Murderer! Seize her," the zombie ogre commander shouted.

Ms. Ellen turned and sprinted back toward the safety of the wall as the army of undead relentlessly pursued her. She saw Kent and Robert poised, ready to let their arrows loose.

"C'mon, Broke Back," Robert urged as he aimed right past

her shoulder.

"God speed," Kent urged as he took aim.

A zombie swung and missed her from behind. Then, another lunged forward. Ms. Ellen felt a dead hand grab her by the shoulder. Its nails dug into her shoulder and drew blood.

"Get off of me," Ms. Ellen yelled as she wrenched away from the clutches of the zombie.

The zombie knelt on its rotting knees. Its sinews were exposed and contracting. The zombie pointed and let loose a terrible laugh.

"You're damned, Axe-Murderer!"

The zombie waited for the change to occur, but it never happened.

"Why didn't you change?"

"As long as I wear my golden tiara, you can't hurt me! Now, goodbye!"

Ms. Ellen sprinted toward the wall.

Another zombie screamed and sprinted toward her at an amazing speed.

Ms. Ellen zigzagged and stutter-stepped, but the zombie was too fast and too quick for her to evade.

Slobber flew from its mouth as it hounded Ms. Ellen. Right then, the zombie reached out to grab the woman.

"Not today, buddy," Ms. Ellen yelled as she drove her palm into the mushy forehead of the zombie, stiff-arming it the ground.

The monster fell face first upon the dusty ground as Ms. Ellen high stepped over its wriggling hands.

"Hurry, Sis," Kent yelled as the zombies closed in on his sister.

Suddenly, Ms. Ellen pointed her axe toward the wall. The

spiked tip of the golden axe ejected. The spike was attached to a small chain. When it smashed into the wall, Ms. Ellen could feel a hidden mechanism speedily hauling her upward.

The zombies screamed as they gnashed at Ms. Ellen.

The mob stopped short of the line of fire and dared not test the range of the archers on the wall. Several zombies hurled spears at Ms. Ellen as she scrambled up the wall.

Fortunately, none ever reached their target.

"You should be in the crazy house," Robert said as he helped Ms. Ellen over the wall.

"This world is the crazy house," Ms. Ellen replied as she caught her breath and wiped the blood from her nose.

"Sis, I think you got everyone riled up," Kent said as he hugged his sister.

"Shhh. It's silent," Ms. Ellen said as she rose to her feet.

Ms. Ellen glanced over the wall just in time to see the zombie ranks part. The Banshee glided across the line of fire where she addressed her foes for the last time. Her long black hair flowed in the wind, and a beautiful smile was on her face.

"I'm your friend. You don't want to fight me. Let me and my friends into your city," the Banshee softly spoke.

The Banshee's voice was almost like music. Those who heard the melody became enthralled. However, Ms. Ellen was not amused. The Lady of the Lake had warned her of the Banshee's evil voice.

"Kent, is today a good day to die?" Ms. Ellen asked as she picked up her bow and pointed the tip of the arrow toward the Banshee's head.

"Any day is a good day to die for freedom," Kent replied as he signaled the Golden Archers.

All across the wall, the archers aimed at the Banshee with sniper rifles and bows, but she was not daunted. She hissed at the archers.

"Then, send this wench and her ugly voice back to the Underworld," Ms. Ellen commanded.

"Fools, I will place your heads on the stakes and pluck out your eyes," the Banshee threatened as she saw the archers aim at her.

Kent snorted and cleared his nasal passages. He wanted his voice to be clear for all ears whether alive or undead.

"Archers, bring the rain," Kent commanded in a loud voice as he drew back his arrow and released.

Hundreds of arrows and bullets were released. As they sped toward her, the Banshee shrieked.

The decibels of the scream repelled the mass of arrows and sent the archers sprawling upon their faces. Only Ms. Ellen remained standing. She looked around and saw her friends trembling in fear.

"Is that all you've got?" Ms. Ellen challenged as she loaded her bow a second time.

"GRRRGGH," the Banshee shrieked as she concentrated her efforts on a specific spot.

The shriek crumbled Ms. Ellen's compound bow as if it were tin foil and tossed her to the ground. A horrible roar went up in the air!

"The Axe-Murderer is down! Take the city," the zombie ogre shouted.

The zombies went into a frenzy and rushed towards the gate, ripping away the stones of the walls.

"We have lost! We have lost," Ms. Ellen sobbed as she felt

the wall tremble from the assault from the undead.

"HHHHOOOOOOOWLLL!"

Suddenly, the howl of a wolf was heard, and the assault of the undead ceased. Surprisingly, Ms. Ellen felt her strength return. Ms. Ellen slowly rose and leaned on the wall.

"Is that a wolf?" Ms. Ellen inquired as she saw a great cloud of dust was on the horizon.

She produced a pair of binoculars from her pocket. She focused the lens. Soon, she distinguished a large black wolf rushing ahead of two school buses. Her father's vision had come to pass! The wolf was coming to Bonanza!

"The wolf is coming! The wolf is coming," Ms. Ellen cried out as she jumped for joy.

"What are you saying?" Kent asked as he cowered in a corner.

"The wolf is coming! The wolf from father's vision," Ms. Ellen joyously shouted as she tossed him the binoculars.

Kent didn't catch the binoculars. He was still in disbelief.

"What?"

"Listen to the howl!"

Kent shook his head as he covered his face. Then, he heard the sound. Kent heard the howl of the wolf.

"HHHOOOOOOOWLLL!"

Kent jerked to his feet and viewed the wolf and the buses.

"Everyone, get up! The wolf is here," Kent encouraged as he helped Robert to his feet.

Ms. Ellen peered back over the wall. The wolf was closer. However, the Banshee had not been idle. She too had heard the howl of the wolf, and she was not pleased.

"Robert, send the Golden Arms to the courtyard and prepare for all out combat! Kent set the Golden Archers along the wall!

We are going to crush this undead army,"

The army of Bonanza reorganized, and Ms. Ellen led the Golden Arms into the courtyard of the wall to the hidden gate. Ms. Ellen waited for the perfect time to strike. As she waited, she prayed for the safety of her people and victory.

7

Midnight beheld the Banshee. Wind rustled her pink robe, and a swirl of dust kicked up around her. He knew she was gathering her energy for a devastating attack.

"Sorry, Danny Boy, but I can't place you in danger," Midnight growled as he transformed into his Shadow Wolf form and increased his speed tenfold.

"What is he doing?" one of the passengers yelled on Danny Boy's bus.

"He is going to bust a head, mon" Danny Boy yelled as the bus slowed down. "Rip her another one from the ruta to the tuta!"

The Banshee let loose her greatest cry. The sound waves of the scream broke the earth and hurled chunks of rocks in the direction of the shadow wolf. Midnight took evasive action, nimbly dodging the flying debris beaming toward him.

"You've got to do better than that," Midnight snarled as he pounced into the air and spun into a rolling ball.

Midnight smashed through the enormous rocks that were being hurled at him.

The Banshee screamed louder, exerting all her energy at the rolling ball. Patches of fur ripped from Midnight's overcoat as the Banshee's voice became a vocal razor. The pain of being skinned alive was tremendous, but Midnight endured the agony and smashed into the monster.

"WHAM!"

The collision sent the two adversaries tumbling onto the ground. The undead watched with great anticipation. Never had anyone silenced the Banshee's scream.

"You've got an anvil for a head," Midnight growled as he reverted to his wolf form and struggled to his feet.

Tendrils of steam rose off the back of the wolf. Patches of fur were missing from his overcoat.

"Ha! Ha! You need a new coat," the Banshee laughed as her smooth skin became warty, and her hair transformed into serpents.

"It isn't over," Midnight growled as he collapsed.

"You are quite mistaken. You are done," the Banshee shrieked at a high-pitched note that could not be heard by any human.

An agonizing ache penetrated Midnight's head, and his body trembled in convulsions. The ground cracked as the Banshee's voice bared down upon Midnight.

"You have to save him, Danny Boy, or her voice will bust his heart," Ms. Pook pleaded as she witnessed the attack on Midnight.

"But he said to protect you," Danny Boy argued.

"Don't worry about me! Save Midnight," Ms. Pook yelled as she clutched the small purse that contained the magical trinket.

Danny Boy leapt off the bus and sprinted to Midnight's aid.

"Aieeee," Danny Boy shouted as he swung his machete at the Banshee's head.

The Banshee ducked but the swing clipped a couple of lashing snakes from her head. Danny Boy froze as the Banshee diverted her scream at him. The force crushed his machete and shred the clothes from his body.

"Fool, I am from the Underworld! No weapon that you possess can harm me," the Banshee bellowed as she grasped Danny Boy by the throat with a warty hand and raised him off the ground. Danny Boy struggled as her talons pricked his neck.

A drop of blood dripped onto her hand. Instantly, she was aware of the battle at the Hole, the heroics of Life and Midnight, Ms. Pook, and the Good Eye!

"The Good Eye is within my grasp! With the Good Eye, I can enhance my scream tenfold," the Banshee whispered as she hurled Danny Boy to the side.

Danny Boy landed on his shoulder. His collarbone snapped!

"Run, Ms. Pook! Lord a mercy," Danny Boy muttered as he fainted.

The Banshee swiftly floated towards Ms. Pook's bus. As she neared the vehicle, she noticed that it had been abandoned. However, she could feel the presence of one poor soul.

"The Good Eye is mine," the Banshee bellowed and tore the door away from the bus.

A black boot kicked the Banshee in the face! The Banshee staggered backwards as a cowboy dressed in black stepped out of the bus.

"I hope you're going to replace that door," Life advised in a comical tone.

"Step aside, cowboy. The Good Eye is mine," the Banshee growled as she rubbed her warty face.

"You'll have to go through me first!"

"My pleasure," the Banshee yelled as she lunged at Life with her sharp fingernails.

Life blocked all of her swings with his forearms and spun around with an open palm. The backhand slap smashed the Banshee on the right side of the cheek and knocked her to the ground. She was startled at the strength of the cowboy and sought another strategy. She transformed into her beautiful exotic form.

"What in the world?" Life mused.

The beauty of the woman enthralled Life.

"You hurt me so much," the woman sobbed.

Life felt disgusted at himself.

"I am sorry."

"Why do you treat me so bad, cowboy?" the Banshee softly asked as glitter reflected on her eyelids.

"I-I didn't mean to hit you so hard," Life spoke as he reached out to help the gorgeous lady.

"Please pick me up," the Banshee requested as she collapsed face first.

Life stooped down and just as he touched the soft shoulders of the woman, her lovely skin tone faded to a warty green.

"Chivalry is dead and so are you," the Banshee growled as she turned around and released a tremendous screech.

Life was thrown against the bus. The impact was so hard that it exploded all of its windows.

"Umm," Life moaned as he struggled to his feet.

"Good-bye, silly cowboy," the Banshee shouted as she screamed louder than ever.

Life felt the intensity of the scream surging across his face. It was like tiny needles prickling his skin. The Banshee drew closer. Suddenly, Life dropped to his knees

The tires of the bus busted, and the frame of the bus bent. The surrounding sand became glass.

"He cannot resist my voice forever! I must get closer," the Banshee contemplated as she placed her face directly before Life's face.

She screamed louder, exerting all of herself as she saw Life's skin ripple. The Banshee had every intention of blowing off Life's face. Suddenly, Life delivered a quick chop to her throat and crushed her larynx.

"Arrggh," the Banshee gasped and bent over.

Life removed two pieces of beef jerky that he had stuffed in his ears.

"I couldn't understand anything you were saying," Life gasped.

The Banshee was startled as she held her throat.

"W-what have you done to my v-voice?" the Banshee wheezed as she staggered from side-to-side.

"I gave you good advice," Life answered as he stood up.

The Banshee lunged at him with her sharp claws, but Life quickly side-stepped and kicked her in the face. Then, he snatched the Banshee by the snakes that were on her head.

Life rammed her head against the bus and spun around with his sword. As he walked towards his friends, the Banshee's body exploded into a fiery heap.

At that moment, a horn was blown. Life wheeled toward its sound. Standing on a hilltop were the Sons of Bonanza.

"Behold the Sons of Bonanza," Life shouted in a loud voice.

Another horn was sounded within the walled city of Bonanza. It was a sound that had not been heard in days. It was the horn of Ms. Ellen responding to the horn of Sgt. Steve!

"The Sons of Bonanza! Impossible," the giant zombie ogre commander with the spiked helmet roared. "Reform the lines, you maggots!"

The army of the undead froze at the sound of the horns. They did not hear their commander. Their undead eyes focused on the hundreds of soldiers surrounding the five generals of the Sons of Bonanza.

"For Ms. Ellen," Sgt. Steve shouted as he held up his battle-axe while charging the ranks of the undead army with his army.

"For Ms. Pook," the residents of the Hole shouted as they rushed to join the fight.

Just then, the giant zombie ogre commander heard a creaking noise that was like a casket being opened after several years of being buried.

He wheeled around as the hidden gate of Bonanza opened. Standing in the gap was Ms. Ellen and the Golden Arms!

"Grggghh! The Axe-Murderer," the zombie ogre commander roared.

Ms. Ellen raised her golden battle-axe into the air and her army roared like a lion.

"For Bonanza," Ms. Ellen yelled as they charged forward.

The army of the undead was trapped. There was no escape.

As the battle ensued, Ms. Pook hobbled over to Life and held his hand in hers. She was full of tears at the fact that Danny Boy and Midnight were greatly injured.

"Life, can you save Danny Boy and Midnight?" Ms. Pook asked as she sobbed.

"Let's see if my water can help them," Life answered as he poured the water from his canteen into their mouths.

After a couple of seconds, Danny Boy regained consciousness, and his wounds were healed.

"Did someone get the number of that train that hit me, mon?" Danny Boy asked as he rubbed his head.

"How is your arm?" Ms. Pook inquired as she comforted him.

"It's good as new," Danny Boy said as he rotated his shoulder.

Life poured a little more water into Midnight's mouth, but he still showed no signs of revival. His condition was worse than Danny Boy's. The Banshee had hit Midnight with some good stuff. Life waited for a couple of seconds. With no signs, Life began mouth-to-mouth resuscitation.

"Hang in there, partner," LIfe slowly spoke as he took a deep breath.

Just as he was about to put his mouth on Midnight's snout, the wolf stirred.

"More beef jerky," Midnight whispered as his wounds healed.

"You ain't nothing but a hound dog," Life laughed as he hugged Midnight.

Ms. Pook watched as they rolled on the ground, oblivious to fact that a war was raging on.

Chapter 4

The Prophecy of the Good Eye

The undead army could not sustain a resistance against the three armies that had converged on them. By sunset, their lines were utterly dismantled. Life, Midnight, and Danny Boy escorted Ms. Pook across the battlefield of burning heaps of gray ashes to where Ms Ellen and Sgt. Steve stood. Life gazed at the woman with great regard. Besides being courageous, Ms. Ellen was also very cute.

"Welcome to the neighborhood of Bonanza, cowboy," Ms. Ellen greeted as she leaned on her golden battle-axe.

"Thank you. You have a beautiful community that is filled with courageous and beautiful people," Life replied as he cracked a smile at Ms. Ellen.

Ms. Ellen thought that the cowboy was handsome. For the first time in years, she allowed the girly side of her to break through as she blushed.

"I am Ms. Ellen."

Life did not shake her hand. He held it and kissed it. This gesture of chivalry sent a unique feeling of excitement down Ms. Ellen's spine, awakening the most powerful bond between man and woman.

The bond was love.

"My name is Life, and these are my friends: Midnight, Danny Boy, and Ms. Pook."

Ms. Ellen immediately straightened her posture. She had literally dreamed of this moment. She rushed to the elderly woman and hugged her.

"The Ms. Pook from my dreams? I imagined you just a little taller," she exclaimed.

"Baby, only when I am leaning on my walking stick," Ms. Pook replied as she hugged Ms. Ellen back.

"Is the Good Eye with you?" Ms. Ellen asked.

Ms. Pook gathered her balance, held up the walking stick, and shouted in a powerful voice.

"The cowboy has returned! The Good Eye is here!"

Everyone who heard the proclamation cheered. The prophecy of Ms. Ellen's father had come true. Freedom was closer than ever, and Ms. Ellen would not wait another day to savor its taste!

"Then you must be brought to the Pyramid as quickly as possible! Transport," Ms. Ellen requested.

Sgt. Steve quickly pulled up in a jeep and assisted Ms. Pook into it. This was one of the few vehicles used only in emergencies due to the scarcity of fuel. Sgt. Steve drove them toward the Pyramid. Soon, they arrived at the Pyramid. All were dangerously silent. Life stared at the rugged sides of the structure.

"Magnificent! This Pyramid aligns itself with the setting of the sun," Life said as he noticed the tip of the structure being illuminated by the setting sun.

"Indeed, it is a wonder of the world, but we do not know what is inside," Ms. Ellen replied.

"Deprivation is inside, and who knows what booby traps he has set for us," Midnight growled.

Ms. Ellen picked up a rock and threw it toward the Pyramid.

The rock vaporized as it came into contact with an electromagnetic field.

"The energy field is deadly. We had to learn the hard way when one of our citizens wandered too close," Ms. Ellen said.

"Life, do you think you can open the way for us?" Ms. Pook asked.

"Let us see, old mother," Life nodded as he walked to where two statues of winged lions stood.

Life held out his hands, feeling the energies of the field. Suddenly, a blue barrier appeared.

"How did you do that?" Sgt. Steve asked.

"The power that gives me the ability to crush the diamonds gives me power over this field," Life spoke.

"It's time we close the screen door and stop these monsters from entering our world," Ms. Pook said.

"Who is going with us?" Life asked.

Silence filled the crowd as all eyes locked onto the cowboy. Who knew what monstrosities guarded the master gate. Ms. Ellen was the first to take the step forward.

"Kent, Robert, and Sgt. Steve, I am leaving you in charge of the forces. Surround the pyramid. When the electromagnetic field goes down, storm it from all angles! For Bonanza," Ms. Ellen shouted as she jumped off the jeep.

"For Bonanza! Sis, take my shield. It was made for a day like this," Kent offered as he handed Ms. Ellen a golden shield.

"Thank you. Set a sentry guard just in case more monsters come," Ms. Ellen ordered as she hugged her brother.

The three captains agreed with Ms. Ellen's decree. Life placed his hands into the field.

Sparks flew as the energy of the field interacted with his body. However, the field had no effect on him.

"H-hurry, I-I cant hold it much longer," Life strained as he stretched the opening wide enough for two people to step through.

One at a time, Ms. Pook, Ms. Ellen, and Midnight bound through the opening. Once they were safely on the other side, Life heaved the opening apart and rolled through. Behind him, the portal sealed. The silent pyramid loomed before them.

"Midnight, keep your nose open and bring up the rear. Next, Ms. Ellen. Then, Ms. Pook," Life directed as he swiftly constructed a makeshift torch out of some nearby brush.

They entered the Pyramid not knowing that they were walking into a trap.

2

Life cautiously led his friends down a dark corridor. His amber colored eyes pierced the darkness as he searched for any signs of booby traps, pitfalls, or signs of ambushes.

"This place needs a country cleaning," Ms. Pook said.

The corridor was dusty, and the walls were smooth without any markings.

"I don't like this. Pyramids are supposed to have some type of recorded history of a civilization on their walls," Life said as he cautiously crept down the corridor.

"Perhaps there is no history," Midnight growled.

"Everything has a history. Even time has history," Ms. Ellen said.

After a while, the corridor forked in two different directions.

"Enie meenie mine mo! The corridor splits. Which way should we go?" Life whispered.

Suddenly, the floor of the corridor trembled, and Life heard a gnashing in the deep ahead of him. At the same time, Life felt waves of absolute hatred. Only a monster from the Underworld possessed such energy.

"Everyone, back up," Life ordered as he peered down the passage into the darkness.

There was a scraping noise along the walls of the corridor. Then, it grew louder.

"What is that noise?" Midnight asked.

"Talons! Big Talons," Life answered as an enormous black claw extended from the darkness and into the torchlight.

Suddenly, the corridor was sealed at the entrance and the intersection. There was no escape for them! Miss Ellen bit her bottom lip as she detected a smell that was like raw sewage.

"Something stinks, and it is coming right for us," she gagged as she tightened her grip on her golden axe.

"It's show time," Midnight snarled as he expanded in size.

Life did not reply. He had only felt such negation during the battle with Death. The scurrying noise ceased and six red eyes glowed in the darkness just beyond the light of the torch.

"It's on now," Ms. Ellen shouted as she lightly jogged in

place.

"Life, what is it? What is staring at us?" Ms. Pook asked.

Suddenly, the flame of the torch lost its intensity and went out. Life and his friends stood in complete darkness as six pairs of eyes stared at them.

"Midnight, whatever happens, do not leave Ms. Pook and Ms. Ellen alone! Take them with you," Life advised as he drew his pistol and cocked the hammer back with his right hand.

"Life, are you going somewhere?" Midnight inquired.

Midnight saw Life's hand shaking. He sniffed and smelled his friend's perspiration. For the first time since the resurrection, Midnight knew that Life was afraid. He would not sit idle while Life was in need. Midnight took a step forward, but Life stopped him without turning around.

"Stay, Midnight. Take Ms. Ellen and Ms. Pook with you," Life ordered.

At that moment, an evil laughter filled the chamber. An apparition of a sky blue flame appeared in the shape of a menacing diamond crusted ram head. It hovered in the air and filled the chamber with an eerie blue light.

"After my gremlins did not return with your head, I devised a crueler demise for you. No one will hear your cries for help," the apparition verbalized in a dreadful voice.

Life stood his ground.

"Deprivation, I will crush you and send you back to the Underworld," Life shouted as he aimed his pistol at the flaming skull.

"Your guns and words are useless here, cowboy," Deprivation warned.

"Deprivation, we're going to put your blue lights out,"

Midnight snarled.

The apparition of Deprivation turned its attention to Midnight.

"Things must be getting bad for you to pick up the elderly and savage to travel with you. You are such a threatening gang," Deprivation spoke in a sarcastic tone.

Life dropped the extinguished torch and drew his other gun. He would not tolerate any more insults from Deprivation.

"Angra, devour them all," Deprivation boomed as his deep voice caused dirt to sift from the ceiling.

The apparition of the flaming blue ram head vanished. There was an explosion of red flames.

Life quickly took off his leather coat and cast it toward his friends. The leather coat stretched across the corridor, blocking the scorching wave of flames. However, Life was left vulnerable. The blast of flames scorched him!

"Midnight, get them away from here," Life cried out as the red and orange flames seared through his black shirt and hat.

Life staggered as his skin bubbled on his face and arms. Suddenly, something darted from behind the wall of flames.

"A fire ant from the Underworld," Midnight growled.

The enormous fire ant lunged at Life with tremendous speed. Before Life could squeeze the triggers of his guns, the pinchers of the ant seized Life by the waist. Life felt the pressure crush his ribs, pelvis, and spine. Life went numb from his waist down.

"Agggh, my back," he yelled.

"Midnight, he's being burned alive! Help him," Ms. Pook screamed as she saw Life being burned beyond recognition.

Midnight pounced at the flaming ant. Angra slapped Midnight with a flaming leg, sending him flying down the corridor.

"Foolish wolf! I was here before the moon was hung in

the sky! You cannot impede me," Angra roared as its flames expanded across the corridor.

Then, the beast jabbed its burning claw at Ms. Pook, but Ms. Ellen somersaulted in front of Ms. Pook with Kent's shield extended.

The flaming talon burst through the shield and began to melt the metal.

"Take this," Ms. Ellen yelled as she immediately slid the shield from her arm and sliced upward with her axe, amputating the tip of the claw from the ant's leg.

The claw dropped to the ground and burned away into ash!

"Arrrgh," Angra roared as it reared backward.

"There's plenty more where that came from, sap sucka! I am the Axe-Murderer," Ms. Ellen yelled as she whirled the axe around her head.

The ferocity of the Ms. Ellen sent the fire ant back into the darkness with Life in its pinchers. Ms. Ellen pursued the beast. Just when she was about to be in striking distance, a hidden door slid across the corridor.

Sparks flew as Ms. Ellen repeatedly smashed the wall with her axe. Life was gone. The fire ant had taken him.

"W-w-why?" Ms. Ellen sobbed as she threw the axe down in frustration and sunk to her knees.

The torch that went out relit itself. Ms. Pook picked up the torch and held it aloft. She hobbled over to Ms. Ellen and consoled her.

"Pull yourself together, Ms. Ellen," Midnight spoke as he limped to the spot where Life was attacked.

Ms. Pook saw Midnight studying the spot. He began to search the ashes with his paws. Something was there.

"What is it, Midnight?" Ms. Pook asked.

"He left me my glaive and his guns," Midnight snarled. "He left his guns and my glaive so that we could finish the mission!"

"Ms. Pook, can you shoot?" Ms. Ellen asked as she refocused on the task at hand.

"Is a chicken wing good with hot sauce?" Ms. Pook replied as she put the torch down and picked up the guns.

To her surprise, the guns were featherweight in her hands. Midnight licked his muzzle as Ms. Pook's aged hands twirled the revolvers like a young gunslinger.

"Put your hands on the nape of my neck and hold onto me. We are about to become shadows," Midnight growled as he prepared to fulfill Life's last request.

Ms. Pook and Ms. Ellen put their hands on Midnight's neck. To Ms. Ellen's surprise, the darkened world transformed to gray and white. To their amazement, several pictographs of an enormous four-legged beast being followed by smaller beasts were etched along the walls.

"What are these pictures?" Ms. Ellen asked as she saw the diagrams on the white walls of the pyramid.

"You have just entered the Shadow World, and that beast is the terrible King of the Shadow Hounds," Midnight said.

"Is he here?" Ms. Ellen asked.

"As long as you hold onto me, you will be in the Shadow World, which is his realm. Hopefully, we will not cross his path," replied Midnight.

They walked through the wall and traveled on the ascending passageway. As the three ventured through the Pyramid via the Shadow World, they were stalked by several shadow hounds who had caught their scent. Now, the signal had been sent out.

The King of the Shadow Hounds would not be merciful for them venturing into his territory. They would pay with their lives.

Sgt. Steve studied the evening sky. The battle was over, but there was still a foreboding presence. He ordered the citizens to be moved into the interior of the neighborhood. Then, Kent reported back on a two-way radio.

"Sgt. Steve, the Golden Arms have mobbed everyone into the interior of the neighborhood," Kent reported to Sgt. Steve.

Sgt. Steve held the button and spoke into the radio.

"I want lookouts in all directions. For Bonanza," Sgt. Steve replied.

"For Bonanza," Kent replied.

Sgt. Steve sat on the rocky hill and let his mind drift. In the past, a person could get stuck in traffic on Tara Blvd, reality television shows replaced sitcoms, summer festivals at Centennial Park lasted late into the night, and the housing market entered a meltdown. Suddenly, his thoughts were broken by a faint cry.

"Agggh, my back!"

"That was Life's voice," Sgt. Steve yelled as he leapt to his feet.

Seconds passed as his heart pounded in his chest.

"BOOM!"

The earth shook. Then, Sgt. Steve saw jets of fire burst from the base of the Pyramid.

"Did a bomb go off?" Sgt. Steve whispered.

There was no response. All was once again quiet. Sgt. Steve bit his bottom lip. There was nothing for him to do, so he did the next best thing. He prayed.

"Lord, have mercy on your servants. Protect them and guide them," Sgt. Steve silently prayed as he bowed his head.

At that moment, the alarm went up from the wall. Bells rang and horns bellowed. Sgt. Steve put his binoculars to his face.

Gathering north of the battlefield was a legion of hideous reptile-men. Reptile-men were the most vicious of adversaries. Their thick scales repelled arrows, and they ate their victims, whether dead or alive!

"Lord, have mercy on us," Sgt. Steve prayed as he gazed on the size of the army.

The day of reckoning had come for the Golden Arms and Bonanza. Today, they would have to stand strong or they would be crushed. Today was the end of the world as they knew it.

The fire had burned Life greatly, but it had not killed him. Life's skin was charred and peeled away. Most of the burns were along his head and chest. Breathing pained him, and his vision was blurred. If Life didn't do something soon, he would die.

"Aaah," Life moaned as he struggled to free himself from the flaming pinchers of the fire ant.

"Quit your nagging," Angra roared as he slammed Life's head into the side of the corridor, hauling him back to its subterranean lair.

Life's burned hat flew off his head. For the first time since his resurrection, Life felt blood trickling down the side of his face. The sensation caused a simple thought to pop in his head.

"N-need w-water," Life moaned.

"Are my flames making you thirsty?" Angra giggled. "Let me give you some air!"

Suddenly, the fiery ant flung Life across the air and watched as the flaming body of his adversary streak across the dark underground chamber.

"Holy Moly," Life cried out as he crashed through a column of rock and into a heap of stones.

A cloud of dust drifted up from the crash.

"Now for your friends! The elderly woman looks so tasty," Angra roared as he crawled away.

Suddenly, Angra felt a positive presence in the room.

"Why are you leaving? The party is just beginning," a voice loudly spoke.

Angra wheeled around and beheld Life standing atop a heap of stones. His sword reflected the red flames that wreathed around the ant. His body and his clothing were fully restored.

"You! I beat you, burned you, and broke you, but you still live," Angra screeched as his red flames became bright orange.

Life polished his fingernails on the jacket of his coat.

"Water improves your appearance, heals your wounds, and makes you feel better," Life spoke.

"Nuisance! This time, I will make sure I burn you to a crisp," Angra growled as he rushed toward Life and was wreathed in a cloud of orange flames.

The ground shook as the six legs of the ant drummed along the ground. Life felt the oncoming heat and knew he could not suffer the flames of the fire ant a second time. Quickly, he formulated a plan.

"Catch," Life said as he kicked an oblong-shaped boulder at the ant.

The rock smashed against its mighty pinchers and formed a small cloud of dust. For a second, the flames died down. Life smiled and swiftly ascended the pile of rubble.

"You have nowhere to run," Angra screeched as he speedily climbed the mound of stones.

In seconds, Angra was on the heels of Life. It seemed that Life's plan had literally backfired when Life's foot slipped. Angra snapped his pinchers with the intent of severing Life's ankle from his leg, but Life nimbly leapt out of his reach.

"You can not outrun me," Angra boasted as Life continued his ascent and made it to the top of the rubble.

Life's cowboy hat touched the ceiling of the chamber. There was nowhere to run. Below him was the fire ant and its hellish flames.

"Ha! Ha! There is no upward mobility for you! You are fired," Angra growled as he opened and closed his flaming pinchers in an intimidating fashion.

"Too bad. I got a promotion," Life replied, whirling his sword over his head, crisscrossing the ceiling with its tip.

As he sheathed his sword, Life uppercut the ceiling as hard as he could, sending a tremor through the structure. Angra lunged at Life and, just as Angra's fiery pinchers were about to clasp Life around his waist, the ceiling shatters.

Dirt and rocks plummeted onto the flaming monster, sending him crashing deeper into the mound of rocks! A great cloud of dust went up, extinguishing the flames of the hellish ant. The ant busted out of the pile of rubble. Life was nowhere to be found!

"Where are you, and what did you do to my flames?" Angra screamed.

The dust prevented the ant from igniting. Angra could not even sense Life's whereabouts. Deprivation had given him specific orders to destroy the intruders. If he failed, a fate worst than death would be reserved for him.

"If the cowboy isn't here, then he must be heading towards the Gallery of Soul," Angra screeched as he searched through the rubble and found nothing.

Angra quickly scurried from its chamber and toward the well shaft that led to the northern portion of the pyramid. Lodged in a crevice of the giant ant's exoskeleton was the tip of a black cowboy hat.

Midnight escorted Ms. Pook and Ms. Ellen along an ascending corridor that opened into a large square room. The room was dimly lit and a wooden podium was erected in the middle of the room. Three beams of sunlight streamed through the ceiling via unseen ventilation shafts. The black hairs on Midnight's overcoat rose as he peered into the room.

"What is it, Midnight?" Ms. Ellen asked as she peered into the dimly lit room.

"This is the legendary Grand Gallery of Souls," Midnight snarled. "Those beams of light are imprisoned souls! Look closer and you will see their pain!"

The two women examined the light beams closer and beheld the misty ghost faces of tormented souls with their mouths gaping open.

"Reeeelease usss!"

The ghost faces moaned to be released from their prisons. In the middle of the room, there was a wooden podium with a parchment on its surface.

"Look! There is a parchment on the podium! Do you think it's the Scroll of Liberty?" Ms. Pook asked as Midnight directed them toward the podium.

"No, that is not the scroll. You will know the scroll when you see it," Midnight growled.

They stood in front of the podium like students preparing to give a group presentation.

"What language is this scroll written in?" Ms. Ellen inquired as she stared at the strange characters.

"Stop before you get a headache, darling. It is Underworld jargon," Midnight snarled as he licked his paw.

"Ooohh," Ms. Ellen said as she pulled her hands away from the parchment.

"It is the language of the undead and only can be read by someone who has been to the other side," Midnight snarled . "Ms. Pook, tell us what the scroll says. The Good Eye has given you the power."

Ms. Pook reached into her small purse and removed the Good Eye. She placed the golden trinket on her forehead. It faintly glowed as Ms. Pook read the scroll. The alien characters became understandable.

"The world is full. Our numbers are as before the sun floated in the sky," she read.

"The sun as in the sun in the middle of the universe," Ms. Ellen said in awe.

Ms. Pook nodded her head.

"Desire has trapped me, but, with Death and the Banshee at my side, I will overthrow her and rule the monsters," Ms. Pook continued to read.

"The drama continues," Midnight snarled.

Ms. Pook paused as she read ahead, skipping lines pertaining to the organization of armies by using the power of the trapped souls.

"Yesterday, Saga the King of the Shadow Hounds decided to make this pyramid one of his many mansions," Ms. Pook said.

At that moment, an unearthly howl was heard throughout the edifice.

The three wheeled around toward the entrance. Standing in the doorway was a giant hyena with giant silvery teeth and green glowing eyes. Ms. Ellen winced at the size of the hound. Black spots covered its tan coat.

"Saga, the Shadow Hound of the Underworld," Midnight gasped as he recognized the overlord of the evil canine spirits.

"It is I, and you shall feel my fury for trespassing," Saga roared as he leapt into the air.

Midnight shook free of his friends, returning them to the real world and pounced into battle. The two canines blended into the shadows and filled the chamber with a terrible noise.

The snarling of the beasts reverberated here and there as they speedily maneuvered about the room.

"Stand close to me," Ms. Ellen said as she extended her Golden Axe in a protective fashion.

Above them, in the Chamber of the Eye, Deprivation ceased his watch of the gathering reptile men. He stood and left the chamber as the sounds of the dogfight enticed him.

"Saga has found a playmate. That pesky wolf is going to be slaughtered," Deprivation spoke as he walked past a podium.

On the podium was the Scroll of Liberty. Little did Deprivation know that the Good Eye had returned to the Pyramid. Not only did The Good Eye contain the power to close all the gates of the Underworld, but it also provided the power to open them wider! If Deprivation discovered the magical artifact, then he would have the ability to immerse the earth into the Underworld! The fate of the world hung in the balance.

Angra traveled at a magnificent speed along the well-shaft. As the fire-ant neared the Gallery of Lost Souls, it became aware of a great dogfight. The snarls, gnashing, and braying of the two beasts was clamorous! Angra slowed to a crawl, enjoying the sounds of terror.

"Saga is really tearing into that mangy wolf, but not like I would," Angra boasted as it crept toward the entrance.

Just then, Angra felt a discomfort beneath its massive thorax.

"You really shouldn't brag. It only makes you half of a person," Life advised as he slid down the ant's body and sliced the beast where its thorax connected to its abdomen.

"Arrgh," Angra screamed as it exploded into a fiery heap.

Ms. Ellen felt a burst of heat swelling within the chamber and took evasive action.

"Duck, Ms. Pook!" Ms. Ellen shouted as she tackled Ms. Pook and shielded her from a torrent of fire that busted through a nearby tunnel.

As they laid on the ground, Ms. Ellen felt a deep coldness enter the room. Sheets of ice formed on the dusty floor of the pyramid.

"Maaaaasssterrr," the tormented souls loudly moaned.

Their tortured cries rose over the sounds of the ferocious dogfight. Ms. Ellen sprung to her feet as Deprivation stood in the doorway at the opposite side of the room. Dark blue armor with shoulder spikes and knee spikes covered the diamond-crusted monster.

"Baaaa! I see that my fire-ant did not do as I asked," Deprivation bleated as he looked upon the two women.

"I got bad news for you, ram head! I am going to turn you into pork chops," Ms. Ellen said as she gripped her golden axe tightly.

Deprivation gripped a spike that protruded from his shoulder blade and pulled it out. Ms. Ellen stared at the end of the spike as it formed a cylindrical shaped iron mace. Behind her stood Ms. Pook. On her forehead was the gleaming Good Eye.

"The Good Eye is here," Deprivation roared as his blue flames grew bright.

"Yes, it is here in the flesh! Them gates will close forever," Ms. Pook replied.

Deprivation was amused by the courage of the foolish woman.

"After I pummel you, I will use the Good Eye to open the gates of hell wider!

Ms. Pook leaned on her walking stick and reached for the guns that she had tucked away along her dress. Her hands touched nothing. The guns were gone!

"Ms. Ellen, the guns are gone! They must have slid across the floor when I fell," Ms. Pook replied.

"Don't worry, honey child. I can take this half-ram, half-man! Take cover, sista girl," Ms. Ellen spoke as she swung her axe at Deprivation.

Deprivation dodged the high swing of the axe, but Ms. Ellen was quicker.

"WHAM!"

Ms. Ellen delivered a smashing knee to Deprivation's flaming ram head and dislocated his diamond jaw.

"Finally, a warrior has come. Finally, a warrior will perish," Deprivation roared as he popped his jaw back into place.

Ms. Ellen ducked as Deprivation jabbed at Ms. Ellen with his mace.

"You're too slow," Ms. Ellen yelled as she nimbly leapt out of the way of the short thrusts.

"CLIK! CLIK!"

"You should stick around," Deprivation spoke in a sarcastic tone as hundreds of spikes protruded from the mace.

"I'm not that type of girl," Ms. Ellen yelled as she spun toward Deprivation, twisting in the air with her axe swinging like a razor sharp tornado.

"Foolish mortal," Deprivation grunted as he swung his spiked mace.

The force of the impact sent Ms. Ellen reeling backward. She was about to fall when something caught her. Ms. Ellen looked down and saw two black-gloved hands holding her up.

"You're back," Ms. Ellen sighed with relief and regained her balance and punched him in the chest. "We thought you were dead!"

"I had to put a fire out. Take Ms. Pook through the passageway to the Chamber of the Eye and close the gate," Life replied.

"Life, I will see your demise is complete, thorough, and has no sequels," Deprivation threatened as the two women warily walked past.

"Deprivation, the only thing you will see is my fist coming towards that ram head of yours," Life said.

Like a prizefighter, Life popped his neck by rotating it to the left and right. He stared at his opponent. Deprivation stared back with his red eyes. He was not afraid of Life, but Ms. Pook was more than she seemed. Only a person tuned to the mysteries of the universe could wield the Good Eye. Deprivation could not wait any longer. He rung the alarm.

"Hobgoblins secure the Chamber of the Eye and have no mercy on whoever comes near. Reptile-men, destroy Bonanza," Deprivation roared in an omnipotent voice.

A horrible screeching, hissing, and roaring were heard throughout the pyramid.

"HEEEYYH! RRRRGGH! IEEEEEYH!"

Suddenly, a breeze of wispy souls rushed through the opening towards the two women. On the outside, the reptile-men heard the order of Deprivation and sprinted towards the city. Robert and Kent let loose the cavalry, intersecting the monstrosities.

"Do you hear that roaring noise? That is the sound of my hobgoblins. They will tear your maids apart," Deprivation said as he stared Life down with his red eyes.

"You will need more than that sideshow to stop them," Life replied.

Suddenly, the shafts of light became illuminated in a fluorescent light.

"Now, you will see my true power. Lost souls, give me your strength," Deprivation said.

Life appeared bewildered as the shafts created a mystic light in the chamber while Deprivation became infused with their energy.

"Maasssterrr, pleeeaaaseee," the souls moaned louder than ever.

In a dark corner, Life saw one of the canines grasping the throat of the other. It was a death move. Unfortunately, Life could not determine if the victor was Midnight or Saga.

"I hope that is you, Midnight," Life muttered as he prepared himself to deal with Saga if Midnight was not the champion.

Without delay, Life threw an overhand right toward Deprivation's flaming head, but his fist was stopped in mid-air as a powerful force seized him. He levitated in the air.

"What is this?" Life asked as he felt the force field surrounding him.

"Inside this Pyramid, I am all powerful! This bubble will dwindle in size until it crushes your bones," Deprivation roared.

The bubble began to constrict around Life. He pushed the constricting sphere with his shoulders and legs, but his efforts were useless. The bubble continued to shrink. Soon, very soon it would be over for Life.

7

Ms. Ellen and Ms. Pook exited the passageway and entered a rectangular-shaped room when a rush of foul air passed them in the darkness. Ms. Ellen skidded to a halt as the wind extinguished the burning torches. The wind was unwholesome with goblin stink.

"Can you turn on some light?" Ms. Ellen asked as she heard evil laughter in the darkness.

"Steady drops of water can put a hole in a rock," Ms. Pook said.

"What?" Ms. Ellen asked as the rush of foul air took shape.

"No time to discern the meaning," Ms. Pook said as she stepped before Ms. Ellen with her gleaming third eye and her walking stick.

The golden light of the Good Eye encapsulated Ms. Pook, and it fell on the host of slimy green hobgoblins barring the entrance to the Chamber of the Eye. The hobgoblins were armed with axes, knives, daggers, short swords, and chains.

"Youse will perrishss, Axe-Murderer," a slimy bald-headed hobgoblin hissed as it shielded its big swamp-green eyes with its green hands.

"Since you know who I am, then you know what I am capable of," Ms. Ellen said as she glanced over her shoulder.

There were hundreds of hobgoblins surrounding them. Some had hair, some had golden hoops in their ears, and some had long crooked noses. Ms. Ellen laughed and the joyous sound bewildered the hobgoblins.

"Whattss is you laughing atsss, Axe-Murderer?" a hobgoblin with a Mohawk and an earring in its eyebrow hissed.

A strand of clear slime dripped from its dimpled chin.

"This is exactly how I envisioned my last stand! Two against hundreds," Ms. Ellen roared as she hurled her knife at the nasty hobgoblin.

The knife plunged the leering hobgoblin in the abdomen.

"Arrggh," the hobgoblin with the Mohawk shrieked as it vaporized into a mound of fiery ash.

"If this is it, Ms. Ellen, then let's set it off," Ms. Pook loudly spoke as the host of hobgoblins went into a frenzy, howling and screeching in their horrible voices.

"Right on, sista," Ms. Ellen replied as she reached into her right boot and handed Ms. Pook a switchblade.

"What is this for?" Ms. Pook asked.

"Cut them from ear to ear if they get too close," Ms. Ellen advised.

Ms. Pook put her back against Ms. Ellen and bashed a hobgoblin with her walking stick!

"BAM!"

Ms. Ellen hacked a goblin.

The two women fought in a sea of foes. However, it was only a mere moment before the tide rose and the monstrous sea overwhelmed them.

Life jerked his head toward the horrible cries of the monsters as the bubble shrunk even more. He had to do something fast if he was going to save his friends and himself. Deprivation became aware of Life's empathy and laughed a sinister laugh.

"Hah! Hah! Hah! You took life from the Banshee, my fire ant, and now I will take it from you," Deprivation laughed as he tightened his diamond fist.

The bubble obeyed Deprivation's gesture and constricted around Life. Life struggled but the bubble continued to shrink, forcing Life's knees to his chest. Life closed his eyes as he embraced himself for the end when he heard the loud howl of a great animal.

"HOOOOOOWWWWWL!"

Deprivation ceased his torture of the cowboy and greeted the victor of the dogfight. Hundreds of leering eyes, glistening claws, and sharp teeth were seen in the darkness. The Army of the King of the Shadow Hounds had come to eradicate his enemies!

"The King of the Shadow Hounds is victorious! Life, behold his army that has come to tear you apart," Deprivation roared.

Suddenly, a larger darker shadow moved in the darkness. This shadow was massive and the fall of the beast's footsteps could be heard throughout the chamber.

"Deprivation, release the cowboy. I want to shred his soul into pieces," the King of the Shadow Hounds growled.

"As you wish, your majesty," Deprivation chuckled as he immediately released Life.

Being shredded alive was more amusing than being crushed.

"Umph," Life said as he fell to the ground and immediately outstretched his hand.

The Glaive of the Moon sped to his hand.

"The King of the Shadow Hounds will not have any mercy on you," Deprivation chuckled.

Life calmly brushed the dust from his shoulders while holding the 'S' shaped knife. Deprivation grew impatient.

"Crush him, Saga," Deprivation commanded.

Instead of Saga pouncing upon Life, the King of the Shadow Hounds nodded his massive head toward Life.

"What nonsense is this?" Deprivation shouted.

"King of the Shadow Hounds, I appreciate you. I will take if from here," Life spoke as he tapped his chest with his fist in a token of friendship.

"Crush the diamond," the King of the Shadow Hounds snarled from the shadows.

Life hurled the glaive toward the beams of lost souls.

The glaive shattered the beams into pieces and boomeranged back to Life's hands.

"Weeeeee'reeee freeee," the souls moaned as they faded away.

For the time being, Deprivation could not harness the power of the lost souls.

"Saga, this treachery will not go unnoticed," Deprivation threatened as he held his spiky mace in the air.

The chamber was filled with an eerie blue light from the broken beams. The light flashed on and off as Deprivation focused on the yellow eyes of the King of the Shadow Hound. Following close to him was his army of shadow hounds. Just as the King of the Shadow Hounds was about to exit the chamber, he addressed Deprivation.

"My name is not Saga! My name is Midnight, the newly crowned King of the Shadow Hounds."

"Impossible," Deprivation gasped as he saw the massive black wolf, its yellow eyes, and large fangs.

"Life, repay me in beef jerky! All shadow dogs forward," Midnight said to Life.

Life nodded and Midnight pounced through the doorway like a general leading his army to the battlefield. Just then, the lights in the chamber went out. The only thing that could be seen was the flaming blue diamond crusted ram head and the amber colored eyes of Life.

"Life verses Deprivation. What a match up," Deprivation spoke in a cold voice.

"All tickets sold out in the arena," Life said as he popped his knuckles.

Deprivation and Life circled one other in the darkness. Today, there would be a victor but who the victor would be remained to be seen.

9

Ms. Ellen kicked a hobgoblin in the abdomen and hacked him in half when a great snarling filled the chamber and ceased all attacks.

"GGGRRGGH!"

"Heh! Heh! Saga has come for you! You should have died while you had the chance," the hobgoblins giggled ominously as they gave way to the King of the Shadow Hounds.

Ms. Ellen's heart pounded in her chest as she saw an unnatural darkness wreath around the beast, leaving only the beast's teeth visible.

"Its teeth are like broken glass," Ms. Ellen said.

She glimpsed the hound's massive shape, shoulder muscles flexing as it walked through the doorway. Behind the massive beast were smaller yet equally intimidating shadow beasts.

"I think the fat lady is singing," Ms. Ellen spoke as she lowered her battle-axe.

"Yes, this is her solo performance," Ms. Pook replied as the smaller shadowy beasts surrounded them.

"Quiet," the King of the Shadow Hounds roared loudly.

The great roar silenced the giggling of the hobgoblins. The massive beast stood before the two women. Ms. Ellen felt the hot breath of the beast. Its breathing was like a finely tuned engine. To Ms. Ellen's surprise, the beast spoke in a scruffy voice.

"Destroy all the slime heads. Let none of them escape," the

King of the Shadow Hounds ordered as he wheeled around and smashed a hobgoblin with a mighty swing of his paw.

The army of shadow hounds leapt into the fray, crushing the goblins with Ms. Ellen and Ms. Pook starring in bewilderment. Ms. Pook focused the power of the Good Eye on the beasts and saw past the darkness that shrouded them.

"Ms. Ellen, its Midnight," Ms. Pook yelled in a voice full of joy.

"Thank God," Ms. Ellen exclaimed as she retightened the grip on her axe.

"Yes, it is me! Climb onto my back! The gate must close if Life is going to be able to defeat Deprivation," Midnight growled as he pounced on a goblin.

"Why is that?" Ms. Ellen asked as she ducked a swing from a goblin's chain and hacked upward, leaving a sizzling mound of burning ash.

"Deprivation doesn't fight fair! He is still drawing strength from the Underworld," Midnight growled as he swung a paw and crushed three hobgoblins.

"Then, let's go," Ms. Pook cried out as she leapt onto Midnight's back.

Ms. Ellen climbed Midnight's shoulder as he plowed his way through the hobgoblins toward the Chamber of the Eye. In the meanwhile, Life was not having such good fortune.

Deprivation squeezed Life by the throat as he pressed his knee into Life's chest. Ice had formed around Life's neck. Deprivation's icy touch spread down his shoulders.

"My icy touch is moving across your body. Soon, your heart will become ice," Deprivation chuckled.

"Y-you can't win," Life whispered as he thrust his knee into Deprivation's lower back.

"WHAM!"

The mighty force sent Deprivation flying across the room where he smashed into the wall. Life sprung to his feet and drew his guns. He cocked them and squeezed the triggers as fast as he could.

"BLAK! BLAK! BLAK!"

Life's revolvers released at least a hundred rounds. However, every bullet was deflected as they struck Deprivation. Life stared around at the tiny holes in the walls. When the smoke cleared, Deprivation was unharmed.

"That tickled me real good," Deprivation laughed.

"Well, if you liked that, then you will love this," Life yelled as he sprinted across the space and dipped his shoulder.

Deprivation took the direct hit but did not budge. Instead, Life was sent sprawling across the room! Life regained his balance and rubbed his sore shoulder.

"Agggh! That hit should have knocked you into next week," Life said as he winced from the pain.

"The strength of thousands of souls can do many things for you," Deprivation said.

"I-I don't understand! I broke the beams and freed the souls," Life said as he staggered.

"As long as the gate is open, I will draw strength. You will never defeat me!"

"That's what you think," Life muttered as he leaned against the wall.

"Now, prepare to meet your maker," Deprivation said as he walked towards Life, sending sheets of ice along the floor and ceiling.

Life leapt into the air and kicked Deprivation three times before landing. As his boots touched the ground, Life spun around and kicked Deprivation in the stomach. Deprivation did not flinch. It was as if Life had never touched him.

"Well, I'll be a fly on the wall," Life softly whispered.

"And like a fly, you will be squashed," Deprivation roared as he seized Life by the collar and tossed him into a nearby wall.

Before Life could spin around, Deprivation punched him from behind.

"You have failed," Deprivation yelled as he punched Life in the face.

Life ducked another punch from Deprivation and swung upward. He missed his target, though. Deprivation sprung backwards and slammed Life's head into the stonewall.

Deprivation thrust his hand on the left side of Life's chest and used his icy touch to the fullest. A sheet of ice covered Life's chest! It was almost over. Deprivation had won.

//

In the meanwhile, Midnight reached the entrance to the Chamber of the Eye. The archway was fashioned like a gaping mouth with four pointy teeth.

"We are here," Ms. Pook shouted.

They passed through the opening to see a stairway and at the top of the stairway was an enormous muscular minotaur that wielded a long bladed whip. As soon as the minotaur beheld them, it snorted smoke from its nostrils and cracked its whip.

"Connivers, prepare for your judgment," the giant minotaur roared as its muscles contracted across its chest and abdomen.

Ms. Ellen glanced down at her golden axe.

"The bigger they are, the harder they fall," Ms. Ellen said as she was about to leap from Midnight's back.

At that moment, Ms. Pook pulled Ms. Ellen back down. She slid off Midnight's back.

"This one is mine! Do not let anything through the doors," Ms. Pook ordered as she limped toward the Minotaur.

"Stop. It's suicide," Ms. Ellen shouted as she watched the old lady hobble toward the monster.

"The power of the Good Eye will protect her," Midnight growled.

They watched as Ms. Pook became illuminated in a golden aura as she sang.

"That's my favorite church song," Ms. Ellen laughed as she heard Ms. Pook's tiny voice soulfully singing.

"If you can't help me, please don't stop me! Move out of my way and don't try not to block me," Ms. Pook sang in her tiny voice as she pointed her walking stick at the monster.

However, the minotaur was not moved by the song.

"Old lady, your song has no power here," the minotaur roared as it drew the whip back and lashed it toward Ms. Pook.

Ms. Pook barely dodged the lash of the whip as it struck the ground and sent out three streams of fire.

"Ms. Pook," Ms. Ellen shouted out.

"This is her fight," Midnight growled.

They watched as the whip recoiled and the Minotaur lashed it again. Suddenly, a blast of light burst from the tip of Ms. Ellen's walking stick.

The beam struck the whip and disintegrated it!

"You shall pay for your insolence," the minotaur roared as he grasped his dagger and stampeded toward the tiny elderly lady.

"I've got a race to run, and I'm running my race to the finish. I'm gonna see his face," Ms. Pook sang as she held her glowing walking stick up in the air.

Beams of light stabbed at the monster like spears, stopping it in its tracks.

"Aaagh! The light hurts! It hurts so baddd," the minotaur screamed as it exploded into a mound of burning ashes.

"That's my Ms. Pook! You go, girl," Ms. Ellen cheered.

Midnight caught the faint scent of something that should have been dead.

"We've got company," Midnight growled as he wheeled around.

"Fulfill the prophecy, Ms. Pook," Ms. Ellen yelled as she flipped off Midnight's back and stood in the doorway.

Ms. Pook hobbled up the stairs to the entrance and thrust the doors open. She entered the Chamber of the Eye. Behind her, she could hear Ms. Ellen grunting as she hacked away at the horde of monsters. Ms. Pook hobbled to the center of the room and performed the last rite to close the Gates of the Underworld.

"Good Eye, shine! Shine on me! Let your light from the lighthouse shine! Shine, shine on me!" Ms. Pook sang in her soulful voice. "Good Eye, close the gates of the Underworld! Good Eye, let your light from the lighthouse shine on the world!"

The Good Eye burst from Ms. Pook's forehead and exploded in a sphere of light. The sphere sped through every stone within the pyramid.

Throughout the world, there was the sound of a rusty gate closing and being locked. Ms. Pook had fulfilled the prophecy, sealing all of the gates of the Underworld! The barrier around the pyramid lowered as the structure became illuminated in a golden light. Sgt. Steve glanced up and saw a brown eye in the illuminated tip of the pyramid.

"Kent! Ms. Pook has delivered the eye! It is the same Eye on the dollar bill," Sgt. Steve cried out.

Kent stared in awe. He reached into his pocket and pulled out his lucky dollar bill. Suddenly, the tip of the pyramid floated above its body, and the golden gaze of the Eye fell upon them.

"Annuit coeptis novus ordo seclorum," a deep powerful voice exclaimed from within the tip of the Pyramid.

"He approves the things which have been begun," Kent translated.

As the light fell upon the hordes of hideous lizard men, they shrank in size and ferociousness. These reptile-men reverted to their natural state.

"Yes! They did it! Sgt. Steve, look below the Good Eye! It's Life's hat," Kent shouted as he saw a blue flaming monster press Life against the wall.

Life heard the Gates of the Underworld lock. The link that Deprivation shared with the Underworld was broken.

"It's hammer time," Life said as he swiftly kicked Deprivation in his knees, breaking the chokehold.

Then, Life whirled around and pulled out his sword in a flash. Deprivation drew back to punch Life, but his forearm slid apart at the elbow.

"Arrrgggh," Desire roared as he glanced at the wound.

"I take only arms and legs," Life said as he squatted low with his sword extended.

"Why you—" Deprivation started as he tried to take a step. His right thigh slid apart from his knee!

Bright white souls streamed out of the two wounds.

"Send me a postcard from the Underworld," Life said as he flipped and sliced downward, letting his blade slice through Deprivation's head.

However, the blade broke.

"Desire," Deprivation yelled out!

Deprivation exploded in a blue light. Life shielded his eyes from the blue glare. When the light show was over, a man, dressed in a dark blazer and dark slacks, was lying on the ground. The man yawned as if he had just awakened from a deep sleep.

"Where am I?" he asked.

"In the land of the living. Welcome back from the Underworld. My name is Life," greeted Life as he assisted the man to his feet.

"My name is Mann," he said as he rubbed his head.

Cheers went up from the army below. Life waived at the people in a show of appreciation. Just then, Ms. Pook, Midnight, and Ms. Ellen appeared below the floating tip of the pyramid. In Ms. Pook's aged right hand was the Scroll of Liberty.

"Midnight," Life shouted as he ran toward his friend and hugged him.

"It is time for freedom to ring," Ms. Pook said as she hobbled toward the edge of the Pyramid.

However, she was the only person with a shadow under the bright light of the Good Eye. Life noticed the sign and leapt to his feet. It could only be a haint, a ferocious shadow fiend from the Underworld!

"Ms. Pook, behind you," Life yelled as he drew his left pistol.

Ms. Pook did not react fast enough. A being with black wings and red eyes levitated from the shadow of the old lady then grasped her by the throat.

"Uggghn...," Ms. Pook started.

The three talons tightened round her throat.

"Let her go, shadow fiend," Life growled as he aimed from the hip.

"The name is Ender, so mind your tongue cowboy."

Behind Life, Midnight expanded in size, and Ms. Ellen gripped her axe.

"Ender, huh?" Life mocked. "If you don't let the lady go, I'll end you!"

"You will learn some respect, cowboy," Ender replied. "This old lady has closed the gates of the Underworld without asking for permission from Desire. She must be dealt with!"

"Desire is about to be put in the dirt, and you're going with her," Midnight snarled as he stood beside Life, ready to take action.

"Ha! Ha! The newly crowned King of the Shadow Hounds! I must confess that I was not betting on you to win," Ender replied in a shrill voice that mocked excitement.

"You can place the bet that you will be sent back to the Underworld," Midnight snarled.

"That is a nice gesture, but I enjoy the Tower of **Wstend** in the old city of Atlanta," Ender replied.

Life lightly squinted and applied pressure to his trigger as a brief opportunity made itself available.

"Easy, cowboy. You don't want to lose your head or someone else's," Ender harshly spoke. "I come with an invitation."

"I am not interested in serving a hellish master and dominating mankind," Life said as he anticipated the next opportunity.

"Too bad! I was looking forward to betraying you," Ender replied.

Life sent a mental command to Ms. Pook. When they first met, Ms. Pook had read his mind as he spoke to Midnight. Hopefully, she could read it again.

"Let me go, you piece of chicken guts," Ms. Pook muttered as she started to struggle.

"Be still or be dead," Ender growled.

"BLAM!"

The bullet blasted the haint at the elbow, freeing Ms. Pook from its clutches. As she broke free, the shadow fiend wrenched the Scroll of Liberty from Ms. Pook's grasp!

"You fool! You will pay dearly," Ender hissed as he gripped his wounded elbow.

"Put it on my tab," Life said as he prepared to get off another shot.

The haint leapt off the side of the pyramid.

"BLAM!"

The shot grazed the left wing of the haint. Life rushed over and aided Ms. Pook to her feet, hugging her at the same time.

"I'm okay. I'm okay," Ms. Pook assured as Life let her go.

Life wheeled around and stared Ms. Ellen directly in the eye.

"Which direction is Atlanta?" Life asked as he sprung upon Midnight's back.

"North but you can't take a tour bus into the city," Ms. Ellen warned.

"Come again?" Life asked.

"The city is damned! The buildings crumbled, and some have fires that never go out! Surrounding the city is an infestation of monsters! For years, we have tried to retake the city, but every attempt has failed to breach the perimeter," Ms. Ellen replied as she stood in front of the wolf before it could leap away.

"We've traveled through thicker briars," Midnight growled as he turned his head north.

"There are other paths to the city," Ms. Ellen quickly advised.

"Listen to her! A hard head makes a soft butt," Ms. Pook said to Life.

Life reconsidered. If Desire were in Atlanta, then that would be the point of origin of the monsters. Atlanta would be considered their capital.

"Where are these paths?" Life asked.

"Hidden underground. One begins under here," Ms. Ellen said as she pointed downward.

"Ms. Ellen, will you guide us on this path?" Life asked.

"Yes, and you need a new sword. You must see the Lady in the Lake," Ms. Ellen responded.

Life nodded his head and dismounted his steed with his black trench coat blowing in the wind. He definitely needed a sword. It was the only effective weapon against these members of Legion.

"Very well, but is her steel strong?" Life asked.

"Her steel is enchanted. That is where I got my Golden Axe and my Golden Tiara," Ms. Ellen said.

Sgt. Steve, Kent, and Robert finally made it to the top of the Pyramid. Ms. Ellen was glad to see them.

"Robert, assist Mr. Mann. Sgt. Steve, implement Operation Sharp Knife," Ms. Ellen ordered as she twirled her golden axe and holstered it to her back.

Life noticed the axe was not strapped to Ms. Ellen's back. It was merely attached to her back. He rotated his head as he saw Sgt. Steve and Kent giving out orders, separating the warriors into an organized fashion. Life knew that the shadow fiend would take the Scroll of Liberty to Desire, and it was a matter of time before she would steal their freedom.

Chapter 5

The Merman in the Cavern

The moon rose in the night sky, but the darkness held no sway over Bonanza as the light of the Golden Eye faintly glowed upon the houses of the neighborhood. The people cheered as they lined the streets, watching Ms. Ellen lead her friends toward the Sanctuary. This joyous celebration was five years overdue, and the heroes engaged in casual conversation, but Mann showed more interest than the others.

"Life, can anyone ever steal your guns and use them to do bad things?" Mr. Mann inquired as they slowly drove the jeep down the crowded streets.

"My guns can only be used by another person who has my permission," Life replied as he waived at the spectators. "No one, including myself, can use my guns for any evil intent."

"Deceit is in the heart of those who imagine evil," Ms. Pook warned as she smiled at a little girl dressed in a dirty pink dress who waived at her from the cracked sidewalk.

No one paid any attention to Ms. Pook.

"Will the Good Eye continue to shine all the time?" Sgt. Steve asked.

"The light of the Good Eye will not stop shining until the land is healed," Ms. Pook replied.

Life noticed the dry ground beginning to bring forth green grass. They walked until they came to the base of an abandoned red-bricked cathedral. The cathedral appeared to have survived a fire.

"Well, here we are. The Sanctuary. Let's go inside," Ms. Ellen spoke.

Midnight was glad. He had felt like someone was watching them.

"Someone is eavesdropping on us," Midnight muttered low enough for only Life to hear.

"The stare of Desire is strong! She has been watching us since we left the pyramid," Life said.

Life gazed at the banners on the tower. The banners were of a lion and a bundle of grapes. However, this tower harbored no evidence of violence.

"This is not a tower where soldiers gathered for battle," Life said as Ms. Ellen led them up the steps.

"No, spiritual soldiers once gathered here. It was once my father's church and had hundreds of members until the fire," Ms. Ellen replied as she opened the door and entered the church.

In the meanwhile, Ender bowed before the throne of his

master with the Scroll of Liberty.

"Master of the universe, Master of all fates, hear my plea. The cowboy has taken my arm! Please give my arm back to me," Ender pleaded.

The throne rotated. Ender glanced upward. Desire was dressed in a purple robe. Her yellow diamond saber tooth tiger head fumed with yellow flames. Desire's red eyes studied the shadow fiend as it clutched its severely damaged arm.

"Why should I restore your arm, Ender?" Desire purred in a soft voice.

"Master Desire, I will use my restored arm to rip the hearts from those who oppose you. Please have mercy," Ender begged.

Desire stretched out her jeweled claw, and the Scroll of Liberty flew toward her hand. Finally, the parchment was hers. Just a couple of months ago, Deprivation had teleported the scroll to the Pyramid and Desire had sent Ender to find a way to steal the scroll back. For months, Ender had roamed Bonanza, waiting for the opportunity to sneak into the pyramid.

"Master Desire, please have mercy! I have served your will," Ender continued to beg.

Desire extracted a glass tube from within the sleeves of her robe. She placed the Scroll of Liberty inside and secured the artifact on the arm of her throne. Ender patiently waited for Desire to tend to his needs. Finally, Desire addressed the shadow haint.

"Ender, do you think that you are different from the ogres, the goblins, and the reptile-men that serve me?" Desire purred.

The question wore Ender's patience thin.

"I did as you asked! I have brought you the scroll! All I want is my arm," Ender snapped.

"If you fight for me, you fight to the death," Desire replied.

"But—"

"Be gone or suffer," Desire commanded as her red eyes blazed.

Ender felt a surge of heat and hurried from the room. He did not want to be destroyed. Desire rotated her throne back around. She gazed out of a shattered window toward the neighborhood of Bonanza. She watched as Ms. Ellen led her friends into a church. Her stare had no power on hallowed ground.

"There is still a pawn to be controlled, and I shall move that pawn to become a king," Desire growled as the yellow flames flickered around her head.

Desire turned her stare from the church and toward the ruined city. Buildings leaned against one another. The streets were littered with paper and mounds of rubble. Beneath the debris were the residents of her city: Ogres, reptile-men, and goblins. Soon, she would have to muster her forces. Humanity had to be crushed.

Life and his friends followed Ms. Ellen down a corridor that was decorated with many photos of children smiling. Life noticed the youthful faces within the photos. He had missed so many technological advances since being starved to death in the cave. Life promised himself that he would take advantage of his second chance.

"These pictures are amazing," Life said as he studied one of a little girl playing basketball.

"Yes, these angels are worth fighting for. Isn't that right, Mr.

Mann?" Ms. Pook asked as she hobbled along.

Mr. Mann did not reply as they entered a large square-shaped room with ten rows of cushioned pews on both sides and a giant cross-shaped stained glass window.

"Truly magnificent," Midnight barked as the light of the Good Eye illuminated the cross.

"We all have a cross to bear. We will bear it together through whatever," Ms. Pook said as she passed beneath the light of the cross and patted Midnight on the head.

Ms. Ellen led them to a door at the end of the room. She stopped at the door and addressed her friends.

"What lies at the bottom of this basement has been kept secret for five years. You are the first to see it," Ms. Ellen announced as she extracted a golden key and unlocked the door. "You are the first to see it."

"What is so important about the basement?" Ms. Pook asked as a curious smile formed on her face.

"My father's works. Follow me and watch your steps," Ms. Ellen replied.

Ms. Ellen led them down a flight of steps. She opened the door, and they walked down a corridor to the basement. They passed several rows of three wheelers and motorcycles equipped with Gatlin guns on their sides. Life could not resist the temptation as he neared a three-wheeler.

"Do the contraptions work?" Life asked as he hopped onto a nearby three wheeler.

"Yes, they work, but it gets better," Ms. Ellen replied as she opened the door of the basement and turned on the light.

The light flickered and then popped on. Life entered the room and saw a spectacular display of graffiti along the walls of the basement. The graffiti was of a cowboy dressed in black and a black wolf leading an assault on a tower located in the center of a devastated city! Behind the cowboy was a pyramid with a glowing eye above its structure!

"Life, your coming was foretold by my father, but I thought he was suffering from dementia," Ms. Ellen revealed.

"Was your father psychic?" Life asked as he studied the mural.

"Yes, he was psychic, and his vision gave us just enough warning to survive," Ms. Ellen replied.

Ms. Ellen walked over to a large oak wardrobe and opened it.

"My father, Mr. Scott, was an artist who was ahead of his time," Ms. Ellen said as she briefly remembered the excitement in her dad's voice once he finished a product.

Numerous modified automatic pistols and rifles lined the walls of the wardrobe. There were grenades, A.K 47's, and modified Uzi machine guns.

"I remember the day he made these for you. It was rainy, and he had been locked up down here for hours."

"What do you mean when you say 'he made something for me'?" Life asked.

"My father knew you were coming so he designed these especially for you," Ms. Ellen answered as she handed him a bag of ball bearings, a bag of tiny silver razor sharp discs, and a modified 12-gauge shotgun with a sharp blade beneath the enlarged barrel.

"Wow," Life exclaimed like a kid opening gifts at a birthday party.

Ms. Ellen giggled as she gave out the specifications of the modified shotgun.

"Take notice of the recoil of the pump action, easy to load, and the barrel with the sharp butcher's blade beneath," Ms. Ellen advised as she rotated the weapon, displaying it from different angles.

"Why are you giggling?" growled Midnight.

"I am laughing because I remember telling him that he was as crazy as a bed bug and the police were gonna take him away for making such things," Ms. Ellen said.

"Ms. Pook, can—"

"Was Mr. Brown the greatest performer?" Ms. Pook interrupted as she hobbled over to Life and took the weapon from his hands.

"AAAWH," Ms. Ellen shouted as she imitated the late godfather of soul.

Ms. Pook began to hum a tune. Her voice grew as she sang her song, and the shotgun became enchanted by the sound of her voice.

"You fight for truth, justice, and honor…You will not be used for evil no matter what others want you to do… Like the heat in the south…Your ammunition will never run out," Ms. Pook sang as a purple aura spread from her to the weapon.

She handed the newly enchanted weapon back to Life. He spun it around, allowing his hands to get used to the weight of the weapon.

"Just what the doctor ordered," Life said as he put the weapon inside his trench coat where it disappeared.

"Midnight, what are you doing?" Robert asked as he noticed Midnight closely studying the wall

"This picture captures my ferociousness but not my more compassionate side," Midnight snarled.

Everyone laughed. It was such a sound that had never been

heard in the basement. Ms. Ellen let the laughter die down before she continued.

"We must leave. Our escorts are waiting," Ms. Ellen said as she strolled over to another door.

"Escorts?" Midnight inquired.

Ms. Ellen opened the door and cocked her head for them to look. Standing beside two dark blue two-seater submersibles was Sgt. Steve and Kent. The submersibles were cigar-shaped with small wings on each side.

"My father designed these mini-subs and coined them the Night Hawks. The earthquakes made a deep underground river that traverses all the way to a large lake on the outskirts of the city," Ms. Ellen said as she led them toward the submersibles.

"We frequently use this secret route to visit the lake where we receive advice from the Lady of the Lake," Robert informed Life.

Mann found all of this absurd.

"Are you serious?" Mann asked. "The Lady of the Lake is make-believe like the Tooth Fairy or Santa!"

Robert shot Mann a look that said, "Shut up and gain some knowledge!"

This gesture made him angry, but he hid his angst toward Robert.

"Too bad your father didn't know one of us was a canine," barked Midnight.

"Au contraire, mon ami. My father designed that one just for you. Your name is even stitched on the seat," Ms. Ellen said as she neared the second submersible that was a little larger than the others.

"Thank you, Mr. Scott, for your service," Life replied as he looked upward, giving a token of respect to Ms. Ellen's father.

Ms. Ellen continued to explain her strategy.

"Once we reach the Waterfalls of Greenbriar which are on the other side of the lake, I will give the signal, and the assault will begin," Ms. Ellen said.

"Just like the artwork," Midnight barked.

"How will the remaining Golden Arms and Sons of Bonanza receive the signal?" Life asked.

"They won't. Ms. Pook and I already share a psychic link. She will use this link to hear my signal, and she will unleash our forces," Ms. Ellen replied as she polished her golden tiara with the end of her shirt.

The flared silver wings sparkled as Ms. Ellen placed the tiara on her head.

"A direct attack is like a bee flying into a thunder storm," Ms. Pook said.

Robert nodded his head in agreement.

"The monsters will be drawn to the attack which will give us an advantage in reaching the tower unchallenged," Ms. Ellen assured.

"Sounds like a plan that has been in development," Midnight barked.

"Yes, Sharp Knife has been in effect for a long time, but we lacked a secret weapon," Sgt. Steve replied.

Suddenly, Mann experienced extreme nausea and vomited onto the ground.

"I f-feel weak," Mann mumbled as he stumbled.

Robert held him up.

"Easy, fellow. You need to rest after being possessed for five years. The infirmary is around the corner. I will get you there as soon as possible," Robert said.

"Robert, get the three wheeler guns ready to rock and roll," Ms. Ellen said as she stepped into the submersible.

Life turned to Ms. Pook and hugged her. Their contact caused Ms. Pook to receive a vision.

"What is it?" Life asked as he saw Ms. Pook's eyes stare off into the distance.

"Life, beware of the lady with two faces," Ms. Pook warned.

Life nodded his head as he walked away and boarded the submersible with Kent while Midnight boarded the other submersible with Sgt. Steve and Ms. Ellen.

Ms. Pook, Robert, and Mann watched them sail away into the distance. Things had been set into motion, but treachery could tilt the balances in either direction.

In the meanwhile, Ender flew from the Tower of **Wstend** towards a group of abandoned buildings and a multi-level parking deck located on the outskirts of the city known as the Station. Since Desire would not restore his arm, he would take the cowboy's arm, but he would need a little help from the werewolves.

"Lupe, wake up," Ender shrieked as he flew through the abandoned buildings.

Red eyes sprung from the shadows of the parking deck, and a beastly snarling was heard.

"Grrrrgh! Grrrgh!"

"Lupe, wake up! I need your help," Ender shrieked.

Suddenly, a slim man with childish face and shaggy hair stepped from the shadows. He was wearing only a pair of shredded jeans. A crooked scar stretched from his ear to chin. This man was known as Lupe, the Ruler of the Werewolves.

"Why do you seek me, shadow fiend?" Lupe asked as he wiped his hair from his eyes.

Ender knelt before the half-clothed man.

"A cowboy took my arm, and I want him dead! Please help me," Ender pleaded.

Lupe looked down at the winged shadow haint. This was the same monster who waved good-bye when Desire had banished them.

"Where is your precious Desire? Go and cry to her. She can kiss it and make it all better," Lupe snapped.

"I have renounced my loyalty to her. I seek a new master," Ender replied.

Hundreds of red eyes lingered behind Lupe.

"I have enough servants," Lupe said.

"But none of your servants know of the Scroll of Liberty. I can give it to you. Then, you could rule all the monsters—even Desire," Ender said.

Lupe took this into consideration. Desire needed a chin checking but not even 1000 monsters could scratch her. Such an opportunity for revenge could not be overlooked.

"Where is this cowboy?" Lupe snarled.

"In Bonanza, the last city of men!"

Lupe rubbed his chin.

"The Axe-Murderer put this on my face. Next time, I may not be so lucky," Lupe said as he rubbed the scar on his face.

The Axe-Murderer had put the scar on his face during an attempt to ransack the city. Ender rose from his kneeling position.

"I know another way into the city. There is a secret way through the Waterfalls of Greenbriar," Ender said.

Lupe did not sense any deceit from the shadow haint. He could kill two birds with one stone.

"Wolf Pack, tonight we ride to the Waterfalls of Greenbriar. Tomorrow, we feast on man-flesh," Lupe shouted as he transformed into a snarling muscular werewolf.

A snarling and braying issued forth as the werewolves rushed from the parking deck, running in a fearsome pack. However, the commotion did not go unnoticed. Desire watched them from the seat of her throne.

"Where are you taking your friends?" Desire growled as the werewolves and Ender left her sight.

She sat in thought. There were things being set in motion that not even she could change. It was time for her to move her pawn. Her throne rotated, and she gazed at the city of Bonanza. Her gaze fell onto a makeshift hospital, down the hallway, and to the room where Mann laid on a bed fast asleep.

"Wake up, Mann," a soft voice whispered.

Mann's eyes flung open. He stared around the room. There was only a bed, a dresser, and a television.

"Wake up, Mann," the voice whispered again.

"Who's there?" Mann frantically asked as he sat up in his bed.

The television came on. On the screen was Jane. She was dressed in a mango colored two-piece bikini, and she was sitting in a lounge chair on a beach with a pink drink in her hand. She put the drink down and talked to Mann.

"It's me. Jane. Look under the bed," the voice said.

Mann's heart pounded in his chest, and the sound affected his hearing. Mann felt as if he was submerged under water.

"Don't be afraid. Look under the bed," Jane urged from the television screen.

Mann leaned over and looked beneath his bed. Lying underneath the bed was Jane. She was dressed in khaki pants and a tank top.

"H-how are you on tv and here? There's no electricity," Mann cried out.

"You know I have connections! I need a favor. If you do this for me, I will make you the King of the World," Jane said.

Mann couldn't believe what he was seeing. He looked Jane in her eyes, but they were not blue. They were swirling cosmos. A comet streaked by as the stars twinkled. Mann gazed into those infinite pupils and became ensnared.

"What can I do for you?" Mann asked.

"Go find the sorceress while she sleeps and sprinkle the contents of this vial in her room. Then, execute Robert in public," Jane commanded.

"I won't fail you."

Mann woke from his sleep and began to get dressed. The last time he checked, Ms. Pook was in the church praying. He was going to set things right between him and his fiancée. While Mann served her will, Desire began to send her thought abroad. She would need all her allies if she wanted to win this war.

Life stared at the lights bouncing off the sides of the sharp scarlet red stalagmites that dropped down from the ceiling like rocky icicles. The air in the cavern became hot as the passage narrowed. Life let his fingertips slightly touch one of the limestone rocks as the submersibles silently navigated the underground river side by side.

"How can the rock be slippery on one side but dry on the other?" Life asked in awe.

"It's the yin and the yang. Everything has two sides," Kent replied.

"Sometimes the first side is not really the real side like a blind date. I am initiating the data link," Ms. Ellen remarked as she pressed an orange button.

Life noticed that the controls became self-guided; the submersible dropped half a foot behind Ms. Ellen.

"What is the data link?" asked Midnight.

The radar in Ms. Ellen's submersible beeped.

"The link lets me control your sub with a remote. Water pools are ahead, and the current is changing. If we don't increase our speed, we will be dragged into them," Ms. Ellen explained as she steered the submersible to the left.

"Hang on to your hat, Life," Kent said as their speed increased.

The two submersibles sped across the water at a tremendous speed. Ms. Ellen steered left, and Life's submersible followed close behind.

The swirling sound of the water was astounding. Life stared at the gigantic swirling pool of water that could swallow a ship. The submersibles increased speed.

Life glanced at the speedometer. The blue digital display read 210 mph! Kent snorted and cleared his sinuses as his radar beeped multiple times.

"Ms. Ellen, the Teeth are ahead," Kent advised as multiple

red dots appeared on his radar.

"The teeth?" Life asked.

"You'll see. After the teeth, there is a Wall that we have to dive under," Ms. Ellen said as she veered to the right.

The submersibles leaned, and Midnight became nervous. He was scared of the water.   "Dive! You mean we have to go under water," Midnight barked.

At that moment, Ms. Ellen veered left. They dodge an enormous pillar of rocks that jutted from the water like a fang. Right after that one, another one loomed ahead.

"Oh my God," Life yelled as he braced himself.

Suddenly, the submersibles swerved left and right in a quick evasive action as Ms. Ellen led them through an area of large pointy rocks. Ahead of them loomed a large wall. Life noticed that their speed had not decreased and the wall was closing fast.

"Watch your head!" Ms. Ellen yelled as a clear glass shield rose over their heads.

The glass shield sealed the cabin, making it air tight. The Wall was closer. Life could see the dark grooves on its surface.

"If we don't do something soon, we are gonna be soaking wet," Life yelled to Midnight.

Just before they crashed into the Wall, the submersibles submerged into the water. Ms. Ellen clicked another button and opened up a line of communication.

"Just sit back and enjoy the under water view," Ms. Ellen spoke through the intercom.

The lights of the submersibles activated as they navigated toward the bottom of the river. After a while, the dark water immediately lightened up to the point where it seemed that they were floating in mid-air! Ms. Ellen turned off the lights of the submersible as they neared a natural wonder. Ahead of them was a pink coral reef that emitted its own light.

"Truly remarkable. Every time I see this wonder it's like the first time," Ms. Ellen said as they hovered in the water.

A school of small white fish dashed by the submersible, and Life noticed the white fish turning pink as they neared the coral.

"I've never seen crabs underwater," Life spoke as the crustaceans crawled among the coral reef.

Suddenly a group of shrimp leapt from the rocks as the fish, the invertebrates, swam in circles, changing to different colors. Suddenly, the school of pink fish scattered in multiple directions as a blue eel streaked from around a rocky ledge.

"There's an electric eel," Sgt. Steve said as he saw the eel target the largest fish in the school.

The fish darted right then left, fleeing for its life. Just then, the fish reversed its direction and headed directly toward the submersibles. The fish darted left at the last moment, and the eel barreled into Ms. Ellen's submersible.

"BAM!"

"Oh no," Ms. Ellen panicked as the power to the mini-subs were drained.

Ms. Ellen pressed the emergency eject button. The floors of the mini-subs opened, and everyone was jettisoned into the water. The eel darted toward the group and stung Ms. Ellen on the leg as she tried to dodge it.

She immediately went unconscious.

"Yooookk," the eel screeched as it went in for the kill.

Kent reached for his knife.

Before his hand could grasp the knife, a silver disc slashed through the water at a tremendous speed. Kent jerked his head to see Life with his hand outstretched, guiding the s-shaped knife toward the slithering blue eel!

"Yoooook," the blue eel screamed as the glaive smashes into its body, leaving a dark spot in the clear water.

"Mmm…mmm," Kent nodded as Sgt. Steve seized Ms. Ellen and swam toward the surface of the water.

Life dramatically pointed his gloved finger toward a gnashing school of blue eels headed toward them as he caught the glaive in his free hand. Life could see their needle-like teeth protruding from their closed mouths.

"Umm! Umm," Life mumbled as he repeatedly thrust his thumb toward the surface of the water.

Just as the eels darted toward them, a deep roar resonated from the water, sending the eels scattering toward the safety of the rocks. In the distance, a massive shadow was moving toward them.

"YOOOKKK!"

A giant eel that had lived for generations in the underwater passage maneuvered toward them, enraged. Sgt. Steve and Kent quickly swam with Ms. Ellen under their arms, but it is too late. The giant eel was upon them.

Life ordered Midnight to swim toward the surface.

Midnight obeyed and swam as fast as he could. The giant eel turned its warty head toward the fleeing wolf.

"YOOOKKK," the giant eel roared.

Instinctively, Life hurled the glaive and watched as the blade scathed the forehead of the beast. The beast jerked its head toward Life; its yellow eyes locked onto its assailant. The s-shaped knife returned to Life's hand.

"YOOK," the gigantic eel roared.

"You need a big breath mint," Life thought as he felt the sound of the roar beating against his body.

Suddenly, Life heard the voice of the monster in his head.

"You will be slowly digested over a one hundred years in the juices of my belly," the beast roared as it hurried toward him.

"I don't go down so easy," Life mentally replied as he floated in the water.

The monster opened its mighty jaws with rows of saber like teeth. Life did not despair.

"CHOMP!"

Kent glanced over his shoulder just in time to see the mighty eel swallow Life.

"That thing ate Life," Kent gasped as he and Sgt. Steve submerged from the water and hurried toward a nearby embankment with pink glowing rocks.

"Lay her down. I am going to do CPR," Sgt. Steve said.

"It ate him! The eel ate him," Kent continued to shout as Sgt. Steve began to administer CPR to Ms. Ellen.

After a couple of short thrusts to the chest, Ms. Ellen coughed as the water was forced from her lungs.

"It ate him!"

"Calm down. He is—" began Midnight.

"BLOOM! BLAM! BOOM!"

Three explosions burst within the water. Kent shielded his eyes as flying sheets of water splashed on them. Kent stared at the pool of clear water as it became a deep maroon color.

"There's blood in the water," Kent said.

The water swirled.

"The beast comes," Kent said as he grasped the hilt of sword.

Suddenly, the head of the eel floated to the surface of the

water. Its pale eyes stared at him. The mouth of the eel trembled as it moved toward the rocky shore.

"I will avenge you, Life," Kent said as he loaded an arrow into his bow.

The mouth of the monster creaked open. Kent could feel his heart pounding in his chest as the eel's head ran ashore.

"For Life," Kent said as he prepared to release the arrow.

Just then, the mouth of the eel opened, and a fang of the eel snapped.

"What in the world?" Kent said as he saw the toe of a black cowboy boot.

He relaxed as Life stepped out of the mouth of the eel. In Life's hand was the modified shotgun. A strand of smoke drifted from its barrel.

"You sly dawg! You blasted your way out the belly of the beast," Kent said.

"This is the new version of the story of Jonah and the whale," Life said as he stepped out of the mouth of the beast.

Suddenly, Kent felt something sharp pierce him between his shoulder blades. The bow and arrow fell from Kent's hand.

"Land Dweller, if you wish to live, be quiet and sit down," a deep voice from behind him said.

Midnight snarled and Kent swallowed hard as he watched Life come ashore, hoping to be rescued.

"I've been buried alive, burned beyond comprehension, and now swallowed. It has to get better," Life said as he staggered onto the wet rocks.

He heard Ms. Ellen cough, but all else was silent.

"Being swallowed is not the only thing you have to worry about," Midnight growled.

Life's eyes darted from Sgt. Steve holding Ms. Ellen at an upright position to Kent sitting down with the point of a golden trident pointing in his back. A scaly blue humanoid creature, dressed in only a brief of woven leaves and silver sea shelled wristbands, was holding his friends hostage. Life stared at the broad shoulders and taunt muscles of the blue man who had a short pointy nose and short black pony tail.

"Good night! A merman," Life said in surprise.

"Not just any merman but, Victor, the King of the Mermen," Victor proudly spoke. "Land Dweller, who are you, and who do you serve?"

"My name is Life, and I serve all men," Life replied as he dropped his shotgun to the ground.

Victor's face frowned. For a moment, Life could see another face behind the blue face! Life blinked, and the thought passed but not the vigilance of the merman. Victor's trident charged itself with electricity.

"You lie! Only the will can serve all men, and it is broken! I was there when it happened," Victor angrily shouted.

Quickly, Life bowed to a knee with his hands stretched out.

"O' King of Mermen, have mercy," Life begged as he began speaking in the gurgled language of the mermen.

Ms. Ellen and her friends were startled to hear Life's voice rise and fall in octave as he produced a deep guttural sound. Victor retracted the trident from Kent's back. Never had he heard a land dweller speak the language so fluently.

"Have mercy, King of the Seas! We only seek the aid of the Lady of the Lake," Life continued to beg as he reverted to the common tongue.

Victor rubbed his hands through his short hair.

"The Lady of the Lake cannot help you," Victor replied.

"Why?" Ms. Ellen asked as she gazed upon the merman.

"The Lady of the Lake is the prisoner of the powerful sorceress known as Lorey the Sea Hag," Victor says.

"How? I just visited the lake three days ago," Mrs. Ellen asked as she leapt to her feet in astonishment.

"The great lake is a now a desert," Victor replied. "Two days ago, I led a regiment of my mermen here to rescue the Lady of the Lake, but Lorey released her giant worm. I was the only one to escape!"

"You waited for someone to come along, so you could poke them in the back," Kent angrily replied.

"Perhaps I should have poked you harder," Victor spoke.

"Then you would be in the next world," Sgt. Steve quickly replied as he pulled his sword from its sheath.

Life could not allow a fight to break out. The talents of the merman would be most valuable in the quest to free the Lady of the Lake. Therefore, he did the only thing that he knew to do. Life stepped into the hostile environment.

"My friends, we need each other," Life yelled as he held his palms outward while standing between the two parties.

"I need no one," Victor yelled.

"Victor, you have no more mermen," Life calmly spoke. "You need our help! We can help you!"

Victor thought about the situation for a moment as he weighed the facts. The cowboy knew the language of the mermen and had slain the giant eel with ease. Perhaps, the cowboy could break the Sea Wall. Perhaps...

"Lorey threatens all underwater realms," Victor said. "Together, we can eliminate this threat!"

"Victory lies not in numbers but in talents," Life replied as he picked up his shotgun and holstered it under his coat where it vanishes.

"Why do you seek the Lady of the Lake, cowboy?" Victor asked.

"My sword broke during my last battle to save the earth. I need new steel," Life answered.

Victor raised his left eyebrow in great regard of Life's claim. He had met plenty of adventurers whose courage was only fueled by the discovery of a lost land or an alluring box of treasure but never had he encountered a man who was willing to save the world. Such a nuisance was a threat and had to be dealt with immediately.

"Then, we shall venture together. Let us not linger here anymore," Victor said as he extended his hand.

Life shook Victor's hand and introduced him to his friends.

"Victor, these are my friends: Midnight, Kent, Ms. Ellen, and Sgt. Steve," Life said.

"I am pleased to meet you," Victor replied.

Life assisted his friends to their feet and glanced around the cavern that was lit by the glowing rocks. With the submersibles destroyed, they would have to rely on the merman to lead them. Hopefully, they could free the Lady of the Lake.

Chapter 6

The Lady with Two Faces

Victor led Life and his friends down a winding cavern that was studded with many glittering red rubies that emitted a red light. As they descended further, the red rubies became fashioned into trees, bushes, and even short blades of grass.

"Wow!" Kent said as he witnessed the magnificent jewels.

"What you see are the outskirts of the dwarf kingdom known as the Red Rise," Victor explained. "Before the earthquakes, this region laid leagues beneath the surface of the earth."

"Dwarves were here? I thought they were only in fairytales," Ms. Ellen said as she squinted.

"Not all magical things are figments of your mortal imagination," Victor replied.

"The dwarves do not care for the upper world as we do, so they fashioned treasures that resembled items in nature," Life said.

"How deep are we in the earth?" Sgt. Steve asked.

"In your measurements, ten thousand feet," Victor replied.

Ms. Ellen scratched her head and giggled.

"And I thought it was hard to grow a tree in the big city," Ms. Ellen laughed.

Victor shook his head. The joyfulness of the land dwellers was annoying and at the first chance he promised himself to toss them into a chasm. Suddenly, they came to a point where the main path branched into numerous different directions.

"Which way now? There are more holes in the wall than a piece of Swiss cheese," Ms. Ellen remarked as she counted at least thirty openings.

Victor did not hesitate. He led them through the third opening from the bottom. They traveled for what seemed like hours, even Midnight became tired and could not hold his silence any further. He broke the peace.

"Victor, how much further?" Midnight asked.

"Land Dwellers are so lazy! We are almost there," Victor impatiently spoke as he ducked under an overhanging rock.

Life noticed the rudeness but said nothing. He was occupied with putting together a sketch of the timeline.

"Just three days ago, Ms. Ellen visited the Lady of the Lake and received advice about the attack," Life said in a low voice.

Kent overheard him and listened closely.

"Victor stated that he had led his mermen through the caverns just two days ago, but Ms. Ellen just passed through without seeing the giant eel...Something isn't right."

Life bent under the overhanging rock and glanced down. He stooped lower and examined the tracks closer.

"His tracks are like a duck," Life muttered as he examined the webbed feet tracks on the cavern floor.

Life glanced up and saw that Victor was wearing a pair of boots.

"What is it?" Kent asked as he saw Life's hand drop near his waist.

"One plus one is adding up to a lie! Keep your eyes opened," Life whispered.

"Like an owl," Kent replied.

Suddenly, Victor held his hand up in a fist, signaling to them to halt. He dropped to a low crouch and beckoned for them to come closer as he placed his first finger over his small lips.

"Shhh!"

Life and his friends moved silently until they were huddled together. Not too far away was an opening that was shaped like the mouth of the eel. Protecting the opening was a water-like energy field.

"There is the Sea Wall," Victor whispered to Life. "I need you to break the barrier so that we can enter the Pink Diamond in the Rough. That is where the Lady is being held captive."

Life nodded and somersaulted over a rock. He thrust his hands through the surface of the seal and began to spread the opening.

"P-patty c-cake! P-patty c-cake," Life strained as his biceps and triceps flexed beneath his trench coat.

There was an electrical arching sound as the opening spread.

"Yes, yes! You can do it," Victor urged.

"B-bakers man! H-how many cakes..." Life strained.

"Go, Life," Ms. Ellen cheered as Life stretched the opening even further.

"Yes! Life, only you can do it," Victor shouted.

Kent noticed Victor's excitement and did not think that it was in their best interest. He had not trusted Victor since he held them hostage on the rocky shore. However, Kent held his peace.

"H-h-hurry! I don't know if I can hold it any longer," Life urged as he stretched the opening wider by stepping inside the opening and using his back to push upward.

"Finally, the Sea Wall has been breached," Victor cheered as he leapt to his feet and rushed toward the opening.

Life's friends followed the merman. Life tumbled through the opening and to the ground. Behind him, the Sea Wall closed without making a sound.

"W-w-wow! I've never felt such a weight," Life said as he slowly rose to his feet, gasping for air.

He glanced to his left at a deep chasm that was filled with a green light but what superseded the green light was the pink glow of a grand structure. Positioned in the cleft of two enormous rocks was a Pink Diamond castle.

"It's so beautiful," Ms. Ellen said in awe as she stared at the magnificent jewel.

"It is the Diamond In The Rough, one of the many places the Lady of the Lake calls home," Victor replied.

Life bent over and a stream of drool dripped from his mouth. His chest was tight, and he was still gasping for air. Midnight became concerned about the health of his friend. Never had he seen him so winded.

"Why is Life so tired?" Midnight asked Victor.

Victor displayed a grin that was evil and diabolical.

"The weight of the Sea Wall has been likened to the weight of the sea crushing down, splintering bone and flesh," Victor replied.

"S-splintering bone and flesh," Life mouthed as he struggled to stand.

"SNAP!"

Life's leg broke from the pressure, and he collapsed.

"Don't bother. Any person who breaches the Sea Wall will suffer from deadly fatigue and broken bones," Victor laughed.

"Did you just say broken?" Midnight growled as he took a step toward Victor.

"You set us up," Kent shouted as he loaded an arrow into his bow.

"Betrayer," Sgt. Steve accused as he jerked out his battleaxe.

Suddenly, Victor leapt into the darkness of the cavern and disappeared.

"Today, you will perish beneath the earth where no one can hear your screams," Victor announced as his voice resonated from everywhere.

While Victor crouched behind two large rocks, numerous small crabs began to crawl from his boots and into the darkness where they began to grow.

"Coward, show yourself," Steve yelled as he glanced over his shoulder and into a nearby precipice where beams of lime green light streaked upward.

"Sgt. Steve, fancy that the glowing precipice would catch your attention. It is a prison that none can escape and will soon be your home," Victor said from the darkness.

Crabs began to scurry through Victor's hair and down his back.

"Come out, Victor. We can talk this over," Ms. Ellen negotiated.

"Be quiet, Axe-Murderer! After I have gained the Crown of Water, I will drain all bodies of water," Victor said.

Life's chest had tightened more, and he collapsed.

"Life is going into shock," Kent said as he stooped down and examined the cowboy. "His ribs are broken, and the pressure is causing his lungs to collapse."

Ms. Ellen suddenly sensed the scent of crabs. She reached into a pouch and extracted a flare. She struck it and tossed it into the darkness. Crouching not too far away was Victor, petting hundreds of monstrous rock crabs.

"Jumpin' Jehosophat!" Ms. Ellen shouted.

"Ms. Ellen, meet my army of carnivorous rock crabs," Victor said as he patted a nearby monstrosity on its flat spiny head.

"Clickket," the rock crab creaked as it exposed its pin-like teeth and snapped its gigantic pinchers.

Ms. Ellen, Sgt. Steve, Midnight, and Kent put their backs together.

"Rock Crabs, have no mercy on the land dwellers," Victor growled as he aimed his trident at Ms. Ellen.

At the vile announcement, the rock crabs began to ferociously click their claws. A nearby rock crab leapt at Ms. Ellen. She easily dodged the mutated crustacean. Before she could hack it with her golden axe, the creature grasped Ms. Ellen by the wrist and heaved her off her feet!

"Clickkket," the monster crab creaked as it prepared to snip her with the other claw.

However, Ms. Ellen was too agile and swift. Ms. Ellen quickly swung her golden axe, smashing the rock crab into a burning heap.

"That's what I call bad sea food," Ms. Ellen shouted.

"Your make-up is fading, fish brains," Midnight growled as he crushed a lunging crab.

Victor's blue skin faded to a pale peach color as a transformation took place. Gills formed along his neck, and his body became clothed in a shirt of dead leaves and brown pants. His black hair transformed into a tangled mass of seaweeds. Victor's cheekbones softened, and he became a woman. Long dirty curvy fingernails sprung from her fingertips.

"I-I was warned about you. Y-you are the lady with two faces," Life wheezed.

Victor let out a shriek of maniacal laughter as he pointed the trident at Life and his friends.

"My name is Lorey, the Sea Hag," Victor said as his trident emitted a large energy bubble that encased his adversaries.

Victor used the trident to levitate them to the side, leaving Life to face the merman by himself.

"I knew you couldn't be trusted," Kent yelled as he repeatedly tried to break the bubble.

"The Power of the Trident of Neptune can not be broken," Victor laughed as his voice transformed from a deep masculine tone to a soft feminine tone.

"W-what did you do with the real Victor?" Life wheezed.

"The last time I was here, I battled with the real King of the Mermen where he hurled me through the seal, but at the same time, I blasted him off the cliff to his death!"

"T-then you assumed his identity," Life finished.

"You're so intelligent," Lorey replied. "Victor released the Guardian, cutting off my escape by water! Victor is still upset that I poisoned King Neptune!"

Life had heard enough. He struggled to stand on his good leg.

"Y-you will pay dearly," Life threatened.

"That is the same thing the true King of the Mermen said before I blasted him," Lorey laughed. "I will use your friends as leverage to gain the Crown of Water from my sister, the Lady of the Lake!"

Suddenly, Life felt as if Ms. Pook was in danger, and she was not aware of it.

"Ms. Pook, wake up," Life cried out.

Ms. Ellen and the others misunderstood his plea. They called out her name also.

"Ms. Pook," Ms. Ellen and the others cried out.

"No one can help you! It is to the depths for you, cowboy," Lorey shouted as she blasted a golden bolt of energy at Life.

The blast hurled Life over the edge and into the green light of the chasm.

"Today, the Crown of Water but tomorrow the world," Lorey shrieked.

On the floor of the chasm, Life laid on his left side. He had several broken bones and his broken right finger twitched as he regained consciousness.

"I-I-I can't move my leg," Life said as he attempted to move his left leg.

Life slowly opened his eyes, and the light gave him a tremendous headache.

"Oh no! The green light is too bright for me to see," Life muttered as he tightly closed his eyes.

As Life laid on the ground, he heard something shuffling toward him.

"UHH! UUUUHHHH!"

Life heard a raspy breathing and reached for his glaive. Whatever it was, it would not catch him unaware. Life played possum, hoping to gain the advantage. That was if there was any to gain.

2

As Life laid broken and blind on the bottom of the chasm, Ms. Pook awoke from a dream where there where super-sized crabs chasing her and people calling her name. She was in the room that Robert had arranged for her in the church. The morning sun streamed through a small window. The sight of the light made her uneasy.

"They should have made it to the Waterfalls by now," Ms. Pook said as she rolled off the bed and picked up her walking stick.

Just before she hobbled from the bed, put on her white sneakers, and took a step, Ms. Pook noticed a brown spider on the floor. Chill bumps formed on her arms.

"Ugly thing," Ms. Pook muttered as she stomped the spider.

As she removed her shoe, Ms. Pook saw another spider. Before stepping on this one, she tipped her glasses closer to her face. The carpet was covered with crawling spiders!

"Help! Lord, help me," Ms. Pook screamed as her arachnophobia set in.

Ms. Pook froze as she heard footsteps on the far end of the room.

"My On-time God!"

The door opened. Standing in the doorway was Mann. He tossed an empty vile onto the floor where it went up in smoke. He held up a fist full of nails and a hammer.

"Save your breath, old lady. Not even God will hear your screams or your prayers. I have dressed your room with a magic dust that attracts spiders and gives them an appetite for old women," Mann said.

Ms. Pook looked closely at Mann. Even from a distance, she could tell he was not himself.

"Whatever was promised to you isn't worth it! Fight it, Mann! Fight off that evil spirit," Ms. Pook said in her feeble voice.

Mann laughed as he slowly closed the door.

"Let me warn you. These spiders do bite!"

Ms. Pook did not let the sound of the hammers distract her. Ms. Pook leapt back as a thumb-sized large spider leapt from the carpet. She hobbled around in a circle as another spider launched from a nearby wall.

"WHAM!"

Ms. Pook slammed her walking stick against the two leaping spiders, leaving slimy stains on the wall. Suddenly, an idea occurred to her. The Good Eye had transformed hundreds of ferocious reptiles into docile reptiles. She could use them to help her!

"Lizards, hear me! Come to me and eat the spiders," Ms. Pook commanded as she hobbled to a safe corner and climbed onto a table.

Ms. Pook used her walking stick to beat the spiders back. If the lizards do not show up, soon she would be a full course meal

Lorey stood on two crabs as they carried her towards the pink diamond castle. Floating at her side was her bundle of hostages. As they neared the castle, Ms. Ellen noticed the signs of a great battle. Broken swords, spears, and shields laid here and there along with many dust-covered skeletons. These skeletons must have belonged to the mermen who had accompanied the real King Victor.

"Whatever happens, I want to thank you for being my friends," Ms. Ellen said as she realized that they were not going to get out of the situation.

"Midnight, can the shadow dogs help us?" Kent asked.

"I am afraid not. The power of the bubble keeps me from changing or calling them," Midnight growled.

Suddenly, they stopped, and Lorey called out in a loud voice.

"Larayne, this is your sister! Come out and play," Lorey shouted.

There was no reply. Lorey raised her trident, simultaneously raising the bubble just above her head.

"Larayne, you will come out to play," Lorey shouted as her trident glowed.

There was no sound. There was no reply. Lorey frowned. Times such as these required a more aggressive course of action.

"Oh no," Midnight growled as his hair rose on his back.

"What is it?" Ms. Ellen asked.

"Electricity," Midnight replied as electrical bolts arced along the trident.

"AAAAHAHHHHHH," everyone simultaneously screamed as Lorey shocked them with the electrical bolts.

"Hear their pain, Larayne! Only you can stop their torture," Lorey shouted above the screams.

Lorey patiently waited for her sister to appear. If the land dwellers don't survive, then she would find another way to gain the Crown of Water. The lives of these Land Dwellers were expendable.

4

Life laid on the bottom of the canyon hurting and in fear of the shuffling and raspy breathing.

The glaive was on his left side and impossible for him to reach. Life laid there, barely breathing as the shuffling and the raspy breathing drew nearer.

"Are you still there, my friend?"

Life heard the weak voice that seemed to belong to an old man. Life held his breath.

"Don't be afraid of me. Only the friends of my enemies are sent here. Only if I could see," the old man's voice said.

Apparently, the light had also affected this so-called old man. Life listened closer, bending all his concentration towards the old man's heartbeat.

"Uhh. Uhhh. Don't go! Don't go! I only wanted water," the old man weakly shouted.

Finally, Life caught the sound of the specter's heartbeat. It was faint, irregular for a human's but far from the silence of the undead or the extreme rapid beat of a goblin.

"Whew," Life sighed.

The old man began coughing as he struggled to breathe.

"Friend, you are still here? Don't be afraid."

Life took a chance and called out for help.

"Here. Over here!"

"Uhhh. Uhhh. Here I come," the old man weakly spoke.

Life rotated his head just in time to feel a shadow descend on him. Life reached up with his right hand and felt a bony hand grab his hand. The bony hand tugged, then released as Life rolled over.

The man fell over. The noise of the fall was loud.

"A-a-are you okay?" Life asked.

The breathing of the old man had worsened.

"I am just weak," the person replied. "The Sea Hag created this canyon to drain the energy of its prisoners. No one can escape."

"L-let's not live up to that expectation. I-I need you to feel for the canteen on the side of my hip and pour some in my mouth," Life replied.

Life could hear the old man crawling toward him. Suddenly, Life felt bony hands fumbling on his hip. At that moment, a loud scream of many voices went up in the air.

"My friends are in danger! Hurry! I just need a large swallow," Life pleaded as tears swelled in his eyes

The old man grabbed the canteen but collapsed.

The canteen tipped over. Life felt the water splash on his leg, and he heard the old man's heart stop beating.

"AAAAAHHHHH," the voices screamed.

Life closed his eyes and stretched for the canteen. Unluckily, his broken finger tipped the canteen over onto the hand of the old man.

"Nooo," Life screamed.

No one heard him. Life laid there with thoughts swirling around in his head as the old man's hand laid on his hip. Life closed his eyes. Hopefully, someone would rescue him. Hopefully.

In the meanwhile, Ms. Pook was batting away the spiders that had crawled up the table with her walking stick. She had smashed so many that the top of the table was saturated with spider waste.

"You ugly things won't get me," Ms. Pook yelled as she

swung her walking stick.

The walking stick smashed ten spiders. As she drew back to swipe away more, her walking stick flew from her hand.

"Lord, remember your servant," Ms. Pook quietly prayed as she backed against the wall.

The spiders swarmed around the bottom of the table and crawled up the legs of the table. Ms. Pook placed her back against the wall and closed her eyes. Just then, something scurried across her feet. She glanced down and saw a brown lizard standing in her defense.

"Good googly goo! You came," Ms. Pook shouted.

"RARRK," the lizard croaked as it lashed out at nearby spider, severing its body in half.

Suddenly, Ms. Pook felt a vibration along the wall and glanced upwards. Hundreds of lizards poured through the opening of a crack and beat back the spiders from the table. The spiders froze as the lizards speedily surrounded Ms. Pook. Some even positioned themselves on her shoulders like soldiers standing guard on battlements.

"Now, what were you spiders gonna do?" Ms. Pook taunted.

Just then, there was a tremendous scratching along the frame of the wall. The scratching maneuvered along the wall and directed itself towards the crack. Then, the crack widened.

"This must be the big one," Ms. Pook said as the crack widened.

Suddenly, a green iguana leapt through the wide crack and landed in the middle of the spiders. The iguana smacked the spiders with its tail and claws. The geckos dove into the fray, severing their legs from their abdomens.

"Watch your back! Behind you! Get that sap sucka," Ms. Pook yelled as she cheered the lizards to victory.

At the first opportunity, Ms. Pook leapt off the table and hobbled to the door. As she picked up her walking stick, Ms. Pook felt something she had not felt before. It was an uplifting sensation. She felt it in her hands, her feet, her eyes, and her eyes.

"I can't believe it! I'm filled with the Charm," Ms. Pook said.

A person was filled with the charm when she reached their magical nirvana and became a supreme sorceress. Sometimes it happened to a person as a child and sometimes during adulthood, but once it happened, the person didn't have to sing her song to make things happen. She only had to command it.

"Uggh," Ms. Pook strained as she pulled the door handle.

The door did not budge. She'd forgotten that Mann had nailed the door shut. Ms. Pook stepped back and stretched out her hands.

"Door open now," Ms. Pook commanded.

The door buckled then exploded from the pressure. Ms. Pook stepped over the debris of the door and exited the church. The sun rose higher in the sky. She could see people moving towards the center of Bonanza. Mann would be there.

"Mann, today you will know the reason to fear Ms. Pook, the great granddaughter of the Shaman," she said as a slight breeze blew through her silvery hair as she vanished in a cloud of smoke.

6

Life's chest heaved up and down as he tried to regain control over his emotions. His friends were dying and he could do nothing to help them.

"If only I could reach the canteen," Life weakly spoke.

Suddenly, the old man's hand moved from his hip and picked up the canteen.

"Good help is so hard to find," the old man creaked as he handed the canteen to Life.

Life noticed that the man's breathing was better but, even more important, was that the man lived!

"You're alive," Life shouted as he grasped the canteen and took a drink.

Instantly, his broken bones were healed. Life opened his eyes and not even the bright green light of the prison could blind him! He looked down. Lying near him was a malnourished bare-chested old man. The old man was dressed in a brief of seashells. Silver bracelets hung loosely on each of his wrists. The old man's large kneecaps and pointy elbows protruded from his sagging skin.

"How did the water bring you back from the dead? I heard your heart stop," Life said to the old man.

The man's breathing became raspy again.

" I-I am a merman," the old man replied. "Just the touch of water will sustain me for a short period of time."

Life knelt down and placed the merman's head on his lap. He rubbed the merman's silky short hair.

"Well, today is your lucky day. Drink and be restored," Life said as he pried the man's toothless mouth open and slowly poured the water from his canteen into it.

"Uhhh. Uhhh. Thank you," the old man replied as he became rejuvenated.

Toned muscle reformed along the bones of the merman, his

stunted gray hair became a nice short black cut, and his droopy eyes became slightly slanted. Life watched as the merman's thin eyebrows became bushy, and a tattoo of a whale swimming upon frothing waves appeared on his broad chest.

"Hail the true King of the Mermen! My name is Life," Life spoke in the language of the Mermen as he knelt before the king.

"Rise, Life! None of my people or my friends have ever bowed to me," Victor said in a noble voice. "However, my enemies will cower before the Avenging Wind of the Seas!"

"Well, let the show begin," Life said as he rose to his feet.

"Hold on to me," Victor commanded as he grasped Life by the waist and pounced from the bottom of the chasm to the top in a single bound.

Life and Victor crouched in the shadows near the lip of the chasm as they viewed the group of individuals being electrocuted. The sight of seeing his friends tortured was more hurtful than hearing their screams.

"We must save them," Life quickly spoke as he leapt to his feet.

"Yes, but first the Sea Hag must be disarmed," Victor advised as he jerked the tail of Life's trench coat.

"But—"

"Safety first," Victor finished. "The Sea Hag wields the power of Neptune, King of the Seas. We need a plan!"

Life bit his bottom lip as he formulated a plan.

"Follow my lead, but stay out of sight. You hit 'em high, while I hit them low," Life said as he drew his pistols and flipped backwards into the gloom of the cavern.

Victor watched as Life sprinted towards the outskirts of the crab army with his guns extended.

"BLAM! BLAM! BLAM!"

The monstrous crabs splattered here and there from the gunshots, leaving burning heaps of ash.

"What is that noise?" Lorey shouted as she ceased the torture of the land dwellers.

Lorey turned around to see her crabs being assaulted by something in the dark. Sparks flew from multiple areas.

"Ingenious," Victor whispered as the army of crabs gravitated toward Life's rapid gunfire.

Victor quickly leapt into the air, silently flying toward Lorey. Life's plan was working!

"Destroy! Destroy!" Lorey chanted as her tangled mass of sea weed swayed back and forth.

She raised the trident aloft and, suddenly, something jerked the trident from her hand. She looked up. Floating above her was King Victor!

"How do you live? I threw you in the chasm," Lorey shrieked in fear.

The trident was brightly illuminated like a ray of sunlight.

"I am alive because you tossed Life upon me. I am grateful, so grateful for your mistake," Victor said as he aimed the trident at Lorey.

"Have mercy, your majesty," Lorey begged.

"Prepare yourself for the Glare of the Sea," Victor said as a wide beam of sunlight beamed from the trident.

"T-the Glare of the Sea! It burns," Lorey cried out.

In the meanwhile, the crabs had discovered Life and cornered him against a rocky ledge. They ceased their attack when they heard the cry of their master. Life hurriedly jerked out his shotgun.

"Please close the door on your way out," Life yelled as he

pumped the shotgun and smashed a nearby crab with the blade of his gun.

"CRASH!"

A group of crabs leapt at Life. Life squeezed the trigger of the shotgun, blasting away the crabs. Life leapt off the wall and fired again!

"BOOM!"

Three more crabs were demolished. Life issued a roundhouse kick at a crab and knocked it into another crab.

"KRBOOM!"

Life blasted those two crabs then slashed two more with the extended blade. However, there were too many crabs.

"Take that! You ain't gonna get me that easy," Life yelled as he fired then twisted half way around, firing the shotgun behind him.

Suddenly, a glare of light exploded toward them. When the glare subsided, the crabs were still. Life looked closer. The crabs had been turned to stone!

"That is a hard hitter," Life whispered as he sprinted toward Victor.

By the time he reached Victor, the King of the Mermen had released Life's friends from the sphere. A gentle beam of light streamed from the trident and restored their strength.

"You look like a real king," Ms. Ellen said as Victor helped her to her feet.

"And you look like a queen," Victor replied.

Ms. Ellen blushed.

"I see you have met Ms. Ellen. This is Kent, Sgt. Steve, and Midnight."

At that moment, the Pink Diamond in the Rough dazzled and

sparkled. Life cocked his shotgun, but Victor shook his head.

"Everything is fine. The Lady of the Lake is here," Victor spoke as the silhouette of a woman appeared in a window of the pink diamond tower.

Immediately, a marble stairway that led to the tower manifested before their eyes. Once the stairway was completely formed, a lady dressed in a glistening white dress strolled down the stairway. She had long blonde hair and eyes that were as green as any emerald on the face of the earth. Floating above her head was a crown of running water.

"Thank you, Victor, for your vigilance. Thank you, Ms. Ellen, Sgt. Steve, and Kent. Thank you, Life and Midnight, for your contributions to save the world," Larayne acknowledged.

She walked past Kent, and an urge to speak to her filled his heart.

"Why didn't you help us?" he asked. "Didn't you hear our screams?"

"I heard you, but I could not save you. Your champion had a charge to keep, and I could not interfere with that," she replied.

"I understand," Kent said.

"I am glad, but there is something that I want you to see," Larayne said as she formed a large sphere of water in her hand. "Your Ms. Pook has reached her full potential. She has received the charm!"

The sphere floated in the midst of them and became crystal clear. Slowly, the image of the forum of the city formed where hundreds of people were gathered. On the stage of the amphitheater stood Mann with Robert gagged and bound before him. Mann gripped a knife in his hand.

"What is Mann doing with Robert?" Ms. Ellen asked.

"He is betraying you," Larayne spoke. "Desire has possessed

him. Watch!"

They peered into the sphere and watched the drama unfold.

7

The people gathered at the amphitheatre after a rumor about a hostage situation had spread around the city. Rumor had it that there was a crazed person on the stage, holding Robert hostage. Four kids had rushed to the amphitheater to see if the rumor was true. They had a valid reason to be curious; Robert was their uncle.

"I don't believe this! We have to help him," Gabriel, the oldest, tallest, and largest of the four children, said.

Before the earthquakes, he was the number high school recruit in his area for defensive tackle. Even though his younger cousins were only ten years old, Jahi, Shada, and Ariel agreed with him but in a more frolicking manner.

"We got to help Uncle Robert," Jahi said in a tiny sincere voice as he jumped up and down.

"I'm gonna hit him in the head with a skillet," Shada said as she did a cartwheel.

"I'm gonna kick him in his ankle if he hurts Uncle Robert," Ariel said as she did a handstand.

"Stop messing around," Gabriel said.

The kids stopped their shenanigans as they heard the seriousness of their cousin's voice. Suddenly, a mist blew past them. Within the mist was the voice of an old lady.

"Stay here, my angels. Ms. Pook is here," the voice said.

Gabriel turned his head as he saw the cloud of fog streaking towards the amphitheater. He stared as the crazed man shouted his demands to the people, oblivious to the strange fog heading towards him.

"I am assuming control of the kingdom, and I am calling a blood truce with the monsters," Mann yelled as he pointed his knife at the bound captain.

"Idiot, they will eat us," the people cried out.

Before Mann could reply, the fog was upon him.

The fog swept around him and Robert.

"What is this?" Mann asked as he stared into the gray mist.

The mist thickened. Mann raised his hand to the front of his face and extended it. The fog was so thick that his hand disappeared. Suddenly, an open palm smacked him across the face.

"Ouch! Who slapped me?" Mann screamed.

"Someone you left for dead," Ms. Pook said from within the fog.

Mann's eyes grew wide at the sound of the old lady's voice.

"Impossible! That room was covered in spiders," Mann cried out as he violently slashed through the fog with his knife.

There was the sound of an elderly lady humming.

Then, a song was heard.

"Plenty of times I should have been dead and sleeping in my grave, but God told death to behave," Ms. Pook sang.

"Where are you, you freak?" Mann yelled as he stabbed here and there in the fog.

Suddenly, a stick walloped Mann across the head!

"WHAM!"

Mann was knocked to the ground. He tried to stand up and something kicked him in the stomach.

"BAM!"

Mann rolled over, trying to catch his breath.

"Hhhh! Hhh," Mann gasped.

The fog around him quickly dissipated. Standing beside the unbound Robert was the old lady he had locked away.

"Take him away," Robert commanded.

Two members of the Golden Arms quickly apprehended Mann and took him away.

"Thank you for saving me," Robert said and bowed to Ms. Pook.

Ms. Pook turned her head and looked toward the west. She concentrated and felt Ms. Ellen's presence. She was safe and she was ready.

"If we survive, thank me later. It is time for the final battle. Begin Operation Sharp Knife," Ms. Pook said.

"Is it time to use the knife?" Robert asked as he pulled out a flimsy camouflage hat from his back pocket and placed it on his head.

"Indeed," Ms. Pook replied.

"We leave immediately to take the city! Hurrrahh," Robert shouted.

At the command of appreciation, those nearby took up the command and its resonance began to spread like wildfire. The Golden Arms and the Golden Archers commenced the operation, bringing out weapon caches that were reserved for emergencies only. The fight was scheduled. Now, all that the Golden Arms and the Golden Archers had to do was show up.

Chapter 7

The Battle of the Silver Vampire Bats & The Dragon

Larayne touched the sphere with her fingertip, and it morphed into an aqua blue aquarium with orange fish swimming. She looked at the people's faces and recognized something that she had not seen since the days of the knights. The people before her had a good purpose that they would not abandon.

"The individual that was created in the image of the creator has one flaw. He can not see the purpose of another's heart. I see your hearts," Larayne said in her musical voice.

"What do you see, madam?" Life asked.

"Your hearts are true, so is your cause. I will help you."

"Thank you," Life replied as he tipped his hat. "Ms. Pook has done her part. Now we will do ours. Ms. Ellen told me you have strong steel."

"My steel is legendary. It will not break or tarnish," Larayne said.

"Then, may I trouble you for a sword? It is the only thing

that will work against these members of Legion."

A waterspout sprung from the ground.

"Reach into the spout, cowboy!"

Life thrust his hand inside the waterspout and retrieved a keen sword with a double edge. Tiny runes ran down the blade to the golden hilt. Life held the sword up for everyone to see.

"The sword that your eyes see is none other than the unbreakable Excalibur," Larayne announced. "This sword will slay anything that is unnatural and defend all that is true!"

"I will return it soon," Life said as he twirled the sword in circles.

"No, it was made for days like this. King Arthur would be greatly disappointed if it was not revealed during this travailing time," Larayne said.

Life performed a flip then slashed at an imaginary adversary.

"Life, quit playing with your new toy! We have to get to the city," Ms. Ellen shouted.

"Sorry, I got a little carried away," Life said. "What is the quickest way to the city?

"Beyond the waterfalls, of course," Larayne replied. "King Victor, I charge you to go with them to represent Atlantis."

"As you wish, your majesty," Victor replied.

"Wait until the tower turns green before following me through the diamond. Hold your breath after you pass through," Larayne warned as she ascended the stair.

Life and his friends waited until the tower turned green before following her through the jewel. Instantly, they found themselves submerged under water. Suddenly there was a forceful current that propelled them along. Life closed his eyes and enjoyed the moment as if it was his last.

2

The evening sky was gray and overcast, and there was an unnatural stillness near the noisy waterfalls. No bird whistled. No chipmunk shuttled through the bundles of green briars. All wildlife had smelled the scent of a mangy dog among in the shadows of a group of large boulders. It was the scent of werewolves. Time passed as the scent grew closer to the waterfalls.

Suddenly, a shadow moved from under the briar bushes. Its wings slightly unfurled as the surface of the lake ripple.

Revenge seemed to be closer than expected.

"Lupe! Here they come! They are coming out of the water," Ender hissed as he extended his talons.

Behind him, the leering werewolves climbed from behind the boulders and crouched with knives, axes, and chains with spikes. Hot saliva dripped from their massive jaws, and their muscular sweaty bodies were tense and ready for battle. They had been promised man-flesh and would take nothing less.

"Ender, we are hungry for man-meat," their leader, Lupe, growled as he crouched in his shredded denim jeans.

"Patience, my friend! There," Ender hissed.

Suddenly, the hand of a woman gracefully emerged from the water.

"Hoooowwl," Lupe roared as he saw the woman's hair that glistened like golden sunshine and her body that seemed to be studded in small diamonds.

A tremendous snarling went up into the air as Lupe shielded his eyes from the glimmer of the woman. The woman stood on the surface of the lake.

"You fool, that is not the Axe-Murderer," Lupe growled as he peered through his enormous claws.

The Lady of the Lake's radiance sparkled as the werewolves cowered before her.

"Who trespasses on the land of the Lady of the Lake," she inquired.

"We go where we please! We are werewolves," Lupe shouted as he shielded his eyes.

"Werewolves, you may be, but you will be prosecuted for trespassing."

Ender felt the power of the Lady of the Lake and became sorely afraid. However, Lupe was not daunted.

"Shut up and go back to your waterhole," Lupe shouted as he twirled a chain that was studded with spikes and hooks.

Lupe twirled the chain. The noise was like the blades of a helicopter. Without warning, Lupe hurled the spiked chain at the lady. The tip of the spiked chain soared toward the Lady of the Lake. She did not attempt to dodge the missile. She caught it.

"How did she do that?" Lupe contemplated as he watched the lady wind the chain around her forearm.

The Lady of the Lake took heed of her adversary's bewilderment.

"Lupe, I am the Lady of the Lake, and I am as strong as the seas," she spoke.

"The Lady of the Lake?" Lupe asked as a remote portion of his human side remembered the legend of King Arthur and his knights.

"Now, your kind will know to fear what lurks in the deep of all bodies of water," she threatened as the steel chain became frozen.

The frozen chain shattered, and the broken particles pelted

against the shore of the lake. The Lady raised her left hand, and Lupe stepped back as hundreds of sharp rocks emerged from the depths of the lake.

"Thank you, shadow fiend, for bringing these werewolves to their funerals," the Lady of the Lake laughed.

"Traitor," Lupe shouted as he wheeled towards Ender.

Lupe's razor sharp claws extended like spikes.

"Don't listen to her, you ingrate! She lies," Ender pleaded.

Ender's pleas were useless.

"If I am returned to the Underworld, then you will be also," Lupe growled as he lunged onto the shadow fiend and ripped him apart.

"Desire, heeeelllp," Ender shrieked as he vanished in a cloud of smoke.

"It is so easy to manipulate shallow minds," the Lady of the Lake said.

"You runt! You tricked me," Lupe roared as he whirled and sprinted toward the lady.

"Lupe, prepare for annihilation," she commanded as she pointed her finger toward the company of werewolves.

A mass of rocks sped towards the werewolves as Lupe dodged the flying debris. Suddenly, a rock smashed into Lupe's knee.

Lupe tumbled on the ground and looked down. His leg was gone at the knee!

"I will get you," Lupe roared.

Larayne smiled as more rocks bombarded the werewolves. Smoke and burning ashes were everywhere.

Lupe waited until it was clear and leapt into the air just as a boulder flew towards him.

The rock smashed into Lupe and sent him sprawling back onto the shore. In seconds, the werewolves were exterminated.

"Who is going to clean this mess up?" Larayne asked as she viewed the burning heaps of ashes.

Larayne raised her right hand, and a wave rushed from the center of the lake to the shore. The wave gently washed onto the land, leaving behind Life and his friends. However, they were bone dry.

"Why are we not wet?" Sgt. Steve asked.

"Within my realms, my will is absolute. Every drop of water is at my command," Larayne replied as she slowly began to submerge within the lake.

"What were those?" Ms. Ellen asked as she pointed at the burning heaps and the scattered stones.

"Just some trash that needed to be taken out," Larayne replied as the water rose above her knees.

Life glanced upward at the obscured sun. Dusk would be upon them soon. It would be treacherous trying to climb the waterfalls in the dark.

"Life, you will not climb the Waterfalls today," Larayne said as she heard his heart.

"I thought the Waterfalls were the quickest way to the city," Life said.

"Time is of the essence. The sun is not obscured by mere clouds but by the will of Desire. She is calling all evil things to her. Armageddon is almost here," Larayne said as she sank further into the lake.

"The end time," Sgt. Steve said as he popped his neck.

"You will travel westward until the sunsets. There, you will see the dragon," Larayne advised.

"The dragon?" Kent asked.

"Yes, it has been asleep for five years. One of you must awaken it," Larayne said as the water rose past her chest.

"We thank you for everything," Life said.

"You are welcome. Take care," the Lady of the Lake called out just as she went under the water.

The water rippled once. Then, it was still.

"Well, let's go," Life said as he took the lead and walked westward. "Midnight, keep your nose open. We are deep in monster country now. Ms. Ellen, do the honors."

"We are moving towards the city," Ms. Ellen said to herself.

Miles away to the south, Ms. Pook heard Ms. Ellen's call and gave the signal to move forward. Robert led the battalions north towards the ruined city of Atlanta. Women, children, and those who had not elected to fight cheered the army until they were out of sight. Then, they returned to the city praying that their loved ones would return to them.

The dim light of the overcast sky beamed down on a cement area with three concentric circles overlapping each other. This was once the site of a beautiful park that hosted the Olympics. A cluster of broken Greek statues was the only thing remaining from that era. Some were missing legs while others were missing arms. Dried up ivy stretched here and there along the cobblestones. A stagnant pool of dark water had formed in a cement fountain and the benches had been smashed. Standing in the middle of this courtyard, draped in a deep purple cloak and hood was Desire.

"Ender, you have passed over," Desire purred.

Just at that moment, a zombie ogre entered the courtyard. Iron spikes protruded from his broad shoulders, and in his hand was a flaming whip that never extinguished. His name was Lud, and he was the general of the monsters.

"Your highness, the gathering is favorable. The humans will run back to their city when they hear our roar," Lud growled.

Desire was not amused by the report.

"I do not want to them to run! I want to crush their bones," Desire caterwauled as she picked up a cement fountain and threw it at the Greek statues.

The statues and the fountain were obliterated from the impact.

"We will overrun them and trod on their bones," Lud growled.

Suddenly, Desire felt something. The feeling was something strange, sincere, and otherworldly. Yet it was something that was very human. The feeling was courage.

"I have not felt a swell of courage since mankind tried to retake the city," Desire said.

She teleported to the pinnacle of her high tower. With Death and Deprivation gone from the physical world, her talents have increased. As she stood on top of the building, the strong winds ruffled her purple cloak. She looked north, west, and east. There was nothing. When she gazed south, Desire saw an army of men and women.

"The entire city of Bonanza has emptied. The Sons of Bonanza are marching here! Mann has failed me," Desire roared as yellow flames licked around her diamond skull.

Desire quickly to dispatched a fearsome ally: The Silver Vampire Bats!

"Silver Vampire Bats, fly and destroy the men!"

At the terrible command, a host of large silver vampire bats rushed from the darkness beneath the city. These beasts were strong enough to carry away a grown man and their mouths had numerous razor sharp teeth.

"Crrrrrkkk," the silver vampire bats screamed as they rushed from within the sewers.

The gathering ogres, orcs, trolls, gremlins, and other gruesome creatures all looked up as the swarm of bats rushed from the sewers. They beat their weapons on their shields, making a terrible war cry. The Silver Bats flew around the ruined city, sending the monsters into a frenzy before streaking south toward their enemies.

"Go my Silver Bats! Leave nothing but blood stains," Desire roared in a hateful tone.

Desire glanced upon the silver storm that she had released. She was so sure that the army of Bonanza would not have a chance that she did not watch the battle. She only wanted to see their bones in the dust.

Life waded through the high golden grass with his friends following close behind. Dusk was setting in when they came to a grove of trees. A warm summer breeze blew through the grass, and Life suggested that they camp under the grove of trees for the night. They made a small fire, quietly talking while dining on roasted meats.

"Victor, was Atlantis a real place?" Ms. Ellen asked as they sat in a circle.

"It was as real as your beautiful face," Victor spoke in his charming voice.

Ms. Ellen blushed and dropped her head in a shy way.

"I remembered hearing stories on T.V about Atlantis. You know the ones with the word 'Dramatization' at the bottom of the screen, but I never thought it existed," Ms. Ellen replied after she regained her composure.

Kent agreed.

"I wish I could have seen that place," Kent replied.

"Your wish is my command," Victor said as he picked up the golden trident and slightly rotated it.

Just then, a projection of an aqua blue sea formed in the air. Three dolphins leapt out of the water as their view zoomed in on several small sandbars in the middle of a blue sea.

"Behold, the Towers of Atlantis," Victor said as the blue light from the sea reflected across his tanned chest.

"But those are just sand bars. Just places to dock your speed boat and have a beer," Sgt. Steve said.

Everyone laughed. It seemed that Victor even had a sense of humor.

"Let's take a look closer," Victor said as the view zoomed in through the aqua blue water, giving them the effect of diving hundreds of feet below.

A fleet of bubbles swirled before their eyes. When the bubbles cleared, there was a magnificent city at the floor of the ocean. Hundreds of oval-shaped boulders have been engineered along a great chasm.

"You would call those oval buildings a neighborhood," Victor said as the view zoomed past the buildings and down a dark chasm.

Suddenly, dim blue and silver lights were seen twinkling in the distance. Ms. Ellen's eyes widened as she saw hundreds of mere-people swimming alongside stingrays and other aquatic life. In the background, the city of Atlantis loomed like a juggernaut.

"It is so beautiful," Ms. Ellen cried out.

"That glowing tower is my home. It is the Horn of the Sea. The crown jewel of Atlantis," Victor said as he shook his head in grief.

Life nodded his head as he patted Midnight on the head.

"The old saying is true: There's no place like home," Ms. Ellen said.

"Atlantis lies approx—"

Victor cut his sentence short as the view of Atlantis faded in and out.

"I'm sorry. This has never happened," Victor said as he checked his trident.

Just then, Midnight detected a rank scent in the wind.

"It's not your trident," Midnight snarled. "Something evil is coming!"

"Help me smother the fire. Let no smoke drift," Life ordered. "Everyone hide!"

Sgt. Steve and Life quickly began to kick dirt onto the small fire. Then, they ducked behind a pine tree. The dusk deepened and twilight came. The stars appeared in the night sky and soon everyone could smell the scent that was like raw sewage. Suddenly, there was a rush of wind that sounded like an oncoming train

"Ahhhh," Ms. Ellen strained as she clapped her hands over her ears.

The great roaring bore down on them, bending even the boughs of the trees. The warriors kept to the shadows of the trees until the wind had passed. When the roaring passed, Life leapt up the nearest tree and peered south. His amber-colored eyes zoomed in on the fell wind.

"Ms. Ellen, tell Ms. Pook that Silver Vampire Bats are headed their way and to take cover," Life shouted.

Ms. Ellen nodded her head and let loose her mental distress signal.

"Silver Bats are headed your way! Take cover," Ms. Ellen contemplated over and over.

Life glanced down at his friends. Hopefully, he had not led them to their funeral. If the Silver Bats discovered them, then they would have been wiped off the face of the earth! Their lives were in his hands, and he had to be more careful.

Ms. Pook rode on a three-wheeler with an attached gatlin gun. Riding beside her was Robert, and behind them was their army. Dark had set in, and a cloud obscured the moon. However, Robert's golden lamp medallion twinkled.

"Robert, where did you find that shiny lamp?" Ms. Pook asked.

"After the earthquakes, my sister and I stumbled across a lake and a lady dressed in diamonds came out of the water. She gave my sister the Golden Axe and me this golden lamp medallion," Robert said.

"Larayne, the water sprite," Ms. Pook shouted.

"I-I guess that's her name," Robert replied. "The Lady said that the golden lamp would shine brighter than silver."

"Shine brighter than silver, hmmm," Ms. Pook contemplated. She knew that Larayne always spoke with a purpose.

"Don't look so ser—"

Robert's sentence was stopped short as Ms. Pook stopped her three-wheeler and grabbed the sides of her head with her hands.

"Silver Bats are headed your way," Ms. Ellen psychically warned.

"Are you ok?" Robert asked as he held his hands up for the army to stop.

"It's time to play Bow and Arrows," Ms. Pook said as she refocused.

"Huh? I don't understand."

"The Silver Vampire Bats are coming," Ms. Pook said. "Call the archers!"

"Battle formations! Golden Archers prepare," Robert shouted as the twenty thousand soldiers reorganized.

"Golden Arms flex! Golden Arms flex," Robert cried out.

The foot soldiers held up their shields, forming a protective dome. Crouching behind the foot soldiers were the Golden Archers.

"Robert, when I tell you to hold the lamp high, do it," Ms. Pook commanded as she took cover under Robert's shield.

Robert nodded his head as he pulled own the face guard of his riot helmet. The soldiers became uneasy as they waited. They waited and then suddenly, a whirring wind was heard.

"What is that noise? Is it a train," a solider asked.

Suddenly, a scream was heard in the wind.

"There are teeth in the wind. You can hear the gnashes," the other replied.

"Something is scraping at my shield," the first soldier shouted.

"Calm yourselves and hold your positions," Robert shouted as something smashed into his shield.

"THUD! THUD! THUD!"

The thuds increased, but the army held their ground. The dome of shields could not be breached. An evil screeching filled the air. The Silver Vampire Bats were upon them!

"Remember the faces of your children and friends! If we fail, then they will be next," Robert shouted.

Suddenly, the screeching ceased, and there was a great roaring as the bats twisted around, forming a tornado.

"Robert, hold up the lamp," Ms. Pook urged.

Robert dropped his shield and held a golden lamp. At that moment, a dazzling beam of white light issued from the golden medallion. The night sky lit up and the silver bats were stunned. They crashed into each other and fell from the sky.

"Golden Archers, send them back to the Underworld," Robert cried out as he fired arrows from his bow.

The foot soldiers dropped to their knees as the archers let loose a blinding shower of arrows. Then, the foot soldiers stood with their shields, protecting the Golden Archers as they reloaded.

"Send the rain," Robert cried out as the golden lamp dazzled.

The foot soldiers crouched again as the arrows were loosed again. On the third series, the sky was cleared, but the ground was littered in smoldering ashes.

"They smell so bad," Robert said as he kicked a lump of ash.

"Have you ever smelled a chicken coup?" Ms. Pook asked.

"Yeah. My parents used to send me to the chicken house to get fresh eggs," Robert said.

"That smell is lemons compared to what you will smell

tomorrow," Ms. Pook replied.

Robert nodded his head. Tomorrow, they would see terrors beyond their wildest nightmares. Some would survive. Some would not. At one time in his life, Robert had been told he could talk a turkey from inside the oven on Thanksgiving morning.

"Golden Archers! Golden Arms! Free people of Bonanza," Robert cried out in his reassuring voice. "These bats are just the first of terrors that we will witness! If any man does not wish to go forward, there will be no shame on his name!"

The warriors did not move. They did not reply.

"Then, we move on tonight. Tomorrow, Bonanza, we retake the city of Atlanta! For love! For hope! For Bonanza!" Robert cried out.

As the cheers went up, ten individuals broke from the thousands. They were the last ten members of the Jonesboro SWAT team. Ms. Ellen had coined them the Sons of Bonanza. Now, Robert put on a pair of night vision goggles and relinquished control to Ms. Pook as he joined the Sons of Bonanza. He was eager to set the tone for the homecoming.

Not too far away, Desire gazed upon the heaps of burning ashes and the success of the Sons of Bonanza. Her overconfidence had betrayed her. Now, she had to take drastic measures.

"All monsters report now," Desire growled.

In the vacant buildings, yellow eyes opened and talons began to scrape the walls of the ruined buildings. There was a howling and gnashing in the dark places of the city.

"Rise from your underground kingdoms! Rise to victory!

Rise to the bondage of mankind," Desire roared.

Sewer tops popped off as hundreds of orcs poured from beneath the city. Trolls were with them as well as snake-men that slid on their bellies. Desire stared down from her tower upon the tiny dots of monsters scrambling here and there among the ruins.

"Armageddon begins tonight," Desire commanded as she triggered the end time.

In a couple of hours, the moon would commence its phases in reverse, signaling all evil that the hour had come to crush mankind.

7

Life gazed from the pinnacle of the treetop. He had seen the sparks in the night and heard the cheers of victory. He knew that there would be no sleep tonight. Life flipped backwards. As he fell, Life grabbed a nearby limb and swung out in a front flip.

"What did you see?" Midnight growled as Life landed on his feet in the middle of his friends.

"Victory," Life replied as he ran his forefinger across the brim of his hat. "We must reach the Dragon soon. There is going to be a big fight tomorrow so drink this!"

Life handed his friends the canteen, and they drank. The water fully restored them as if they had slept for the entire day. They followed the cowboy into the underbrush. As they traveled, Life glanced upward at the night sky time after time. It was not until their midnight break that he saw a sign of the times.

"Everyone, look at the moon," Life pointed as he climbed a grassy slope.

The glistening moon was high in the sky, but it was going through all of its phases from waning crescent to new moon. Never had anyone seen such lunation on the face of the earth!

"Life, what is happening to the moon?" Ms. Ellen asked.

"Desire is declaring Armageddon," Life replied.

"But the seals have not been broken," Midnight growled as he stared at the evil omen.

"Are you referring to Revelations?" Kent asked.

"No. Desire is using the moon to signal all evil minions to eliminate mankind," Life replied as he bit his bottom lip.

"Well, let's hurry before the party is over," Midnight growled as he leapt up the grassy slope.

Midnight let out a loud snarl when he made it to the top of the slope. Life hurriedly somersaulted to his friend's side with a revolver drawn. Life did not see any hulking monstrosities but a group of metal contraptions.

"This is a graveyard, but what kind?" Life inquired as his eyes searched for any signs of the living or undead.

However, Sgt. Steve, Kent, and Ms. Ellen knew exactly what they were looking at. They were staring at the Dogs of War!

"My friends, you are looking at the last machines that some of us saw before the earthquakes," Ms. Ellen said. "I remember army helicopters and jets flying towards the city. Their objective was to bomb the city to keep the diseases from spreading!"

"Yes, that junk heap used to be a Black Hawk helicopter," Kent said as he pointed at a helicopter that was sitting sideways!

"The operators must have abandoned these machines. There are no bones," Life replied.

"Or they could have been eaten," Midnight growled.

Sgt. Steve walked away from his friends. What he saw made

him shout for joy. Of all of the broken rusty military vehicles, there was one that was still intact.

"A Sherman Tank! That must be the dragon," Sgt. Steve yelled.

'What does it do?" Life asked.

"It kills," Sgt. Steve replied.

"I have seen these machines, and they can cause fierce fires that can destroy hundreds," Victor confirmed.

"Follow me," Sgt. Steve instructed.

Life and Midnight followed them. When they reached the Sherman Tank, Sgt. Steve quickly inspected the outside then hopped into the driver's console.

"And let there be light," Sgt. Steve yelled as he flipped a switch.

The bright lights on the tank came on in a flash and the 105mm gun swiveled from right to left. There was a loud clicking noise as the 75mm turret guns automatically loaded.

"Everyone, hop on," Sgt. Steve cried out as he began to maneuver the tank around.

Life leapt onto the side of the tank with Midnight where he manned a turret gun. The tank slowly turned around and rumbled toward level ground. When they reached the city, the meaning of the phrase "blaze of glory" would be put to the test.

Chapter 8

Armageddon

Giant broken pieces of concrete and abandoned cars laid in crisscrossing patters across the overgrown expressway that once led into the city of Atlanta. Tall grass and weeds had overcome this roadway within the last five years. On the top of a crushed mini-van was a crumbled sign that read "Langford Parkway". Tonight, fifty dangerous snake-men armed with sharp spears and swords laid on their bellies among the tall grasses, abandoned vehicles, and slabs of concrete. They had one purpose— to ambush anyone approaching.

"The humannss will perishs tomorrows," a black cobra snake-man hissed as he laid on his belly behind the rear passenger tire of an eighteen-wheeler with a crescent axe in his hand.

"Yesss, they will screams for mercies," a brown snake-man hissed as he rose up from behind the front driver tire of the eighteen-wheeler with a curved scythe in his hands.

Two car doors slammed and something scuttled through the tall grasses. The snake-men were aware of the disruption. The snake-men came out from hiding.

"Someone issss sneaksy," hissed the black cobra snake-man as his hood opened up.

Just then, a shrub shook.

The movement of the shrub caught the attention of the black snake-man. He cautiously tapped his crescent axe on the side of the eighteen-wheeler and pointed towards the bush.

"There issss the sneaker," the black cobra snake-man hissed as his red tongue flickered back and forth.

The brown snake-man took a deep breath through his pitted nostrils.

"It isss a man," the brown snake-man hissed.

At that moment, the bush moved again.

"He is minesss," the black cobra snake-man hissed.

The transitioning moonlight softly beamed below, as the black cobra snake-man slid forward from the brush with his crescent axe extended. The black cobra snake-man slithered lower to the ground flicking his forked tongue back and forward. Suddenly, the bush moved again.

"Diiiieeeess, humannn," the black cobra snake-man cried out as it speedily slithered towards the bush, bashing it repeatedly.

The thrusts of the snake-man's axe tore the bush apart. The black cobra snake-man's pupils widened as he saw a stuffed teddy bear in the bush. He grabbed the bear. Tied to the leg of the bear was a small rope that looped around a nearby tree limb. It was a trap!

"Egggaaaad," was all that the black cobra snake-man could manage as a blast of arrows come from all directions.

The lingering company of snake-men was obliterated. As the smoke cleared, a man covered in a mesh of grass and weeds and wearing a pair of night vision goggles slid down the slope.

He waived his left hand two times, and nine other people covered in the grassy mesh moved forward. The Sons of Bonanza quickly secured the area. However, not too much could escape the stare of Desire as she sat on her throne. She had seen the attack and the fierceness of the Sons of Bonanza.

"I am here, master," Lud said as he entered the room.

The ogre stood before his master with an iron spiked mace in his hands and the flaming whip at his side.

"Lud, the Sons of Bonanza are coming. Prepare them a surprise," Desire commanded as she stared out the window of her throne room.

"I have something in mind," Lud replied.

Lud left the throne room. He would not fail his master.

The man with the mesh of leaves covering his body scuttled over the rugged terrain with a bow in his hand. The Sons of Bonanza were one hundred yards behind him. Soon, the once popular baseball park known as Turner Field came into view.

"Take me out to ball game," the man quietly sang to himself as he passed the silent stadium.

He sprinted around a parked SUV, a red convertible, and a van. The night vision goggles had been very helpful. He moved forward. Even in the darkness, he could see the abandoned buildings. Never before had he been so close to the city. It was strange. It was bizarre.

"The Tower of Wstend," he said as he glanced upwards at the abandoned tower looming above the other buildings.

Suddenly, a ball and chain swung from around a pick-up truck.

"Almost got me," the man said as he performed a backwards handspring and landed on top of a car.

He tossed aside his mesh of grass and weeds. The man was none other than Robert! The ogre dropped his ball and chain, picked up cars, and began to throw them at Robert. Robert dodged the flying cars. They crashed into other cars and caused an explosion.

"BOOM! BOOM! BAAMM!"

The flames shed a dim light onto the dark area. Robert jerked the night vision goggles off of his face. Standing before him was an ogre with hexagonal shaped spikes traveling down his spine.

"Puny human! I will smash you," the ogre roared as he picked up his iron ball and hurled it at Robert.

The iron ball smashed into the windshield of a car as Robert leapt to the ground. The ogre heaved the chain from the wrecked vehicle and whirled it over his head. Robert rolled on the ground, loaded his bow, and fired. The arrow struck the monster through the bottom of his chin and into its brain.

"Smash that," Robert said as the ogre busted into flames.

Suddenly, a giant black scorpion leapt from around a school bus and lashed its pincers at him. Robert ducked and dodged the claws of the beast.

The black scorpion lashed its deadly tail at Robert.

The poisonous barb barely missed as he leaned to the left. Unfortunately, Robert tripped over on his own feet and fell to the ground.

"It's a trap," Robert shouted as he saw the numerous scorpion legs and ogre legs running towards him.

He struggled to his feet as an ogre with a large golden hoop in his nose stomped forward, waiving an iron hammer.

"Smash, infidel," the ogre screamed as he heaved the hammer high, aiming it towards Robert's back.

Suddenly, a warning was heard. He only heard this warning during combat drills. His highly trained body instinctively reacted as he dropped flat down on his stomach.

"Robert, fire in the hole!"

Arrows whistled through the wind.

The ogre's hammer hit the ground beside Robert's head.

However, he was not out of danger. The exoskeleton of a giant scorpion was too thick for speeding arrows. Now, the scorpions rushed towards Sons of Bonanza.

"Tikk! Tickks," the scorpions screeched.

Robert leapt to his feet and ran away, but a scorpion seized him by the shoulder with its pincher and heaved him from his feet.

"Ahhh," Robert screamed as the claw dug into his skin.

The scorpion rotated him around.

"Trrrkkk! Trrrkkk," the black scorpion screeched.

"You're ugly," Robert said the black scorpion, drawing back its poisonous tail with the intent to impale him.

Suddenly, something silver crashed into the black tail of the scorpion and then ricocheted against the pincer that was crushing his shoulder. Robert fell on the ground and wrenched the claw away from his shoulder.

"Raggghh," the scorpion screeched as it flipped on its back, wriggling in agony.

"BLAT! BLATT! BLAATT!"

The sound of heavy rapid gunfire erupted.

Robert laid on the ground. It had been years since he had heard automated gunfire of that magnitude. When the gunfire ceased, Robert raised his head. Rolling towards him was a Sherman Tank!

"Good golly, Ms. Molly," Robert said.

Robert pulled out his walkie-talkie.

"Recon, perimeter is secured. Charlie is at lunch," Robert reported as the Sons of Bonanza took position around him.

"The bird is about to nest," recon replied.

"Who is driving the tank?" one of the Sons of Bonanza asked as he peered into the darkness.

"I'm not sure, but they saved our lives," Robert responded as he shielded his eyes from the glare of the lights of the tank.

Soon, the tank stopped. The top popped open and out stepped Ms. Ellen.

"You need to watch out what types of women you attract," Ms. Ellen shouted as she leapt off the side of the tank and hugged her brother.

Kent and Sgt. Steve joined in on the celebration. Life leaned on the gun turret as he gazed towards the ruinous city. He looked past a blasted building that leaned against another and towards the tallest building. There was a glint of red. He knew it was Desire.

"Midnight, the Golden Arms will never defeat Desire. She possesses the Map of Liberty," concluded Life.

"They are sitting ducks, and Desire has the shotgun," Midnight growled.

Life tipped his hat at Midnight.

"Shall we get the party started?" Life asked as he slid off the side of the tank.

"Quickly," Midnight growled as he leapt off the side of the tank.

The two heroes disappeared into the darkness. It was the hour of dawn, and all except Ms. Pook, mistook the stare as the warmth from the up coming sun.

"They have forgotten that I possess the Map of Liberty," Desire harshly spoke as she picked up the magical parchment. "I will take away their freedom during their greatest moment of victory!"

Desire stared at her enemies gathering on her doorstep. On this day, she would be victorious.

Shortly after Life departed, Ms. Pook arrived on her three-wheeler. As soon as she saw Ms. Ellen, she leapt from the cart and hobbled to her. Ms. Ellen was glad to see her as she rushed to her and hugged the elderly lady.

"Are you okay? Where are the Golden Arms and the Golden Archers?" Ms. Ellen asked.

"Don't worry, child. They are headed towards the city by another route. I just had to take a quick detour," Ms. Pook replied.

"I can't believe that you heard me! Does that mean you hear all my thoughts?" Ms. Ellen asked as she scratched her head.

"Nawh, baby, it means that you have a touch of what I have. One day, you will receive the charm," Ms. Pook replied.

Ms. Ellen did not know what to say. Ms. Pook lowered her

voice so that only Ms. Ellen could hear it.

"I won't tell anyone about your love for Life."

Ms. Ellen's brown cheeks became flushed. The time that she had spent with Life had been so compelling, so riveting, so rejuvenating.

"I've felt like this from the first time I saw him. I would die for him," Ms. Ellen said.

"Young love is always fresh, and it makes me proud. There are too many broken relationships," Ms. Pook said as she leaned on her walking stick.

Ms. Ellen looked around. Sgt. Steve was conversing with Robert and the others. However, Life and Midnight were nowhere to be found.

"Where is Life?"

"He has to make it do what it do," Ms. Pook replied in her tiny voice.

"Huh?"

"He and Midnight are our only hope."

"The Map of Liberty! I forgot about the Map! We have to retreat," Ms. Ellen stressed as she ran her fingers through her curly hair.

"If we leave now and hide in our city, the end will come. It will be like a hammer smashing a pecan!"

"We can't win," Ms. Ellen said as she began to fret.

Ms. Pook grabbed Ms. Ellen by the arm.

"I need you to be strong, Axe-Murderer! She is watching us now," Ms. Pook warned.

Instinctively, Ms. Ellen switched to battle mode. Her hand dropped to the hilt of her golden axe at her side.

"Who is watching us?"

"The lady with the diamond cathead! That heat that you feel is not from the sun, sista! It is her stare," Ms. Pook whispered.

Ms. Ellen felt a chill travel down her spine. Who in the world had a stare that was like the heat of the sun?

"Desire," Ms. Ellen stated as she glanced towards the tower.

"Life is the only person who can stop her from possessing the earth," Ms. Pook advised.

Ms. Pook pointed her crooked finger towards the tower and shouted in her tiny voice.

"The great-granddaughter of the Shaman is here!"

Ms. Ellen was enamored by the elderly woman's pizzazz and spunk. She put her hand on Ms. Pook's frail shoulders.

"The Sons of Bonanza and the Golden Arms will give the world a fighting chance," Ms. Ellen loudly spoke in a proud voice as she turned her head toward the city.

Miles away, Desire frowned at the defiant stance of the two women but even more at the elderly lady.

"Sorceress, you will pay dearly," Desire roared as she pounded her yellow diamond fist on the arm of her throne.

She would make sure that she dealt with them personally.

In the meanwhile, Life and Midnight were crouched in bundle of thickets and small trees located right outside the city. Ogres, giant scorpions, orcs, and snake-men were moving in and out of the nearby buildings, making it hard to maneuver without being detected. Soon, the dawn would break and the darkness that was concealing them would be lifted. They had to do something quick or else.

"Midnight, I need you to turn into the Shadow Hound and cause a distraction," Life requested as a giant red scorpion crawled nearby.

Midnight began to fade as he took his shadowy form.

"You are about to witness shock and awe shadow wolf style," growled Midnight as he crept from the thickets.

Life waited for a moment and doubled back towards a giant boulder they had just passed. Life snuck forward then jerked back behind the boulder. Two slimy green-faced orcs with stringy black hair were resting on the other side. Life took a step and his boot snapped a stick.

One of them heard the thickets rustle behind the boulder.

"Did you hear that, Gully? It sounded like footsteps," one of the orcs croaked as he pulled out his curved scimitar from his leather belt.

The edge of the scimitar was serrated and was designed for ripping things apart. Gully did not answer; he was too busy eating a beetle that he had just dug from under the boulder. The orc slapped Gully up side the head, knocking the chewed up beetle on the ground.

"Gilly, I should cut you like a fish," Gully shouted in his monotone voice.

"Shhh! Something is behind the rock, my darling! I bet it's a bigger beetle, one with skin, hair, and legs," Gilly spoke as he smiled, displaying his rotten teeth.

Gully's dark gray eyes lit up.

"Big beetle," Gully whispered as he slobbered.

"Big beetle with bones and gristle," Gilly said as he nodded his head.

They both crept around the boulder. Crouching low with his shotgun extended was Life.

"Come here, big beetle," Gilly harshly spoke.

A green slimy hand reached out and touched the side of the boulder. Life grimaced as he studied the three-inch black nails and sprouts of hair protruding from the orc's knuckles. He placed his finger on the trigger and was ready to blast the orc when a great unearthly howl went up.

"HHOOOWWWWWLL!"

The green hand jerked back around the corner.

"Whew," Life quietly sighed as he relaxed.

Gilly and Gully wheeled around as the harrowing sound of the howl broke the silence of the early morning.

"Did you hear that beast?" Gilly asked as he put his hands over his ears.

"Big beast. Underworld," Gully slowly spoke.

"HHOOOOOOOOWWWWWL," the beast howled again. Only this time louder.

"Yep, it's the king of the Shadow Hounds! Those mangy men are about to get slashed, my darling," Gilly shouted as he cheered.

The monsters stared into the darkness searching for the champion of the howl. Desire even ceased her watch of Ms. Pook and searched for the owner of the howl.

"Saga, the King of the Shadow Hounds is here to fight with me," Desire cried out as she rushed to a nearby window and gazed onto the battlefield!

What Desire witnessed only infuriated her. There was no hound braying at her enemies, daring them to come any nearer. There were only heaps of burning ashes exploding here and there in the morning darkness. Only a shadow hound could move through darkness without being detected. The maneuver was crafty and had dismantled her army of thousands in a matter of seconds.

"Traitorous shadow hound, I will punish you," Desire screamed as her yellow diamond head became engulfed in a golden flame.

Suddenly, the morning sky lit up. Dawn had come and, like the truth, the light made everything visible to the naked eye. Desire peered at the swirling shadow that swirled around the hound, protecting it from the naked eye. However, the artful movements of this shadow hound did not mimic the blundering movements of Saga.

"Who are you?" Desire asked as she gazed past the withering darkness and shadow.

Her red eyes zoomed in and detected an enormous black wolf with yellow eyes. His teeth were gallant blades, and his massive paws were crushing hammers!

"The wolf of the cowboy! If he is here, then the cowboy is here! Lud, secure the entrance to the tower," Desire roared.

Desire became desperate and seized the Map of Liberty from the arm of her throne. The golden flames about her jeweled claws unlocked the power within the parchment. Its ink letters glowed brightly as Desire claimed dominion over the earth.

"Liberty, you are mine," Desire commanded as a beaming light emitted from the parchment, shredding the purple robe from her diamond crusted body.

The sunrise paused as a deep silence filled the land. The monsters felt stronger and more empowered while the Army's of Bonanza became doubtful. Ms. Ellen's hands shook, and her heart pounded in her chest. She was very afraid.

"What is happening?" Ms. Ellen fearfully asked as she glanced at the soldiers.

The Army's of Bonanza seemed troubled, dazed, and confused. Some gripped the sides of their helmets while trembling as others laid on the ground, too scared to get up.

"She is using the Scroll of Liberty against us," Ms. Pook cried out.

Ms. Ellen dropped her Golden Axe as a gnashing was heard from the monsters.

They madly dashed towards the crippled people.

"Ms. Pook, do something," Ms. Ellen pleaded as she dropped to her knees, and her belly began to ache.

Ms. Pook was already two-steps ahead of Ms. Ellen, causing a mist to form along the ground. Hopefully, the mist would give them a chance to escape.

Life had not been idle. As soon as Midnight began the stellar performance, he sprinted towards the city. Now, he was running through the city with his trench coat flowing in the wind. His destination was the only standing building: a blasted tower with the faded words, **WSTEND**, at its pinnacle.

"Desire, ready or not, here I come," Life said as he sprinted up a hill of fallen debris.

Life landed on a car door and surfed down the opposite slope of debris where he crashed onto a severely cracked street. He glanced at a sign that was attached to a building that read:

Peachtree St. Standing guard at the entrance of the tower, no more than one-hundred yards away, were five trolls armed with large machetes.

"The cowboy is here! Get him," a troll roared in a deep voice.

The trolls sprinted towards Life. Life did not hesitate as the towering monsters rushed him. He sprinted towards the trolls and leapt into the air with his sword extended. The cowboy glided through the air, his blade shining silver. His adversaries swung their heavy machetes.

The sound of the sword crashing into the machetes was crisp. The five machetes shattered, and the five trolls exploded. Life landed and crouched. The tail of his trench coat fluttered around him like the cape of a count from a foreign land.

"RRRRGGH," another troll roared that leapt from behind a mound of rubble.

The troll wildly swung a rusty axe.

"SWWOOOSH!"

Life dodged the powerful slash that would have slain five men. Then, he punched the troll in the elbow.

"SNAP!"

The bone broke and protruded on the opposite side of the thick hide.

"Agggh," the troll roared in agony.

Suddenly, an enormous ogre busted out of the nearby debris. Life stepped back as metal beams fell here and there. Standing before him was Lud. His broad warty shoulders were covered in iron padding. He twirled a large hammer. At his waist was a flaming whip.

"What big orange eyes you have," Life said as the troll drew the hammer back.

"Prepare to be bludgeoned," Lud roared.

"Not today! Not ever," Life replied as he leapt to the left as the hammer fell.

"Noooo," the troll with the broken arm screeched as the hammer crashed into his head, causing him to burst into flame.

"Look at what you made me do," Lud roared as he dropped the hammer and grabbed his flaming whip.

With a flick of the wrist, it lashed at Life.

Life barely dodged the evil weapon as it licked past his head. He glanced down, and there was a fiery cut on his shoulder. Life knew he had to end this battle soon or Desire would use the Scroll of Liberty.

"You shouldn't play with fire," Life said as he flipped backwards and hurled a fist full of razor sharp discs.

Lud's fiery whip lashed out, but the silver discs shredded the whip and struck him in his claw.

"Agggh," Lud roared as he clutched his injured appendage.

"Ahhh yahh," Life bellowed as he leapt in the air. His trench coat fluttered in the wind.

The orange eyes of Lud quaked with fear as the cowboy swung his sword in a silver arc.

"FOOM!"

A burst of blue flame jetted upward as Life's blade cleaved through the metal shoulder pads of the troll. Suddenly, the troll busted into flames, but the flames did not burn.

"What in the world?" Life said as he stared at the fire that didn't burn.

At that moment, an ominous voice was heard. Life snapped his head upward as beams of light busted the windows in the tower.

"Liberty, you are mine," Desire proclaimed.

Jets of yellow flame burst from the pinnacle of the structure.

"It is now or never," Life said as he glanced around.

Nearby was a large slab of concrete lying at an angle with the opposite end tilted in the air. Above the beam on a deteriorated building was a crane. Life extracted his lasso and hurled it high into the air. The hoop wrapped around the edge of the crane and tied itself into a knot.

Life somersaulted onto the end of the concrete slab and jerked as hard as he could. The crane crashed over the edge.

"Up, up, and away," Life yelled as the crane crashed onto the tilted end of the column, catapulting him to the ninetieth floor of the Tower of Wstend.

Life crashed through the window and jerked out his shotgun. Desire wheeled around, engulfed in a searing orange flame. Only the darkness of her catlike skeleton could be seen like a burning shadow.

"Cowboy," Desire roared.

"Play time is over. It's back to the Underworld for you," Life threatened as he pumped the shotgun.

The cowboy crouched before the flaming abomination.

"When I am finished with you, cowboy, there will be nothing left to resurrect," Desire roared as her orange flames transformed to a scarlet red.

"Been there, done that," Life yelled as he repeatedly fired the shotgun.

"BOOM! BOOM! BOOM!"

The blasts hit Desire on the claw that clutched the Scroll of

Liberty and loosened her grip. Life quickly whirled his lasso at the parchment. The rope wrapped around it, and Life jerked it into his possession.

"You have failed the world, cowboy! The parchment is useless! I have drained the power within the scroll," Desire purred.

Life holstered the shotgun. They had only one chance to save the world.

"Midnight, catch me," Life screamed as he dove out of the window headfirst.

Desire hurried towards the window to see Life falling ninety stories. She also saw the fleeting shadow of a wolf moving along the ground at a tremendous speed. Suddenly, the shadow of the wolf leapt into the air, pouncing off the sides of the derelict buildings and caught the cowboy on his back.

"Hey, hothead! I forgot to tell you something," Life yelled as he held up the parchment in a taunting fashion. "The power of the parchment can be reversed by a person who has the charm! The great-granddaughter of the Shaman just received it! Thanks!"

"Then, I will destroy you both," Desire roared as she leapt out of the window.

"Go! Take me to Ms. Pook," Life cried out Life as he placed the Moon Glaive in Midnight's jaws and extracted his revolvers.

"Hang on," Midnight roared as he sprinted towards the battlefield at a tremendous speed.

At that moment, there was a loud explosion as dust and debris flew into the air. The tower of Wstend and the surrounding buildings were leveled. Life glanced over his shoulder to see the flaming specter rise from the cloud of dust. Desire had grown ten feet taller!

"Midnight, I need you to run like the wind," Life shouted.

Midnight increased his speed. The buildings became a blur.

"Fools, there is no escape! I can be in more than one place at a time," Desire cried as she vanished and appeared right before Midnight.

"How in the world did she do that?" Midnight mumbled as he quickly changed directions.

"Death's and Deprivation's demise must have given her more power," Life assessed as Desire appeared again, but this time, wielding an enormous flaming sword.

"Hold on to your hat," Midnight growled as Desire swung the flaming sword, creating a searing arc of fire.

Midnight sprinted towards a group of abandonded buildings as the arc of fire sped towards them. He pounced up the side of a building just as the arc of fire crashed into the buildings around him.

Midnight leapt through the air, just above the flames and skid to a halt on the ground.

"Whoa! My coat," Life shouted as he quickly patted his left coat sleeve that had a patch of fire on it.

"We have bigger problems," Midnight growled.

The flames that had just crashed into the buildings did not die out. They became alive.

"Fire Stalkers, incinerate them," Desire bellowed.

Life knew that the longer it took for him to get the Scroll of Liberty to Ms. Pook, the quicker the monsters were going to slaughter his friends. Midnight would have to get the job done while he faced Desire alone.

"Midnight, go to Ms. Pook, and whatever you do, don't open

your mouth. Be careful, you will have to keep your physical form to hold the map," Life warned and stuffed the parchment into Midnight's jaws behind the Moon Glaive.

Life leapt from Midnight's back and faced the flaming monsters. Midnight darted away, moving along the shadows of the buildings. Life glanced around and quickly drew his guns. He commenced firing his guns at the Fire Stalkers. Each bullet passed by the gang of fiery creatures and smashed into a weathered wall.

"You need to improve your aim," Desire purred as she watched Life's futile attempts.

"Who said I was aiming at your friends?" Life asked as the wall fell upon the fiery creatures, creating a great cloud of dust that extinguished their fires.

"Nuisance, I will deal with you myself," Desire growled as she sprinted towards him waving her flaming sword.

The ground trembled, but Life did not lose his balance.

"A classic match up. Man verses fire," Life replied as he sprinted towards Desire with the tip of his sword scraping the broken asphalt, sending tiny sparks flying.

Life swung Excalibur in a sideways motion, and it crashed into the burning broad sword of Desire, sending a great explosion of fire within the ruined city. The ravenous monsters ceased their maddening dash toward the helpless people as plumes of smoke and jets of fire erupted into the sky. Suddenly, there was a shadow and a glint of silver rushing from the city.

"It is the shadow wolf! Reorganize," a troll grumbled with a single fang that protruded over his upper lip.

Before the other monsters could readjust, the shadow wolf plowed into the ranks of the monsters. Ms. Pook ceased working her magic as she felt Midnight's presence.

"Ms. Ellen, I need you to rise to your feet," Ms. Pook commanded.

"I-I can't," Ms. Ellen weakly responded as she leaned against the wheel of the three-wheeler.

"You can, and you will. Prepare yourself to lead your soldiers! The picture your father painted on the wall is at hand," Ms. Pook said.

Midnight leapt into the air and shook his head.

The parchment flew from Midnight's mouth and soared above the heads of the monsters. They reached for the parchment, and it glided over the tips of their talons.

The parchment fell right into Ms. Pook's outstretched hand. Midnight crashed into the monsters and transformed into his shadowy form, but he had nowhere to run. His only option was to fight for his life.

"Stab the dusty shadow," a red coral snake-man growled as he thrust his spear at the shadow.

Midnight blocked the thrust with the Moon Glaive and sliced the snake-man across his scaly belly.

The snake-man incinerated and left a mound of ash. Midnight quickly pounced to his left and slashed a green orc with his paw. Just then, the monsters surrounded Midnight with a circle of spears.

"The last dance is supposed to be slow, but this one may be fast," Midnight snarled.

Suddenly, there was a shift of momentum. The change was felt within the earth, the people, the monsters, and even the sunrise. The monsters became dumbfounded as the rooster crowed at the coming dawn. Liberty had been restored to all free beings!

"Fight for freedom! Fight for love! For Bonanza," Ms. Ellen shouted as she stood to her feet and fixed her golden tiara with the silver wings.

"For Bonanza!"

"Golden Archers, make it storm," Ms. Ellen requested.

"Right on, sista," Midnight growled as he busted out of the ranks of the monsters.

The archers loaded their guns and bows, then they fired.

The arrows smashed into the monsters, and they began to flee.

"Golden Arms, crush, grind, and stomp," Ms. Ellen roared as she rushed towards her enemies.

Ms. Ellen swung her axe and bashed a scorpion across its back. "CRUUNNCH!"

She stepped through the burning ashes and swung her axe again. This time it hacked through an orc as it tried to spear her.

The Golden Arms rushed around her. An all out battle broke out. However, Ms. Pook was concerned about Life.

The sounds of the explosions and blasts within the city were louder than any thunder! Ms. Pook glanced upward at the sky, oblivious to the battle cries of the Golden Arms and the screeching of the monsters. She swallowed and realized that she had not had anything to drink since leaving Bonanza.

"Water! He needs water! Midnight, go and by us some time," Ms. Pook commanded as she held up her hands.

Dark clouds began to swirl in the heavens as Midnight streaked towards the flaming city. Just then, a figure levitated from the battle and flew behind the shadow of the wolf. The figure was none other than Victor, the King of Atlantis.

6

Life dodged the flaming debris of a crumbling building by

quickly rolling along the pavement. Desire had cornered him
into an area of deserted condominiums and was demolishing the
nearby buildings by wildly swinging her flaming sword.

"Surrender, and I will make you the greatest of my officers,"
Desire offered as she swung her flaming sword.

Life ducked the swing and pounced backwards as Desire's
two laser beams blasted from her eyes.

"You are swift but quiet," Desire roared as she cornered Life
between two blasted office buildings.

Life was quiet because he had been thinking of a plan to end
the madness of the monster without being destroyed, but nothing
had come to his mind. He backed up and found himself against
a wall of debris. This time there was no escape.

"You have nowhere to run, cowboy," Desire chuckled as her
flames exploded in orange and red colors.

"If you ever served the true king of old, serve me now," Life
whispered to Excalibur as he pointed the tip at Desire in a defiant
stance.

"Now, you are speaking to swords as is if they are alive! What
a loss of talent! Surrender to me or suffer the consequences,"
Desire ordered.

"Never will I surrender to you, Desire! Mankind may
struggle, but they will prevail," Life replied.

"Then, your fate is sealed," Desire yelled as she swung her
flaming sword.

Life swung Excalibur with all of his strength. The force of
the impact shattered Desire's sword. Desire stared at the broken
shards of her sword that began to form small pools of lava along
the broken pavement. For the first time since the battle had
started, she was afraid.

"Now, for the icing on the cake," Life said as he swiftly advanced toward Desire with Excalibur raised above his chin.

However, Desire had more than one weapon. Now, she released the deadliest weapon, one that no man could survive.

"Dead Star," Desire roared as she formed a circle with her left fiery talon.

The circle became a ball of fire and then the energies collapsed upon itself. Suddenly, a black hole formed.

"Noo," Life yelled as he was jerked off of his feet by the tremendous suction of the black hole.

"This hole will be your eternal tomb," Desire said.

In an act of desperation, Life stabbed Excalibur into the ground. His black coat fluttered in the wind like a flag as he grasped onto the sword. Desire was amused at the plight of the champion of men and began to taunt him.

"Let go! Be free! You are the savior of men," Desire taunted.

"Agggh," Life strained as he retightened his grip.

Desire was amazed at the strength of the man. However, if she could not have him physically, then she would have his soul. She touched the black hole with the tip of her talon and its power intensifies.

"This black hole will take your soul. No man can live without a soul," Desire said.

Life glanced down at his hand as it withered away. The force from the black hole drained a significant amount of his life force. Life closed his eyes as he tried to concentrate

Life's eyes flung open. Rain was falling from the sky!

"Water, quench my thirst," Life whispered as he opened his mouth.

Suddenly, Desire whirled around to see Victor, the King of

Atlantis.

"Fire-Demon, your tyranny ends here," Victor advised as he pointed the golden trident at Desire.

"Fish-man, I will fry you for your intrusion," Desire roared.

Victor was undaunted by the threats of the monster. His trident became illuminated.

"Behold! The Glare of the Sea," Victor loudly spoke as he blasted a wide beam of light from the trident.

Desire shielded her eyes from the glare. At that moment, a shadow of a wolf leapt through the air with a silver S-shaped blade and cut off Desire's left hand. Instantly, the portal closed.

"You will pay with your lives," Desire growled as her flames stretched outward like wings.

"Shut your sewer hole," Life said from behind the fiery monster.

"Imbecile," Desire shouted as she leapt backwards.

"It's time for you to go home! The street lights are on," Life gleefully responded as he flipped toward Desire and pulled out his shotgun.

"Burn! Burn," Desire shouted as her fires became blue.

Victor noticed the sand on the ground as it crystallized from the intensity of the heat.

"He's committing suicide," Victor cried out as the blue flames swallowed Life.

"Don't give up yet," Midnight growled as the rain fell harder.

Suddenly, Life reappeared, hacking through the blue fire with the shotgun. The flames had consumed him, reducing him to a raggedly clothed skeleton armed with a shotgun.

"You should be dead," Desire gasped as Life waded through the blue fire as if it were water.

"Even during death, there is Life," the severely burned cowboy cried out.

Life reached upward with his bony hand and clutched the burning apparition by the collar. There was strength in his dry bones, and he jerked Desire down to his level and, at the same time, placed the barrel of the shotgun right below Desire's chin.

"Close your eyes. This could hurt," Life replied as he squeezed the trigger and blasted Desire at point blank range.

The blast from the shotgun separated the yellow diamond from the body of young woman known as Jane Wright. Jane collapsed on the ground still dressed in her t-shirt and khakis. She was unharmed and seemed to be asleep. Beside her was the yellow diamond of Desire. Victor rushed to the woman and checked her vital signs.

"The woman lives," Victor determined.

"Giver her some of this," the severely burned Life spoke as he handed Victor his canteen.

Even as his bony hand stretched out, the rainfall quickly healed his wounds and clothing. By the time Victor received the canteen, Life's hand was completely restored.

"Finally, we can close the chapter of the diamonds of Legion," Midnight growled.

"Desire, I know you can hear me inside your prison," Life spoke as he reached down and grasped the yellow diamond.

Just then, the voice of a little girl called out from within the diamond.

"Life, I need you. You need me! Don't destroy me!"

"Crush her, Life," Midnight urged.

"You are everything! I am everything! Together, we are the universe," the little girl continued.

Life's fist began to glow. Victor gripped his trident as Life struggled. Midnight could see the power of the diamond taking hold of Life.

"Life, snap out of it! Crush the diamond," Midnight snarled as Life dropped to his knees.

The yellow diamond dazzled. A tremendous temptation had fallen on Life. Even though his eyes were open, Life could see the cosmos unfolding, universes collapsing, and time becoming space. The power of Desire was unyielding.

"The world! The universe is mine," Life screamed as the ground began to tremble.

"Desire is overpowering him! We have to do something," Midnight growled.

"Yes! Give into me! Open your hand cowboy and put me on," the voice of the little girl continued.

In an act of desperation, Victor dashed the water from the canteen into Life's face. Suddenly, Life stood to his feet and held his glowing fist high in the air. The water had brought him back to his senses.

"Desire, tell all of your friends in the Underworld that Earth is free. Tell them that the hunter of monsters is free," Life said.

"You need me! You neeeeee—," the little girl cried as Life crushed the diamond in his bare hands.

The heavy rainfall became a light drizzle. Life turned to his friends and showed them his gratitude.

"Thank you for not giving up on me," Life said as he knelt before them.

"Who can ever give up on Life?" Victor asked as he placed his hand on Life's shoulder and helped him to his feet.

Life patted Midnight on the head and then remembered Ms.

Pook and Ms. Ellen.

"Ms. Ellen," Life shouted.

"The battle is over! Thanks to you the city is once again ours," Ms. Ellen said as she leapt up a mound of rubble.

Life wheeled around. Standing at the top of a nearby mound was Ms. Ellen. Life stared at the beautiful strong woman. His heart was moved. His heart was in love.

"You make the day so much brighter," Life replied as he pounced onto the mound of rubble in a single bound.

"Life, you sure know how to treat a woman," Ms. Ellen said as she embraced Life.

They kissed. A warm breeze blew around Midnight the Shadow Wolf, Victor the Merman, Ms. Pook the great-granddaughter of the Shaman, and the last organized army of men as they surrounded the couple. Suddenly, Sgt. Steve shouted out as he stood on the Sherman Tank.

"Life, Ms. Ellen! You have to hear this!"

Sgt. Steve clicked on the P.A system and tuned it to a military frequency. Everyone became silent. Sgt. Steve turned up the volume as a lady with a sultry Louisiana accent was broadcast over the airwaves. There was panic and fear in her voice as she jumbled broken English and French words. Terrifying sounds of beastly screams were heard in the background of the broadcast.

"Is dere anyone out there, cher? This is Jaylous, broadcasting from New Orleans, the Crescent! We need help! The coni Voodoo King has returned with beaucoup creatures! Hurry!"

There was a round of machine gun fire.

The broadcast ended. All eyes became fixed upon Life as the tail of his black trench coat fluttered.

"Who is going to New Orleans with me?" he asked.

Ms. Ellen smiled, and Midnight wagged his tail. Thus began a new chapter in the world's existence. The world's new champion stood for hope, justice, and freedom. His name was Life the Cowboy!

The End...for now

G.S.CREWS

Another Title by G.S. Crews

www.ingramcontent.com/pod-product-compliance
Lightning Source LLC
Chambersburg PA
CBHW050025180626
46810CB00002B/583